Myster
St Andrews

W.P. Lawler

Paperback ISBN 978-1-78092-464-9
ePub ISBN 978-1-78092-465-6
PDF ISBN 978-1-78092-466-3

Published in the UK by MX Publishing
335 Princess Park Manor, Royal Drive,
London, N11 3GX
www.mxpublishing.co.uk
Cover design by www.staunch.com

Grateful acknowledgment to Conan Doyle Estate Ltd. for the use of the Sherlock Holmes characters created by Sir Arthur Conan Doyle.

Table of Contents

Dedicated to My Friends, Family

&

The America I Love

Preface

Long a fan of the writings of Sir Arthur Conan Doyle, particularly the exploits of his world-famous detective, Sherlock Holmes, I decided to attempt a pastiche of my own as a tribute of sorts to that wonderful mystery writer. Having read all of Conan Doyle's adventures of Holmes and Watson several times over, I thought I might attempt to emulate, certainly to a much lesser degree, his artful storytelling style.

Fully realizing the scope of what I was trying to accomplish, I had no delusions that my writing could ever favorably compare with his creative ability in writing such captivating tales. Rest assured, however, that every effort was made to do the best that I could.

As my friends and family know, I'm the type of person who likes to challenge myself. Whether it's on the golf course trying to shoot a score, composing or learning a new piece of music, or even undertaking the task of writing a club history, I find I enjoy projects that require large amounts of time and many hours of effort.

For example, as a young lad, a friend introduced me to stamp collecting, a most curious hobby. While I primarily stuck to the outdoor sports, baseball, basketball, football, etc., there was something about stamp collecting that captured my interest. I vividly remember contacting stamp companies around the country to request free sets of stamps. Naturally, along with the free ones, came other sets "on approval." This was the way the companies promoted their products. Once you saw them, you had to have them.

With my small allowance, I had to learn to save in order to acquire "mint" sets, those unused stamps that were worth considerably more than used stamps. While this activity held my interest for a short time, I quickly found that every time I applied for the free stamps, the company sent more and more sets on approval that had to be purchased or returned. Sadly, I had to pay postage to return the packages and often it would be cheaper to just buy the entire selection.

This pursuit went on for a number of years until, I became occupied with other interests. To this day, however, I still have my collection, though I haven't looked at it in years!

More recently, I have been blessed with time, having retired from teaching in 2001. Certainly, anyone who pursues an activity requiring large blocks of time must have the necessary interest, passion and patience to pursue any such time-intensive endeavor.

I wondered what I should write about this time? Silly fool, the best writers write about what they know. Maybe I'll put together another book about golf. . . Well, at least I've played enough golf to know something about it. Also, I have documented evidence to that end, having compiled a brief history of my club, Fox Hill Country Club, in Exeter, Pennsylvania.

Not immodestly, I am also proud of two, self-published books, <u>Rank Amateur, A Selection of Musings</u> and <u>Vague Recollections of a Passionate Golfer</u>, and <u>Rank Amateur II, The Saga Continues</u>. While they haven't exactly been flying off the bookstore shelves, I have had a great deal of enjoyment writing them. Both books are autobiographical accounts of my experiences playing the game, the interesting people and situations I've encountered. They chronicle my continued attempts to improve my play in tournaments for over 45 years.

Those books are collections of my travels around the eastern United States, competing in as many quality golfing events as I could fit into my summer golfing schedule. Many of these tournaments had qualifying criteria. Either you had demonstrated the skills prerequisite for an invitation, or you were provided with an opportunity to qualify for the events.

All of the tales in these two compilations are true, even though some may seem very difficult to believe. Those of you who play this great game know that strange things can happen on the golf course. These books are chock full of bizarre events. Still, most golfers will relate to them.

Many of the people whom I have met, have had lasting effects on me, and I have been truly blessed having gotten to know them. Some were more memorable and influential than others, and many were extremely talented individuals. Others, far from being tournament strong, left me greatly impressed when I had learned of their backgrounds. These golfers played for the sheer love of the sport, not for the success it could bring them.

When I write, I try to involve the reader in my adventures. My stories take them to courses where I've experienced some near misses in trying to qualify for major events. I describe the crazy bounces and bad breaks that far outnumbered the good ones. I also attempt to relate what it felt like when I finally qualified for a national event, the 2006 United States Senior Amateur Championship at Victoria National Golf Club. The year 2006, as Sinatra sang it, was a "very good" year.

So, in addition to the challenge, beauty and addictive lure of golf, what other areas in my life have been able to hold my interests? Well, certainly my wonderful family and all of the great times we've shared together would make a most enjoyable read, at least for our family and friends. I continue to spend a great deal of time at the piano for I enjoy music.

My interests in music range from the progressive Bluegrass songs of New Grass Revival, Alison Brown, and Bela Fleck to the smooth jazz piano musical compositions of David Benoit. I have written over 25 musical compositions, all in various stages of completion, that crave my time and attention. But my own musical expressions are probably best appreciated by Bill Lawler, himself.

I've always loved to read, and while my areas of interest vary from political writings, golf books(by other writers of considerable skill), "how-to" books, and lately, the classics, I still love mysteries the most.

Hmmm....I know what I'll do. I'll write a golf mystery that combines what I know, or what I think I know about golf, and a great plot with fascinating characters to describe. Then, I'll follow through to a striking conclusion that will have the readers truly shocked! Yep, that's what I'm going to do. Well, that's what I'm shooting for. It remains to be seen if we'll accomplish that lofty goal.

I also want to thank my wife, Gloria, who continues to support and aid me in my efforts. A special thanks to my team of proofreaders who have been invaluable assets in my continued efforts at writing.

Hope you enjoy this, my latest endeavor.

Bill

N.B. There is a glossary in the book to decipher certain Scottish words and phrases. They may be coded with ***

Part I

The Range
May He Rest In Peace

My name is John Watson, actually it's Doctor John Watson. For those among you who have read my compilations of the various adventures of Mr. Sherlock Holmes, the world's foremost consulting detective, you know from following these tales that Holmes never wanted the prestige and notoriety that my humble accounts served to bring him. Still, he did admit, in his later years, that he was touched by my steadfast attention to detail in chronicling his many cases. I, for my part, was grateful for his approbation and continued my documentation of so many of his noteworthy successes.

Mind you, not all have been triumphs by any means. Yet, all have demonstrated his dogged determination to seek and interpret the most unfathomable clues as only his mind might serve to conjecture.

Many of you have been faithful followers of the exploits of this intriguingly brilliant and wonderfully eccentric criminal investigator. Indeed, quite a few complimentary missives have made their way to my door and for those kind words I am truly most appreciative.

Some readers, though, may be quite surprised to learn that there were many cases that I was not permitted to detail for fear of grave repercussions that might result from disclosing the particulars of certain investigations. Many of those adventures could have put national security at risk had they been revealed, so of course it made perfect sense to keep them out of the public eye.

Other accounts might have unnecessarily embarrassed innocent parties and since they would have served no other purpose, have also been omitted. In cases such as those, testimonies were never required to successfully prosecute the guilty, so Holmes and I agreed to protect identities. Hence, those tales were likewise shelved.

As of this writing, however, I had not formally put down any further cases, for I naturally believed they had ended with my dear friend's recent passing. For the rigors of such a busy schedule and, sadly, a regression to some of his former habits, finally took the life of this truly exceptional man.

Yes, he has left us, and this time, it is forever. I can still recall his amazing "resurrection," for I was convinced that he had died after his furious struggle with Professor Moriarty on the ledge at Reichenbach Falls. I was certain that I had seen him fall to his death in those treacherous, swirling currents. I also remember how I fainted when he surprised me several years later in our old rooms. His explanation of how he had cheated death gave me, dare I say it, goose bumps. Yes, I was delighted to have him back, once again most privileged to accompany him as he continued to pursue his chosen profession. Those wondrous days, alas, are now truly gone forever.

Friends, this time Sherlock Holmes is finally at peace. His passing, though shocking to us all, was not totally unexpected. I was informed by his brother Mycroft that he had lapsed into a drug-induced coma from which even he could not escape. A small but select circle of friends, while ever vigilant, had misread some of the signs that he had returned to his 7% solution. We were all led to believe that everything had been going well in his life. Yet, one can only ponder what may have driven him back to that infernal, life-altering addiction.

Perhaps, he sensed the slow demise of his sterling intellect. While a natural component to the aging process, it might have been too much for someone so brilliant to bear. Some speculated that the many strains and aches he had experienced in his career had become too painful for him to endure. Others surmised that he had simply had enough of all that this life had to offer. He was merely "moving on" and doing so on his own terms.

We may never be certain as to what might have moved him to this end for an addiction is what it is. Still, of one thing we can be certain, our dear friend and bosom companion Sherlock Holmes is no more! Sadly, a great loss for good people everywhere, and at the same time, an open invitation for criminal minds to once more ply their evil trades.

Having said all of that, I do believe that Holmes would have been pleased by the solemn, private service held in his memory. Arias from his favorite operas were tastefully rendered by some of London's finest contraltos. Scotland Yard sent its most decorated detachment of kilted bagpipers to the service. The chief inspector, too, along with many of his colleagues honored his memory by their presence. It was nice to see that they finally acknowledged that organization's gratitude and appreciation for the exceptional help Sherlock Holmes had provided over many years.

Mycroft, his faithful brother, provided a most fitting eulogy. Thanks to his eloquent talent for storytelling, those in attendance were privileged to get a brief glance at Sherlock's youthful days. In his remarks, he indicated that his brother was a mischievous lad, a most inquisitive youngster with little time for the conventions of the educational practices employed by the public schools of England.

He then added, "I'm sure that this information comes as no surprise to all of you who have been fortunate enough to have known my dear brother. Sherlock was never a great student when it came to 'traditional' learning. He was, however, exceptionally brilliant when his attention was directed to the many things that were of interest to him." His kind comments brought both smiles and tears from those acquaintances and friends present at the funeral.

At the conclusion of the church service, our dear friend's shiny mahogany coffin was transported to one of his favorite spots, the Tinturn Cemetery. He had long ago confided to me that he had spent a great deal of time meandering among those quiet tombstones as he sought solutions to many of his greatest challenges. There, under a stately oak, was laid the remains of the world's greatest detective!

Holmes, for all his considerable accomplishments and talents, was a most humble and private individual. He left this world in a most fitting ceremony. Never an outwardly religious man, Sherlock believed in a Supreme Being, not in the church-going way, but as someone who had observed logical consequences in the unfolding plans of an orderly universe. No doubt he has, at last, personally experienced and come to understand that eternal mystery which still remains for those of us still looking for the answers to life's questions.

I must confess that my own life has been naturally much less complicated with his passing. I say this not with any great joy but simply as a matter of fact. Of course, I will always miss his friendship and his deductive brilliance. Though I am semi-retired, I still see a few old patients now and again. I, too, am starting to feel the years and am actually beginning to enjoy my free time. My children, Ian and Barton, two successful young physicians, now have families of their own and I frequently play my role as grandfather.

Sadly, I miss my Mary, a wonderful wife and an exceptional mother to my boys. It was on one of our earliest cases that we met. I was quickly swept away by her beauty and grace. I suppose that that's just one more reason I have to thank Holmes for including me in his cases. Had I never gone with him as he unraveled the mystery in <u>The Sign of the Four</u>, I most likely would never have met the love of my life!

Still, always, always in the back of my mind are all the many wonderful adventures I was fortunate enough to have shared with my dear friend. They continue to sustain me and, thankfully, I know that they will never fade from my memory.

All of this background information leads me to the purpose at hand. For as you will soon learn, there was another case that even I, his closest companion, was never privy to for the longest time. So friends, allow me to relate this most curious tale, that in many respects, may be one of the most interesting of all. But that remains to be determined. . .

Hole 1 Burn

One evening along the Firth of Forth, Scotland, 1894. . .

    A dense fog had been steadily moving in from the North Sea along the coastline of the tiny village-town of St Andrews. Ordinarily, the links would still be teeming with golfers who were able to play very late into the August twilight at this time of year. Yet, the thickening fog made the "Old Course" very unsafe for those who loved to chase the "gutty" as the gutta percha golf ball is called.

    Looking out over the fabled golf course, one could barely see the flag on the eighteenth green; a distance of only twenty yards! Still, such weather could actually be a good thing for the course could always use a brief rest now and again. A few extra hours to restore itself and grow some more blades of grass to test the skills of the hundreds of players sure to appear at first light certainly would prove beneficial to that storied parcel of land.

    As the sky continued to darken, the ever-present calls of the terns and sea eagles could be heard through the incoming clouds. The frequent splashing of the cormorants diving for their meals echoed off the stark headquarters of the Royal and

Ancient building, home to a distinguished group of individuals whose commitment to the game of golf knew no bounds.

On this stormy early evening, townspeople could be observed scurrying about in this quiet corner of Scotland, putting the finishing touches to another workday. Drays and various other types of wagons heading here and there all added to the quiet excitement of this murky summer night. There were still all kinds of other sounds that made their way through the approaching mist. Strange sounds, too, they were, arriving on the still mild northeast zephyrs.

Yes, they seemed somewhat unusual but, upon closer scrutiny, they were most familiar to those who play that infernal, demanding, addicting game believed to have been devised by Scottish shepherds. With the shifting wind, breaks in the fog provided the listener with a view to validate what his auditory faculties had been telling him. For in the near distance, someone could be seen striking golf balls out along the beach. That person was striking them with a remarkably solid and predictable cadence. A solitary figure, braving the best that nature could issue, was dutifully working on his game.

There he stood, taking his stance in the now soaking, soggy, gritty sand that was the shore. The howling of the wind and the incoming tide tried to muffle the loud clicks made by his irons as he sent each ball to some unseen target further down the coastline. His iron of choice for this bizarre practice session was a mashie-niblick. It was probably his favorite club. The pace of his swing was a thing of beauty. He took very little time in squaring up and sending ball after ball into the low-lying fog.

The contact was unmistakably pure, as golfers know the sound made by a well-struck ball coming off the sweet spot of an iron. This scenario went on for over an hour with conditions ever worsening. Surely, increasingly darkening skies now accompanied by a blowing horizontal rain, would drive this golfer to seek shelter. One must certainly succumb to those elements or be deemed queer indeed!

Such was not the case. For only after the sun had finally set, did the constant barrage cease to echo along the shoreline. Only then did beams from a lamp appear, flickering through the weather and moving slowly southeast along the water's edge. A few minutes later and the light was carefully lowered to the ground, alarming the small gathering of gulls that had been attracted by the appearance of some 50 golf balls. All of the golfer's "eggs" lay in a tidy circle of less than 5 yards.

Shortly thereafter, the last glimmer of light slowly disappeared and there were only the repetitive sounds of waves breaking over the dunes during a Scottish summer storm. . . .

- - - - - - - - - - - - - - - - - - - -

"E-e-e-o-r-r" creaked the Kelly-green, weather-beaten door that opened into MacTavish's tavern. That squeaky annoyance heralded the arrival of a rather thin, tall middle-aged man. He quickly wiped the "weather" from his Mac, much to the displeasure of some of the nearby patrons who had gathered for their nightly refreshments in that fine old establishment. On his way to the ornate old bar, a very loud "ker-blam-m-m" shook the room as the heavy door returned to its proper position.

"Andy," spoke Angus MacTavish, the proprietor of the tavern, "would ye try to remember not to let that door slam? Ye scared three of me customers into a visit to the loo!"

Half laughing, Andy Kirk turned a bright red and replied, "Then it's a good thing I did let it slam for some of these lads would just as soon leave their work in their trousers!"

"And, my good friend," Kirk continued, "enough about the bloody door. Have ye had a look out across the "Old Course" toward the firth?"

"Not lately, no," answered the short, round tavern owner. "Ye ken I've seen it afore, several times too, as you might imagine. Why do ye ask?"

"Well, on the way over here, I heard some peculiar noises a comin' from the direction of the shoreline. I decided to perambulate over and investigate the situation," Andy reported.

Before Angus could reply, another resident of the town of St Andrews interrupted what had been a private conversation. This rather large redhead wearing a rain-soaked jacket still dripping from the precipitation had ignorantly stepped in front of the proprietor to join the party.

"And ye found what?" inquired Mike Mullen.

"Mullen," MacTavish raised his voice, "he wasn't talking to you, you old bearded eavesdropper."

Andy smiled a nervous smile and continued, "Why, when I arrived there, I ducked behind a small dune, peered through the scrub grass, and what do ye think I saw? Why there was a tall, thin, gangly old man hunched over and smashin' a pile of guttas. He was really smashin' them along the water's edge."

At that remark, there was dead silence. Andy, mouth agape, anxiously waited for some reaction from the assembled patrons.

"Well?" he inquired of the two men.

"Well, what?" Angus answered. "What's so unusual about that? It'd be right next to the golf course, now wouldn't it?"

That response set off a raucous round of guffaws and rowdy laughter from those assembled in one of the many quaint, comfortable dining establishments in the tiny village.

"Angus," Kirk continued, "it's rainin' sideways and it's God-awful cold outside. So, I want to know what in the world a man's doin' hittin' balls out in that weather?"

MacTavish smiled and slowly wiped the bar top with a well-worn rag. He approached Andy slowly and began his response.

"Arrgh, it's no mystery to those of us who've come to know the man of whom yer speakin'," said Angus. "He's been around here for probably over five or six months and he's got himself hooked on the game. He claims he's going to learn to play golf better than anyone that played before him, he is!"

"That so? Well, what would be his name?" asked Andy.

"Dunno," the tavern owner continued, "we all refer to him as 'the Quiet One.'"

"You mean ye don't know who he is?" Andy added. "Has nobody gone and asked him for his name?"

"Would do no good, now would it? Him bein' a mute," interjected Mullen, taking a large gulp from his mug.

"A mute? Ye mean he can't speak?" offered Andy incredulously.

"Well, now, aren't ye the bright one? Of course, he can't speak. Mutes can't speak now, can they? That's why they're called mutes," chided Mullen, tugging his unkempt beard. "All he does is grunt and shake his head this way and that."

Andy scratched his noggin and began again, "Well, ye must ken something about the man? After all, you say he's been here for several months."

The look on his face was priceless as Andy began a veritable litany of questions, "Do ye know what he does for a living? Where might he be stayin'? Does he have a family? Is he Scotch, Irish, British? Why, he could have come here from almost anywhere!"

"Will you shut yer yammer before I do it for ye?" a now much-annoyed Angus MacTavish responded angrily.

At that last remark, the "grand inquisitor" paused, looked around the pub, picked up a tankard of freshly poured ale and sat down at his usual place at the bar. There was a brief pause in the evening's doings as a few more patrons required additional refreshment. The barkeep had enough time to calm down some and slowly made his way back in Andy's direction.

Kirk was a cooper who spent his time golfing when he wasn't working on barrels for the townspeople. He was a little over twelve stone and well over six feet tall with thin, loosely strewn brown hair surrounding a longish, angular face. His blue eyes seemed to twinkle when he smiled and he loved to smile. He was known by all to be a fine broth of a lad.

"Andy, to tell ye the truth, none of us can tell ye too much about him," continued Angus. "Ye see, when he first set foot in this establishment, he kind of took us all by surprise. We didn't know what to think of him. Still, if ye got some time to listen, and if you're that curious, I'll tell ye the little bit I've been able to glean about him."

After buying a round of drinks for his clients, Angus began to detail his initial encounter with "the Quiet One."

"On a particularly rare sunny day in March, this strange gentleman walked into me tavern, found himself a seat at the bar, smiled and began to grunt while pointing to the Guinness tap. Of course I was only too happy to help him slake his thirst, and while he sipped his brew, I tried to help pass the time with some of our polite Scottish conversation. After my first inquiry as to his identity, he shook his head and waved me away.

The look I received from him, I must admit, put me off. Subsequently, I judged it best to leave him alone to his own amusement. Still, I decided to keep an eye on him. As I watched, I tried to imagine what his story was, thinking perhaps that he was just another sad character whose wife had left him. Maybe he was enduring a chronic health problem and was on his way out, so to speak. Perhaps, he was just some old tar who had recently found fishing on the North Sea to be beyond his aging body's ability to cope. You see, I didn't know but could only surmise what he was about.

So I went on about me business, but every now and then, I'd sneak a peek to see if he needed any additional liquid refreshment. He seemed to be a rather tall man. I'd guess him to be over six feet. He had the most piercing eyes I'd ever seen. His nose was hawk-like, but it was difficult to see his features clearly for all of the thick hair on his head; that, and the beard and mustache he seemed to be a-hidin' behind.

Anyway, I continued to tend bar, still creating all kinds of possible backgrounds for this gent in me mind, when he grunts for a second drink. Again I tried to get something out of him. So I ask, 'Well, mate, what brings ye to the quiet village of St Andrews?'

He took a sip from his drink, looked me straight in the eye, and slowly rose from his stool. He smiled and then began to perform a few golf swings, doin' a bit of groanin' as he 'hit' each imaginary golf ball. Furthermore, upon completin' his swing, he acted like he was watchin' its flight, holdin' his finish like he was actually waitin' to see where it landed!

'Oh,' I says to him suspiciously, 'ye be a golfer then?'

He thought about my remark, made a strange face, and turnin', proceeded to 'hit' a few more shots whilst me and me patrons watched him. I have to tell ye, while the first impulse was to laugh at this codger, his intensity was such that the lot of us could almost 'see' him actually strikin' them gutties!

After each ball had 'landed', he'd go to his 'bag' and prepare to take another swing! He kept doin' this until he had finished his imaginary round. I swear he was keeping score!

After that session, he looked around the room, smiled at us and returned to his bar stool for a large sip of stout.

'Ah, yes,' I said, 'I can see that you're a golfer.'

'Ungh,' I think he said, 'Ungh' as he moved his noggin up and down, expressing his response in the affirmative.

As I looked around the bar, most of my clients had a most bedazzled look upon their faces, and frankly, I couldn't blame them. This stranger had us all thinkin' things about him. It

couldn't be helped! We'd never seen his like before that day.
He continued to enjoy his drink. Then, pushing his chair away
from the table, he stood up, took out a quill from his pouch
and grunted; this time pointing to the ink well and a stack of
writing parchment he spied sitting on me desk behind the bar.

I quickly got the gist of his actions and returned with the
needed materials. Apparently he had noticed all of us were
sneakin' peeks at him whenever we could, and he decided to
provide us with some details about himself.

After pullin' some paper from the pile, he clasped the quill
in his left hand, dipped it into the ink, and in a clumsy,
crabbed writin' style he scribbled these lines:

> I have no wish to identify myself.
> It's none of your business. Don't be askin' me!
> I'm here to become a champion golfer.
> Lost the ability to speak many years ago.
> If it's anythin' important, I'll write it out!
> Do you serve food?

At that last line, he slid the paper to me, gruntin' audibly,
what was to become his familiar 'Ungh.'

I quickly scanned the page and informed him that our
specialty of the night was brisket of beef. The answer seemed
acceptable to him as he shook his head and moved to a table
by the window lookin' out over the links. He took his time
gazing out on the 'Old Course' that late afternoon. It was like
he was in a daze. After he had finished eating, he paid his
expenses and quickly disappeared into the night.

Everyone in me tavern was mesmerized by his actions. I
have to admit when he finally left the building we were quite
exhausted from just watching him! The strangest thing was
that all of us who were witness to this 'practice session' swore
that we could actually 'hear' a ball bein' smashed by one of
them imaginary irons that he was a-swishin' before our eyes!

I'm tellin' ye, I had to shoogle meself to get me wits back after he put his 'clubs' away. ***

That was our first meetin' with 'the Quiet One' but it wasn't the last. He's been favorin' us with his presence many more times over the last several months."

MacTavish paused to catch his breath and then added, "Andy, now that ye've got me goin' on about him, I have to confess that I, too, wanted to find out more about him. So I asked around and checked up on him. Surprisingly, many had taken an interest in him and in several conversations with the locals I was able to discover some additional information."

"First, he came by train from London one evening carrying his clubs and two suitcases. I learned that from one of the conductors on duty the night he arrived. He was turned down at the first rooming house he visited. The owner said that the man's ragged appearance scared the livin' snorks out of him.

The Robbies took him in soon afterward. They're fine people and Mrs. Robbie said 'the Quiet One' looked so sad and mournful that she had to take pity on the poor soul.

Sarah Robbie informed him that she and her husband, Carlyle, were the proprietors of the rooming house and that they would need a deposit if he wished to stay with them. She said he opened his pouch, gave her enough money for 6 months rent, bowed and headed to his room.

With that meeting, 'the Quiet One' had found a place to stay. He told them, well, actually, he wrote down, that it was his dream to become a champion golfer. Argyle Street was a mere 2½ blocks from the golf course, making it a short trip back and forth each day.

It didn't take long for him to receive special attention, not that he ever wanted any. He was just so different from the locals. He actually was 'the Quiet One' and more than lived up to the part. Here was someone who truly minded his own business. That's a rare commodity in a small town where everyone knows all about everyone else.

He wouldn't dress in the traditional Scottish manner. A kilt would be out of the question for him. In fact, he was never seen without his baggy old black sweater and ribbed trousers. As we mentioned, his long hair and ragged beard made it very difficult to actually tell what he looked like! His eyes were his best feature. Usually, he was seen wearing a pair of tinted spectacles which made him seem even more mysterious.

So what were his neighbors able to gather from such a person? Very little in the way of personal information was ever put forth by him and he liked it that way. Some citizens had suggested that he was hiding from a past life. Perhaps he was a criminal of some sort, a thief, robber or worse. . . Others suspected that a bad marriage had soured him on women. He was rarely seen in the presence of the fairer sex.

Close friends? Not one of his contacts, be they golfers or fellow rooming-house residents, could ever be counted as a close friend of this very strange recluse. He always treated them courteously, though never overly friendly. To say that 'the Quiet One' was somewhat aloof would most certainly have been considered understatement."

When MacTavish had finally finished, there was dead silence in the room.

"Well, ye got more out a me tonight than I planned, Kirk," spoke the tavern owner.

Andy shook his head, grabbed a swig of his brew, squinted his eyes and voiced, "Incredible! Well, what in the world did ye make of it all?"

It was Mullen's turn again, "What did we make of it? What do ye, yourself, make of it, Andy, ye old foozler? We don't ken much more than that what ye've just heard. We've problems enough of our own!"

MacTavish tried to ease the tension somewhat, offering, "Now, Mullen, Andy's a curious man. 'Tis no crime to be that way, is it? After all, 'the Quiet One' is a stranger in these parts and a bit of a mystery at that!"

Mullen, still in a vile humor, merely shrugged his shoulders and slammed the door on his way out.

"What's with Mullen?" Andy whispered quietly.

Angus answered, "Oh, it's just Mullen bein' Mullen. Take no offense for his mood. He'll be his regular gregarious self come tomorrow evening."

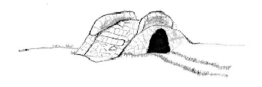

Hole 2 Dyke

A few weeks had passed since Andy Kirk had first witnessed the golfing prowess of the man known as "the Quiet One." He, being on the curious side, continued to walk daily along the shoreline watching the odd, reclusive stranger hit ball after ball with the remarkable precision one might expect of a trained archer shredding the red "bull's-eye" on a hay bale. He made no overtures to the golfer, but, truth be known, he took great pleasure in watching and studying the man's fluid golf swing.

As Kirk would later relate, the man had a very unusual golf swing. He remained flat-footed throughout the entire motion. That is, he was solidly balanced from take-away, through his backswing, and even through impact and into the follow through! That kind of swing would place enormous pressure on a golfer's lower back. Possibly, Kirk surmised, that was the reason for his poor posture. This odd stranger always seemed to be "bent over" with a pained expression on his face. That could be one explanation.

He would never be considered well-dressed in anyone's judgment, for his choice of apparel was, at best, horrid. For one thing, "the Quiet One" always seemed to wear ill-fitting clothing, donning oversized sweaters and pants that appeared far too loose to be comfortable.

Sadly, the man's grooming habits left much to be desired, as well, what with his unkempt beard practically obscuring his facial features. His long hair hadn't been particularly well-cared-for either, and to be blunt, the man truly needed to bathe more regularly.

These realities had not gone unnoticed by the residents of this quaint historic town. It was understandable that some people might be put off by a person having such little regard for his appearance.

Still, Kirk for some reason, wanted to get to know this strange golf savant and he reasoned that if he followed him on a daily basis, a meeting would be inevitable.

Finally, on one such occasion while Kirk was strolling along the North Sea, "the Quiet One" stopped abruptly and looked his way. Apparently, he had polished off his daily quota of iron shots and was gathering the balls. He suddenly turned toward Kirk and, beckoning with his club, invited him to come closer.

Somewhat embarrassed by having been seen, Kirk, at first, was going to turn and walk away. But, looking up, he saw "the Quiet One" waving with even greater agitation. Reluctantly, he decided to accept the man's request and slowly walked over to the stranger.

When he was within arm's distance, "the Quiet One" extended his right hand. After this initial meeting, he presented Andy with a small frayed card that simply read:

Charles Hutchings
London

That was it. That was all Andy saw on the card. Kirk looked up at the man and saw that Hutchings was grinning at him as he gave him the once-over.

"Mr. Hutchings," Andy said smiling, "I'm very honored to make your acquaintance, I'm sure."

"Ungh," was all Charles Hutchings of London replied.

"Beg pardon?" Kirk offered. "What did you say?"

"Ungh," Hutchings repeated with some mild agitation and then suggested with his hands that Kirk turn over the card.

Kirk immediately understood his meaning and flipped the card to find the following words:

> I can talk, but I choose not to do so.
> Please keep this our secret!
> Take no offense at this. It is my chosen way.
> My communication will be non-verbal.

Kirk, after reading the card, looked back at Hutchings, who was smiling at him, shaking his head up and down.

"I see," Kirk responded. "Well, I think I see. Hmm, I guess it'll have to do, won't it?"

Hutchings shook his head in affirmation.

"Well, Mr. Hutchings, I'm a cooper by trade and I play this infernal game every chance I get," explained Andy Kirk.

"I say, old man," Kirk continued his inquiry of the silent stranger, "do you mind me watching you as you practice?"

Hutchings, who was now on about the business of gathering his practice balls, picked up his head and shrugged his shoulders.

"So, it's acceptable to you?" he reiterated.

The response was a positive shake of the head, followed by a resounding "Ungh!"

As he helped Hutchings gather the practice balls, Kirk realized that their meeting had been planned by "the Quiet One," for he had printed that card prior to that occasion. Andy didn't know why he was selected to keep Hutchings's secret, but he thought Hutchings would explain the reason when it was time for him to know.

This was the beginning of their strong friendship. Kirk spent many days and weeks getting to know "the Quiet One." While to most residents of the town, Hutchings was a bit of an outcast, in Andy, he had found a true friend. They could be seen shagging balls along the shoreline whenever the weather would permit.

These men loved the game and Hutchings worked to get Andy to change his swing. He wanted him to flatten his backswing and learn to release the clubhead freely into and through the ball. Sadly, it was a waste of time and effort, for Kirk's barrel-making had made him extremely muscular.

Oh, how he loved the game, its civility and its traditions. Yet, he struggled to play a consistent round. Lesser souls might have tossed it all in, you know, given up. But not Andy Kirk, and perhaps, that was one of the reasons that Charles Hutchings had been drawn to the fine man.

At any rate, they became fast friends, and would play many rounds together, often teaming up against much more balanced opponents. Yet, they rarely lost a match, largely due to the almost daily improvement in Hutchings's play.

After one such outing, Kirk and "the Quiet One" decided to visit MacTavish's Pub for a few draughts. By now, Angus was well used to the foibles and peculiarities of Mr. Charles Hutchings and loved to tease him, as he did to all of his regular clientele. When the duo entered the establishment MacTavish started on them, being careful to use his pet names for two of his favorite customers.

"Well, look who's here," he bellowed. "If it isn't me two favorites, Guinness Andy and his friend, Mr. Grunt!"

Andy and Hutchings smiled, knowing MacTavish treated all of his best patrons to some seemingly harsh but friendly barbs.

"Ungh," Hutchings remarked, quickly raising his thumb to his nose and wiggling his fingers.

At that, all of the pub regulars began to laugh along with Angus MacTavish as he brought them their first round of fine Irish brew.

"So," Angus began, "whose money did the two of ye take today, ye bloody thieves?"

Again some mild rolls of laughter echoed through the smoke-filled bar at the tone of that remark.

"Never ye mind, Angus," Kirk continued, "it's here we'll be spending some of it, that is, if you can keep your mush quiet for a few minutes. My God, man, you're a nosy thing."

"Hmmm," the pub owner sighed, smiling broadly, "I guess I'll get back behind me bar and take care of them that I really cares about."

While Andy and Hutchings sat and conversed, (well, not really conversed in the traditional manner), the broad tavern door swung open and a tall figure wearing a black top hat emerged from the afternoon sunlight. He slowly made his way over to the bar and found a stool. After removing his hat, he smoothed his locks and took a quick glance around the large open-beamed area.

Business was brisk that afternoon and the barkeep had all he could do to keep everyone's tankard full. The newest customer sat patiently waiting to be noticed. MacTavish was still supplying drinks for his regulars, but he nodded to the newcomer, acknowledging his arrival.

The mysterious, tall man had dark bushy eyebrows that gave him a most foreboding appearance. His huge grizzled mustache was neatly trimmed and his deep blue eyes flashed this way and that as he studied the locals who were enjoying this well-established bar. His clothing showed a tasteful elegance and the quality of the material left no doubt that this man spared no expense in his choice of clothier.

Finally, when things quieted down, he caught MacTavish's eye once more and, with a wave of his hand, called him over.

"Give everyone in the house a drink on me, old man," he announced loudly. Cheers rang out, and many of the patrons walked over and clapped the stranger on the back to thank him for his generosity.

MacTavish was equally impressed and after pouring out whiskey and beer for all present, introduced himself. "Sir, my name is Angus MacTavish. I'm the owner and proprietor of this establishment and on behalf of all present, I welcome you and thank you for such a kind gesture."

"You're all quite welcome," the benefactor replied, adding, "my name, by the way, is Colonel C. M. Sebastian and I'm here to play golf."

That introduction produced the expected response, as one old whiskey drinker said with a smile, "Bless you, kind sir, and let me assure you that if that's what you like to do, then you've certainly come to the right place."

"Here, here," the others all joined in.

Sebastian smiled and offered a toast, "Gentlemen, I'll take you at your word. Let's raise our glasses to the town of St Andrews and the 'Old Course,' the finest test of golf in all the world!"

With that being put forth, all concurred, declaring yet another "Here, here!" which led to another round of drinks.

At that point, one of the village elders produced an old squeeze box and began to regale all present with a fine Scottish melody, setting the mood for what would become a long night of drinking and storytelling.

Sebastian smiled and finished his whiskey in one gulp. He looked around the fine old wooden-beamed barroom once more, nodding here and there to those who met his measured, steady, confident gaze. When he spied Kirk and Hutchings seated near the large bay window, he ordered another drink and sauntered over to join them.

"Excuse me, gentlemen," he inquired, "would you mind if I kept you company for a while?" Leaving them little chance to reply, he quickly pulled over a chair and sat down.

"Hutchings, I believe," Sebastian stated extending his hand. "My name is Colonel C. M. Sebastian. I've heard a great deal about you, sir."

Hutchings squinted his dark eyes and slowly took Sebastian's hand and gave it a firm shake offering his famous "Ungh!" as he did so.

At that response, Sebastian stood up and backed away seemingly offended by the remark .

"What? What did you say?" he inquired angrily.

"Mr. Sebastian," Kirk spoke, moving quickly to head off a possible misunderstanding. "Please, sir, my friend, Charles, meant no harm with his remark. He doesn't speak. Virtually all of his communication is by hand gestures or the written word. Please take no offense."

"Is that so?" Sebastian replied in a much more subdued voice. "And you, who are you, sir, if you don't mind?"

"My name is Andy Kirk, Colonel," he offered. "I consider myself one of Charles's best friends and I can vouch for his character, if it comes to that."

"Forgive my reaction," the tall man implored. "I didn't know what you said, Mr. Hutchings. I do beg your pardon."

Hutchings stood up, smiled, bowed, and issued another "Ungh." After shaking hands with Sebastian and Kirk, he quickly bowed to both parties and, waving to all, walked out of the front door and into the late afternoon light.

Sebastian stared at the closed door, somewhat confused by what had just transpired.

"Please understand, Mr. Sebastian," Kirk suggested, "my friend, as you have seen, travels to the beat of a different drum. I can assure you, he bears you no ill will. It was simply time for him to go back to his practice."

"Practice?" Sebastian inquired, "do you mean that man is a medical doctor in addition to being such a dedicated golfer?"

Kirk suddenly burst out laughing. "Please excuse me, Mr. Sebastian," Andy continued, "Charles is certainly not of the medical profession. When I said 'practice', I meant he needed to practice his golf."

C.M. Sebastian still seemed a bit perplexed, twisting his head and curling his lips.

"You see, sir," Kirk continued, "Charles Hutchings, while a bit on the eccentric side, is, as you may have heard, one of the finest golfers in Scotland or anywhere else in the world, for that matter."

"What? That man.....a championship golfer?" Sebastian asked with incredulity, scratching the top of his head.

"Yes, indeed," Andy reaffirmed his previous statement. "Despite his appearance and his inability to speak, I have come to know and respect him as a truly fine, honorable human being who possesses a true aptitude for golf."

"Well, that's good to hear," Sebastian continued almost to himself. "I dare say I"ll wager that people think him a bit off-putting when first they meet him. . . ."

Suddenly, changing the subject, Sebastian asked, "Say, do you think there's any chance that he might join us, you and me, for a game tomorrow?"

"Thank you for the invitation, Mr. Sebastian," Kirk replied. "I'm afraid that we'll have to decline your kind offer. You see, Charles and I have already scheduled matches for the next several days, but I thank you for asking us. Perhaps we can get together sometime in the future. How may we contact you to arrange a match?"

"Mr. Kirk," Sebastian responded, "I'll be staying at the Old Course Hotel directly off the wonderful seventeenth hole. I look forward to hearing from you and your friend. Hopefully, we can get together soon."

Both men rose from the table and shook hands. Sebastian waved to MacTavish on the way out, and walking briskly, left the quaint tavern.

Andy Kirk returned to his table and ordered another Guinness. He was somewhat perplexed about the afternoon's events. He had no idea how "the Quiet One" would react to the invitation. He also had many questions about this new acquaintance, C. M. Sebastian. It struck him as very odd indeed that a perfect stranger would immediately offer a golfing invitation to two individuals he had newly met! It was considered very presumptuous in these parts.

After he had finished serving an older couple next to Kirk, Angus MacTavish pulled out a chair and joined him.

"Hey, Andy," he asked, "what de ye think about that man?"

"Angus," Kirk continued, "what would you be thinkin' about a stranger who just bought a round of drinks fer people he had never met before?"

MacTavish put down his wash towel, crossed his arms, fashioned a quizzical expression on his face and replied, "Andy, Andy, Andy.... I, too, have only just met this fellow. What can I possibly be thinkin' about him, 'ceptin' for the fact that he just spent a good amount of shillings at me establishment!"

Kirk shook his head in agreement but quickly added, "Aye, that's true enough, Angus, but did ye' form any opinion of him, if even for just havin' met him?"

"What are ye' gettin' at, Andy?" questioned the proprietor of MacTavish's pub.

"Nothin' really," spoke the other. "It's just that there does seem to be somethin' peculiar about him. I dunno why I feel this way. He just seemed a little too sure of himself. Ya' know, buyin' everyone drinks and comin' over to Charles and me, uninvited and all..."

"Lad, I can see what you're tryin' to say about the man," said Angus, "but I don't see any harm in a newcomer introducing himself in such a 'friendly' manner. I wouldn't spend too much time analyzing his actions. I'm sure they were done out of genuine good intentions."

At that, MacTavish rose and headed back to tend to his customers. Andy Kirk finished his drink and started for his apartment. He only lived "a good spoon's distance" from the Starter's shed, as he often told his friends.

There was still some daylight remaining when Andy left the tavern. He took about five steps, then suddenly stopped. For out across the dunes, he could see his friend Charles Hutchings and his familiar swing, practicing long and hard, as he always did after a day's golf. That routine was to be expected. What was not expected, was the presence of a tall man in a top hat crouching behind a grassy hillock, observing "the Quiet One's" every move!

That struck Andy as a bit strange. Kirk was concerned with what he saw, but he hardly had any need of worrying for his friend's safety. Charles Hutchings could take care of himself. Of that Andy was certain. Kirk had witnessed his strength on many occasions. Most recently, they had seen a Clydesdale straining to pull its milk wagon out of a very muddy section of Church Road. The rear wheels were stuck halfway up the axles and the poor horse was having a most difficult time.

Kirk and Hutchings happened upon that poor animal on the way to the golf course. There they saw the horse snorting and bucking as it tried to pull the wagon from the mire. Hutchings quickly dropped his clubs and ran over to the rear of the wagon, himself sinking deeply into the mud. Quickly rolling up his sleeves, he grabbed the left rear section of the wagon, filled with the day's delivery, and raised that end of the conveyance up and out of the mud.

The delighted milkman cracked the whip, and the fine old horse gave a mighty pull, extricating the cart from its condition. Soon, the wagon started up again, safely conveying bottles of milk to the anxious villagers of St Andrews. Hutchings, now covered in muck and mire, picked up his clubs, signaled to Kirk, and continued walking to the course.

News spread like wild-fire about the amazing feat of strength performed by "the Quiet One," and this little community would never forget him for that kindness.

Remembering that early morning show of strength helped Andy to decide to leave the situation as it was. He knew his friend could fend for himself. Turning for home, he picked up his pace, for he realized the evening winds were beginning to strengthen. That usually signaled a storm. While rare, you didn't want to get stuck in a summer tempest that close to the North Sea. . . .

Hole 3 Cartgate Out

The morning air was fresh and sweet as the players
approached the first tee of the venerable "Old Course" at St
Andrews. Long gone from this tranquil town were the fierce
lightning strikes and thunderous storm clouds that had roared
through the region the previous evening. Aside from a few
puddles on the adjacent roadway, one might have never
guessed just how much rain St Andrews had received, such
were the absorbent qualities of the linksland. Summer storms
of such violence were rare in this part of Scotland, but, that
said, all golfers appreciated the benefits rain afforded in
keeping courses healthy and in the finest condition possible.

The foursome readying themselves on the first tee was
anxious to play that day, for this had been arranged many
weeks prior. It was one of the more popular formats played
on the "Old Course," alternate shots by teams of two
gentlemen. Normally, there would be a polite wager to keep
things interesting, but nothing outrageous, for the golfers
involved were more concerned with bragging rights than in
visiting their opponents' purses. This match, however, would
be different. There were some hard feelings carried over from
an earlier match. Today's round was to settle a score, or
perhaps not. . .

Mike Mullen and James Tolliver were competing against the
team of Andy Kirk and his partner, Charles Hutchings, "the
Quiet One." Mike and James were lifelong residents of the

area. Andy came here from Tunnykirk in 1870, but his partner
was still a relative newcomer to the Kingdom of Fife.

Today's match had been put together several weeks ago,
while sitting in the "Old Course" clubhouse. It seemed that
Kirk, Mullen and Tolliver had been discussing the particulars
of the round they had just completed, when Mullen suddenly
raised his voice displaying the kind of emotion evident when
someone's honor has been challenged.

"Kirk," Mullen offered, "I'll tell you what we're going to do.
We'll play another match, this time a foursome. Tolliver and I
will compete against you and any partner whose services you
choose to employ. We'll soon put a stop to your whining, you
miserable turd!"

"Easy now, Mike," interjected Tolliver, "Kirk here only
suggested that we had played uncharacteristically well today."

Mike turned on his partner Tolliver, now questioning him,
"What are you sayin', man? Why, the miserable squint accused
us of cheatin' now, din't he?"

"I only suggested that the two of you played much better
than your handicap would indicate," replied the squint.

"What I meant, Mr. Mullen," continued Kirk, "was that we
played today's match with you and Tolliver each receiving a
stroke a hole, when clearly that was far too generous an offer,
seeing as how ye both scored 97 and myself an 89. I'm
looking for a little fairness in our next match. That's all I'm
saying. . . Let's just agree to a half-one." (Players would
receive one shot on alternate holes)

Tolliver and Mullen conferred quietly at the corner table
and after some small discussion responded to Kirk's offer.

"Done. We'll play you and your partner, whoever it may be,
and we'll only take the half-one," Mullen thundered. "But,
we'll be playin' for more than the day's libations. How does
five pounds a hole sound to you?"

Kirk scratched his head for a moment and then nodded his
approval of the match as well as the time and date.

"I'm agreeable, gents," said he, after which Mullen stormed out of the room.

The date for the match had finally arrived. When the parties first appeared at the starting house, only Kirk knew whom his partner would be. Upon realizing that "the Quiet One" was their fourth, both Mullen and Tolliver seemed relieved. They feared that Kirk would select one of the area's finest players as his partner, and that could have spelled disaster for them. Little did they know. . .

Tolliver had chided Mullen the day after the match had been arranged, for Mullen had not specified the type of player Kirk would be allowed to select. Had he so desired, Kirk could have chosen any of Scotland's finest players, a golfer much more skilled than any of his opponents, thereby claiming the match before it had ever begun. But that was not his way. Kirk only wanted a fair match, one that would be closely contested, for he truly enjoyed a challenging golf match.

"Gentlemen," spoke Kirk, "I'd like you to meet my partner. You've seen him before, but you've never formally met him. Shake hands with Mr. Charles Hutchings of London."

A smile came to Mullen's face as he offered his hand, "So, you're his choice? Glad to formally make your acquaintance, though your choice of friends I do question."

"Don't mind my partner," James Tolliver offered. "He's only jestin'. I'm James Tolliver and I'm very glad to finally meet you, I'm sure."

Charles Hutchings bowed to both men, producing his well-known, "Ungh."

The rules for the day were discussed and it was determined that Tolliver and Mullen would have the honors.

As Kirk and his partner watched, Tolliver began his practice ritual, a rapid series of swings followed by pinching an exact amount of sand upon which he carefully placed his golf ball. He next would back away from his ball, stand some three paces directly behind the target line, turn his head sideways, closing one eye while he studied his shot.

After lining it up, he would step up to the ball, take one waggle and proceed to launch his low-flying slice toward the hole. As expected, Tolliver's ball ended up in the middle of the fairway, though never as far as he wished.

Mullen was already smoothing his teeing-sand before his partner's ball had stopped rolling. Before you could say "Old Tom Morris", Mullen's ball was on its way, splitting the fairway with his low draw, some 80 yards short of the Swilcan Burn.

Kirk and his partner watched both of their opponents play their tee shots and said nothing. They nodded to each other. Judging by their opponents shots, they knew that they would be in for most interesting and challenging day of golf.

Kirk asked his partner, "Charles, would you like to start us off?"

"The Quiet One" shook his head in the affirmative, responding, "Ungh!"

At that reply, Mullen looked at Tolliver and rolled his eyes, unaware that he had been seen by Mr. Hutchings as he was addressing his ball.

Hutchings slowly stepped up to the ball and executed a smooth balanced swing, launching his shot high and straight, right down the middle, a mere forty yards from the pin.

Kirk clapped his partner on the back and praised the shot, "That was nicely executed, Charles."

Taking a brassie from his bag, Kirk took his stance, waggled the club and proceeded to foozle his shot a mere hundred yards into the right rough.

"Nice one, Kirk," Mullen chimed in, "I guess your partner didn't know what he was getting himself into! Ha! Ha!"

"The Quiet One" gave Mullen a dirty look but said nothing. He just winked to Kirk and they strode down the first fairway.

Andy Kirk pretended to be worried about the match. He knew that he was not a good golfer, but he also knew how fine a player his chosen partner was, having watched him hit balls along the shoreline at low tide. His main purpose for challenging his opponents to this match was a bit selfish. Both men loved to brag about their golf games and, to be fair, they were not bad players, not bad at all. Still, Kirk was tired of their self-praise and wanted to teach them a lesson.

When Kirk arrived at his ball, he realized that he couldn't fly his gutta long enough to carry the only water hazard on the course, so he wisely laid up short of the burn. His opponents quickly seized the opportunity to comment.

Tolliver, tipping his tam, spoke first, "Mr. Mullen, did you see how nicely Mr. Kirk played his second shot? Now, why do ye' suppose he's gone and done such a thing?"

Smiling as he responded, Mullen growled, "Why, maybe Andy's afraid he might lose his brand new ball!"

Both men laughed at the remark with Mullen clapping Tolliver on the back as they strode past Kirk.

Hutchings pretended not to hear their calloused jesting, but the scowl on his face indicated that he, indeed, had heard their teasing. He mumbled to himself as he took the niblick from his golf bag and took a practice swing.

Kirk reassured him, "Charles, don't let them get your goat. That's their way. They mean no harm."

Tolliver's second shot had found the rough to the right of the first green while Mullen's mashie stopped rolling a mere two yards right of the flag.

"Let's see ye' get inside o that 'un, Hutchings?" challenged the ever-annoying Mullen.

Hutchings took two practice swings and knocked his approach ten feet past the pin, and then spun it back to tap-in range for a birdie!

Winking at Kirk, he replaced his club and waited for his partner to play his shot over the Swilcan Burn. Andy waggled and quickly played a conservative pitch shot that rolled out fifteen yards past the hole. It was a decent shot, but his partner had already been conceded his three, so he picked up his ball.

As Tolliver approached the green, he knocked Hutchings's ball back toward him, remarking, "That was a fine shot, sir, a fine shot!"

His chip shot stopped four feet short of the hole and so it was up to Mullen to tie the hole.

"I guess I should be able to handle this one, gentlemen," he offered as he stroked his ball toward and directly into the cup. With the stroke they were getting, Mullen's 3 -1 =2, beating Hutchings's birdie.

"Fine stroke, Mullen. You've always been a great putter," Kirk offered as the men moved to the second hole.

On their way to the tee box, Kirk saw Hutchings waving to someone near the dune on the right. When Andy turned to see who it was, there was no one in sight. He was just about to ask "the Quiet One" whom he had seen when C. M. Sebastian appeared coming over the dunes.

"Good morning, gentlemen," he said. "It seems that you have a wonderful day to play. By the way, I hope you don't mind if I tag along to observe the match. It's always a treat to watch better players."

"Why, who the hell are you?" Mike Mullen asked sullenly. "Who invited you to our little match?"

Kirk quickly interjected, "Mr. Mullen, Mr. Tolliver, let me introduce you to Mr. C. M. Sebastian, a fan of the game and an avid golfer, I've been told."

"Thank you, Kirk," Sebastian responded. "Mr. Mullen...Mr. Tolliver...It's a pleasure to meet you both. I promise that you'll not even know that I'm around. I merely want to see how you gentlemen play this game, you know. Perhaps I can pick up some pointers!"

"Sebastian is it?" inquired Mullen. "Well, if that's your plan and you keep your word, Tolliver and I will certainly have no objections."

C. M. Sebastian bowed in acknowledgment and quickly began to walk up the left side of the fairway. While the foursome waited until Sebastian had moved out of range, Mullen tapped Andy on the shoulder.

"Hey, why is that Sebastian fellow here?" questioned Mullen. "Did you bring him along to help find your wild shots?"

"Ungh!" growled Hutchings at the wild accusation offered by one of their opponents.

"What kind of answer is that, Hutchings?" spoke Mullen again, responding to the angry tone in "the Quiet One's" reply.

"Mike," interjected Andy Kirk, "my partner and I have no idea why that gentleman decided to observe our play today. Your implication is totally lacking in merit, so I must ask you to retract it. . . "

Clearly, Hutchings and Kirk were angered by Mullen's suggestion and the match could have ended then and there, had it not been for Tolliver's calm demeanor.

"Gentlemen, let's forget about this stranger and get on with our match," he offered. "Mullen, it's none of our business if this Sebastian person chooses to walk the golf course. It is open to the entire community, after all."

"I guess I was a bit put off, surprised to see this fellow come out of nowhere to observe us," Mullen offered in a much more subdued voice. That would be as close to an apology as Mullen could ever advance, but it was good enough for play to continue.

For the next several holes, the match remained even. It was marked by consistent drives from Mullen and Tolliver, less-than-ideal shots by Kirk, and some brilliant play by Hutchings. Sebastian, for his part, remained well away from the golfers, but clearly he was paying close attention to one individual in particular.

With each hole, it became obvious that he was studying the style and golfing ability of "the Quiet One," and he was not disappointed. After a close match for thirteen holes, Kirk and

Hutchings were still down one hole, although they played very well. Things were not looking too good for them when Hutchings's drive on the 14th caught one of the "Beardies". Kirk had done even worse, foozling both his tee-ball and his second shot, the latter ending up out of bounds.

Their opponents had both laced their drives in the fairway and had successfully hit their second shots in play. Both opponents would easily reach the green in regulation figures. Hutchings's terrible lie in the bunker only allowed him to advance his ball a short distance. When he prepared to play his third shot, he realized that he still had 270 yards to the green and his lie was not the best.

Knowing his partner was out of the hole, he considered laying up short of the green, but that would mean an "up and down" from there for a par. As he studied his shot, he looked at his partner, shrugged his shoulders and placed his hand on his mashie-niblick. Clearly, he was planning a lay up!

Kirk knew that "the Quiet One" was looking for advice and turned to check the distance to the green. When he looked back at Hutchings, he saw that his partner had returned the iron to the bag and was now holding the brassie in his hands.

Catching Kirk's eye, Hutchings offered his familiar, "Ungh?", this time with a questioning manner of grunt.

Kirk peered at his opponents, re-examined the distance, returned to his partner and said, "What the hell, Charles, why don't ye go fer it!"

With that, Hutchings took the fairway wood and launched a beauty that soared high into the cloudless blue sky; the ball drawing into a left-to-right breeze, landing and skipping up to and on the putting surface. Their opponents were stunned at the shot and even Mullen had to applaud the effort, "Hell of a shot, Hutchings.... simply magical..."

When the players had reached the green they were amazed to see Hutchings's ball a mere foot from the cup! It was too close to make him putt it. Mullen and Tolliver reluctantly conceded the birdie 4. After witnessing Hutchings's incredible shot, both golfers were so shaken up that their own efforts came up woefully short.

C. M. Sebastian was seen scribbling some notes as the group proceeded to the 15th tee. He seemed genuinely interested in the outcome of the match, but no one really understood why he was so concerned.

With the match all-square, there were four holes to play. Clearly, the momentum had swung in the direction of Kirk and Hutchings, for the play of Mullen and Tolliver began to suffer. They lost number 15 to a bogie, even with a 1-shot deduction, and they lost number 16 when "the Quiet One" birdied the hole, sinking a 40 yard putt from the far edge of the adjoining double-green 2nd hole!

Up two holes with but two holes to play, Kirk and Hutchings were now dormie. That meant that the best their opponents could do was to tie them! It was do-able, but most improbable, especially the way Hutchings was playing.

Apparently, Sebastian had had enough, for the players saw him trudging slowly off the course and straight into the front door of the Old Course Hotel.

The penultimate hole was tied with bogey, including the stroke that was given! That was that. Begrudgingly, Mullen and Tolliver doffed their caps and congratulated the duo.

"Fine play, Hutchings," offered Tolliver. "Your practice sessions have really paid off, man. Why your play even seems to have rubbed off on old Kirk there..."

That remark brought a smile and some hearty laughter from the entire foursome. The group had only one hole to play and, even though the match had been decided, they agreed to play the eighteenth anyway.

All four players settled for par on that famous finishing hole that brought them right back into the middle of St Andrews. There were always townfolk watching the players finishing up on the last hole and occasionally some mild applause would issue forth if a particularly excellent shot was properly executed.

When the last putt had been holed, the weary golfers shook hands and quickly retired to the tavern directly across the road to settle their bets and share drinks. Yes, the nineteenth hole was a wonderful place for golfers to discuss the good and bad shots of the day and today would prove to be no exception.

As the golfers entered MacTavish's tavern, drinks were already poured and waiting for them at the bar.

"Wonderful golf, gentlemen!" praised Colonel Sebastian, appearing out of nowhere. "I took the liberty of ordering libations to celebrate the great play I witnessed out there today. Also, I wish to thank you for indulging my presence and allowing me to accompany you on the course."

"Well, now, Sebastian," spoke Mullen slugging down his ale, "thank ye kindly. I guess I'll need to have a different opinion of ye after this. . ."

Sebastian smiled, but he wasn't amused. Apparently, he didn't care for the tone or content of Mullen's clever barb.

"Yes, Mr. Sebastian," added Kirk, "very decent of you. Thanks!"

"Ungh," mumbled Hutchings, raising his tankard.

"Guess it's my turn to show my gratitude, friend," uttered Tolliver. "How about you, Sebastian? What'll ye have?"

"Mister.....ah....Tolliver, is it?" Sebastian responded. "I believe that I'll take you up on your generous offer if you, gentlemen, will allow me to join you for a few minutes. What say you, all?"

Kirk sensed the apprehension of the group and decided to take the lead.

"Why Mr. Sebastian," he stated, "speaking for all of us, if I might be so bold, we would be honored to have you visit with us. Pull up a chair."

After a polite, but sincere "Splendid", Sebastian pulled his bar stool closer to the foursome, now a fivesome.

It had been a long day on a crowded golf course, but with the addition of several rounds of drink, it soon grew into a long evening!

During the course of the golf conversation, four of the men talked on and on about this most recent match, the great shots and the poor ones as well. As time wore on, Sebastian became more comfortable with the men and proved to be a skilled raconteur. His golf tales were the equal of any that had been told that day. His understanding and appreciation for the game was easily observed and heartily acknowledged by those who had gathered to listen.

When asked about his own level of play, he stated, not immodestly, that he considered himself a better than average golfer. He further stipulated that he had plans to improve his play so as to compete for the Open this year.

At this, there was some "eye-rolling", accompanied by mild guffaws. Suddenly, he realized that he had indeed said too much.....much too much, for these men had only his word to rely upon, never having seen him play.

"Please forgive my bragging," he implored. "You fellows have just met me and just listen to how I've gone on about my playing ability!"

Charles Hutchings had been silently watching for a while now, sipping on his scotch. Sensing the disquieting mood that had suddenly arisen, he grabbed his pencil and pad and printed the following question for Sebastian.

Rising to his feet, he walked over and handed the paper to the newcomer.

As Sebastian read the question, he read it aloud as Hutchings had requested:

> "Colonel Sebastian, we have enjoyed your company
> and your tales immensely. Please tell us, if you
> would, more about yourself to help us get to know you
> better. . . "

"Ah, yes, Hutchings," Sebastian replied, "that would be the proper thing to do now, wouldn't it?."

He took a long sip from his tankard and began to relate the following narrative:

"Gentlemen, I apologize for not having had the decency to properly introduce myself, especially since we've had such a great afternoon together. I am Colonel C. M. Sebastian, a rank I achieved while serving with the 1st Bangalore Pioneers in the Indian campaign. A native of London, I was born in 1840, raised as the stepson of Sir Augustus Moran. You may have heard of my late stepfather. He served at His Majesty's pleasure as the Minister to Persia. My schooling took place at Eton and Oxford."

He continued:

"At the moment, I am currently self-employed. Most recently I penned two books; <u>Heavy Game of the Western Himalayas</u> in 1881 and <u>Three Months in the Jungle</u> in 1884.

I hold memberships in the Anglo-Indian, Tankerville and Bagatelle clubs, all of London. As you might gather from that list, I enjoy gambling. I am currently still a citizen of London, living on Conduit Street. I dearly love to travel and, most recently, I have become relatively infatuated with this marvelous game. That, gentlemen, will give you a better idea as to who I am and I thank you for your kind attention."

"That's quite a mouthful, Sebastian," mouthed Mullen. "From what ye've told us, I'm glad you're on our side!"

Mullen's attempt at humor was greeted with polite laughter, but they'd all had a long day and the conversation was turning bland.

Shortly, thereafter, the gentlemen rose as one, and bid one-to-each a friendly handshake before departing for the night. Another golf match had been played with winners and losers sitting together to drink and replay some of their memorable and maybe not-so-memorable shots. These men had done their best, win or lose. They were heading home from their day's play, none the worse for wear, but so much the better for the game.

The streetlights were just being lit and a bright moon shone steadily through the evening mists that made their way to shore. A mild breeze echoed through the quiet little village and another beautiful day on the links would soon have come and gone. . .

Hole 4   Ginger Beer

A mild, foggy mist was accosting the sleepy town of St
Andrews on one particular Sunday morning. It was the kind of
weather, chilly and damp, that was better used for rolling over
and staying in the "sack" for a few more minutes, or even
hours. The gulls didn't mind, though, and their continuous
shrieking made it quite uncomfortable for many of the
inhabitants who were trying to enjoy some extra rest, safe and
snug in their warm beds.

Also, it being a Sunday, churchgoers needed to "rise and
shine," requiring many of the faithful to tend to their spiritual
sustenance. It certainly wouldn't do to miss the Church
service. For one thing, the minister, as well as your fellow
parishioners, might notice your absence. Put in more familiar
parlance, people would talk.... That was the way it was... and
the way it still is, at least in most parts of Scotland.

Charles Hutchings hated Sundays. Oh, it wasn't because he
was an atheist, or even an agnostic, for he did believe in a
Supreme Being. It wasn't because he disliked to go to the
Sunday service, because he usually did attend the local
Presbyterian proceedings. It most assuredly wasn't because
he cared a rodent's arse about what others might say if he
failed to appear. As a matter of fact, his intense dislike for the
day wasn't about religion at all!

Can you guess? Think you know? Well, "the Quiet One"
detested the "day of rest" simply because golf was not allowed

to be played on the "Old Course" on that day of the week! That's correct. Years and years ago, the locals who governed the land had determined that on one day in each week, their fabled golf course would be closed to golfers. They specified that this edict was proposed and made into law, so that the grounds had a chance to recover from all of the play it normally received the other six days.

The course and surrounding natural areas were also considered public property and on Sundays, residents of St Andrews used the land for walking, conducting picnics and playing with their children. Every local golfer knew that was the case and accepted it without making too much of a fuss. Every local golfer? Well, every one except Charles Hutchings, lately from London, England. As a matter of fact, some of his fellow golfers still talk about "the Quiet One's" minor "run-in with the law" when he first came to St Andrews.

It seems that on Charles's first Sunday in St Andrews, he was particularly eager to play golf. The problem for him, was that it was Sunday. Actually, he had gotten up "before the roosters." After washing and slipping into his Sunday best, he made his way to one of the kirks in the region and attended services. Immediately upon returning to his room, he quickly changed into his golf togs, grabbed a piece of a Scottish scone and headed for the course, golf bag over his shoulder.

The sun was shining brightly, the air crisp and clean and only a mild zephyr to influence the flight of a golf ball. In short, it was a perfect day to golf, but then again, in Scotland, every day's a perfect day to golf. It's the weather that sometimes complicates the slogan!

Charles was grunting a melody of some kind when he turned the last corner around the building belonging to the Royal and Ancient Society of Golfers. As he placed his clubs along the bag rail, the rugged beauty that was linksland golf stunned his senses. He felt humbled by the experience. Immediately, he was struck by his unbelievable good fortune.

For when "the Quiet One" looked out over the first tee, turning toward the starter's shed, he found not one player anywhere in sight! There was not another golf bag to be found!

As he later informed his friends, he was shocked, to say the least. His mouth was wide-open and he grinned perhaps the widest grin he had ever grinned. He couldn't believe that there were no golfers out to play on a day like this one!

Here he was, at 9:45 A.M., on the first tee at the "Old Course" at St Andrews, and no one to be seen anywhere! He couldn't imagine such a scenario at this time of day. Where was everyone? There were no clubs, no caddies, no starter....He was both confused and elated beyond measure...

Still dumbstruck, he looked over the two adjacent holes, numbers one and eighteen, and he became a bit agitated at what he did see. For many groups of townspeople, their children and friends were making their way across Granny Clark's Wynd, a road that ran from the downtown to the dunesland and the North Sea beyond.

"What the hell are they doing?" he wondered aloud in one of his familiar grunts, "Ungh?" This would not do. How could anyone golf with so many people heedlessly walking across the fairways? It was wrong. He would remedy this situation posthaste. Charles decided to loosen up things by launching a few warm-up shots off the first tee into the midst of the oblivious citizenry. The nerve of them, disrupting a game of golf by ignoring the golfers while they tried to play.

Quickly and vigorously he moved his clubs to the first tee and stretched with a few agitated practice swings. A minute later he was teeing his ball on a tiny packed pinch of wet sand, still beaming grandly at his unparalleled good fortune. He was lining up for the shot, when, just as he started his backswing, a loud whistle split the sweet morning air. It sounded like a police whistle, so he stopped and turned.

Sure enough a town constable, dressed in black, came dashing over the rail, down the slope and running over the closely manicured teeing ground, device in mouth, whistling of course, and pointing directly at Charles Hutchings.

"Stop, man," yelled the policeman spitting the whistle from his lips. "What in the world do ye think you're doin'?"

Hutchings, dropped his head, looked around to see if the officer was speaking to someone else, and shrugging his shoulders voiced, "Ungh?"

"What did you call me?" the constable offered as he grabbed the "grunter" by the arm. "Did you call me an oaf? Why I oughta..."

Charles Hutchings shook his head indicating that he did not call anyone anything and quickly took out his writing pad and pencil. He hurriedly scribbled his response and carefully handed it to the official. It read as follows:

> "Officer, I humbly beg your pardon. I didn't call
> you any name at all. I do not talk and what you
> actually heard was my voice expressing surprise at
> what I was experiencing. Oh, and why did you
> put your hands on me?"

"What's this?" the policeman asked when he received Hutchings's note. As he read the short message, the lawman grew even more agitated.

"Oh, is that what that noise was, eh?" the officer responded. "Well, you're going to have to come with me anyway. A golfer trying to play the "Old Course" on a Sunday. The nerve of you, sir!"

Hutchings gave the law officer a strange, quizzical look, as if he couldn't believe what he was hearing."

Before he knew what was happening, three more policemen made their way towards him, the whistling having caught their attention. One "copped" him by the collar, another grabbed his golf clubs and the initial "whistle-blower" began to fill out an arrest paper.

Thus, unceremoniously, the constables removed "the Quiet One" from the first tee and, crossing the street, led him to a holding cell in the headquarters building.

It was only blind luck that Carlyle Robbie, Hutchings's landlord, was passing by with his family on their way for a day at the beach.

Surprised and appalled by what he had just witnessed, he explained to his wife that he'd be back in a few minutes.

"Look, dear," he said, "the police have poor Charles. I've got to go and see about him."

When Mr. Robbie finally caught up with the police, they had already entered the office and moved to the sergeant's desk. Indeed, they seemed to be filling out a report.

"Gentlemen," he cried, "please hold on for one moment, if you would."

"Beg pardon, sir?" the sergeant inquired of the recent intruder. "And why, now, would we stop what we're doing, as if it's any business of yours?"

"Officer," Carlyle Robbie explained, "this man is Charles Hutchings. He's a fine man and I'm of the belief that he's not guilty of having deliberately committed any crime. I can't think of any reason for you to be charging him."

"Don't be so sure about that, laddie," responded the policeman in no uncertain terms. "He called me an oaf when I arrested him for violating the 'Old Course' Sunday curfew."

Another officer joined in, "What do ye think of that Mister, ah, Mister. . . What's yer name?"

"Pardon my manners, officers," the landlord offered. "My name is Carlyle Robbie. I happen to run a boarding house and I've come to know Mr. Hutchings and I believe there must be some misunderstanding that we can resolve amicably."

At these remarks, the officers sat Hutchings down on a bench and began to talk quietly among themselves. As they spoke, they would occasionally look over at Hutchings and turn to examine his spokesman. This went on for a while when they were interrupted again.

"You see, sirs," Robbie continued, "he doesn't speak. He only grunts and gestures to communicate, he does. As far as the Sunday curfew violation is concerned, I'm of the opinion that he never heard of it. You see, Charles is new to Scotland. He only arrived here last Monday. If I may be so bold, gentlemen, I don't believe this man would ever willfully break this law or any law, for that matter."

At that last comment, the sergeant held up his hand, paused, and spoke, "Mr. Robbie, ah, that's yer name, right? Well, we'll take you at your word and release this Hutchings fellow. Be advised, that should this happen again, we'll double the fine and jail time. Is that understood by the both of you?"

"Certainly," Robbie answered. "Thank you, officers!"

"Ungh. . . Ungh. . .", replied Mr. Charles Hutchings, doffing his cap and shaking the sergeant's hand as he left the precinct house.

Once outside, Hutchings opened his tablet and scribbled, a quick note, handing it to his landlord:

> "Mister Robbie, thank you so much for interceding on my behalf. Everything happened so quickly. I was stunned, truly stunned. That was the first that I had ever heard of that law and, as strange as it appears, it does make sense. The course does see a lot of play."

After handing him the note, Robbie read it, clapped him on the back and addressed him, "You're welcome, Charles. Don't give it a second thought. I'll see you later at the house."

With that the landlord dashed across the fairways and joined his wife and family for a fine afternoon along the Scottish coastline.

That had been the first time Charles Hutchings ever heard of the Sunday curfew and his rude introduction to it could have been even more embarrassing had it not been for the intervention by his landlord. While he didn't particularly like the ordinance, he would not break the law. He decided to reserve Sundays for getting better acquainted with the lovely old town and surrounding areas.

At first, he had great difficulty being away from the addictive sport he had come to love so much. He believed that every minute away from the game was a minute of practice lost. When he thought of all the time he missed practicing because of the curfew law, it made him physically ill. . . at first!

Little did he know that the Sunday ordinance was a blessing in disguise, especially for someone so caught up in the addictive aspects of the game.

When he finally resigned himself to accept the law, his life became much more balanced. Each Sunday was a day for Charles Hutchings to become more familiar with his adopted home. Before this change in lifestyle, he was totally one-dimensional. He was Charles Hutchings, the golfer. There were very few people in his early days at St Andrews whom he could properly call "friends," just not many at all!

Then one Sunday, he decided to visit the ruins of the famous old cathedral overlooking the North Sea. Up bright and early, Charles packed a light lunch, filled his flask with some tea and headed up along North Street, passing the University until he arrived at the ruins of the historical edifice.

As he trod the hallowed grounds, he tried to imagine the picturesque majesty of what had once been the largest and most important church in Scotland. Hutchings was to learn that the first cathedral buildings were completed in 1144. It surprised him to find that it had taken from 1160 to 1218 to be completed. The main church must have been huge, for that structure's interior worship area was reported to have been over 357 feet in length!

The ruins are located on the east side of town and, sadly all that remain are the foundations. Yet, they symbolize the grandeur of what was the center of a deep Christian faith. It was here that Charles Hutchings found time to concentrate on the meaning of his life, at least one aspect of it.

While there, he visited the grave of Young Tom Morris, a man whose great golfing ability made him famous at a very early age. The tragic loss of his young wife and their infant child was said to have led to his death at the early age of 24, a death many Scots believed could have been attributed to a broken heart. Hutchings sat down at the base of the young man's monument, and he felt tears welling up. It was then that Charles finally was able to put the game of golf in proper perspective. He knew that he had let it have too much control over his life, and he needed to change.

Golf would no longer mean "everything" to him from this point forward. Oh, to be sure, it would forever hold a special place in his heart. The infinite challenges the game presented to him would never quite leave. Such was the lure of golf, and such was the make-up of "the Quiet One." One thing was certain, Charles knew that his visit to the young champion's grave had had a profound effect on him.

The following Sunday's excursion had him visiting the town's University. St Andrews was Scotland's first, founded in 1413. That same year it received full University status by the exiled Pope Benedict XIII. He was one of two rival Popes, Boniface IX, being the other, who were proclaimed pontiff when the Catholic Church was divided by groups supporting their own respective leaders.

Charles examined many of the University buildings. He was impressed by the records that were kept in the University library. As a matter of fact, the library was the building which held the greatest interest for Charles Hutchings.

Among all of the historical references contained on the well-documented shelves, the University had a wing reserved for the history of the town, from its origins through its continued development.

As he leafed through the pages, he stopped abruptly when he came to articles about the beginnings of the ancient game of golf. One of them was a book entitled <u>A Keen Hand</u>, written by Henry Farnie.

His attention was immediately focused upon that publication. He quickly recognized the frontispiece engraving of Allan Robertson. A broad smile came to his face as he sat down at the nearest table and began to scan through the manual. Robertson was renowned as one of the finest players in Scotland, and "the Quiet One" had heard and read of his many accomplishments.

The one that stood foremost in Hutchings's mind was Robertson's record breaking performance at St Andrews. He was reputed to have been the first golfer to have broken 80 on the "Auld" Course. Charles always admired achievers. It mattered not what occupation they had chosen; It only mattered that they had done their best. From what he was able to glean, Robertson, called the "Father of Professional Golf", had been such a man.

Farnie, the author, according to town records, was a journalist and librettist who worked at a Fifeshire newspaper when he wrote this golf manual.

While it described the history of the game, it was of interest to Charles because it was one of the earliest instruction books for the sport! Writer Farnie detailed the various types of clubs, when and how they should be used, styles of shot-making, appropriate behavior and proper golf attire. He also included a glossary of golfing terms and an appendix of the rules of the game and a list of the links in Scotland.

When the Honourable Company of Edinburgh Golfers first put together their rules for the game, they started with thirteen. Hutchings was aware of them but wanted his own copy. Taking his pencil and pad he carefully copied them as they had been written:

Rules of Golf (Honourable Company of Edinburgh Golfers)

1. You must tee your ball within a club's length of the hole.
2. Your tee must be on the ground.
3. You are not to change the ball which you strike off the tee.
4. You are not to remove stones, bones or any break club for the sake of playing your ball, except upon the fair green, and then only within a club's length of the ball.
5. If your ball comes among water, or any watery filth, you are at liberty to take out your ball and bringing it behind the hazard and teeing it, you may play it with any club and allow your adversary a stroke for so getting out your ball.
6. If your balls be found anywhere touching one another, you are to lift the first ball till you play the last.
7. At holing, you are to play your ball honestly at the hole, and not to play upon your adversary's ball, not lying in your way to the hole.
8. If you should lose your ball, by its being taken up, or any other way, you are to go back to the spot where you struck last and drop another ball and allow your adversary a stroke for the misfortune.
9. No man in holing his ball is to be allowed to mark his way to the hole with his club or anything else.
10. If a ball be stopped by any person, horse, dog, or anything else, the ball so stopped must be played where it lies.
11. If you draw your club in order to strike and proceed so far in the stroke as to be bringing down your club, if then your club should break in any way, it is to be accounted a stroke.
12. He whose ball lies farthest from the hole is obliged to play first.

13. Neither trench, ditch, or dyke made for the preservation of the links, nor the Scholars' Holes or the soldiers' lines shall be accounted a hazard but the ball is to be taken out, teed and played with any iron club.

Over the years that followed, changes to these original rules had been made to better meet the needs of the golfers and the changes in course construction and maintenance.

Charles was fascinated by that manual and he read Farnie's book that very afternoon. It would be the first of many times he would do so.

Sundays provided Charles with the break from the game that he really needed, although he never would have agreed with that sentiment. Still, he longed to play on that day of the week, and it really bothered him to no end that he couldn't play the "Old Course". His golfing friends were supportive, but so were his neighbors.

Though not golfers, they came to know and appreciate this simple man. They invited him to attend Sunday plays and concerts in a fruitless effort to get him to think about something other than golf. For a short time, it seemed to be working. Charles hadn't raised the issue for weeks.

Then, early one Sunday morning, he failed to meet them for an "agreed to" luncheon at the Royal Hotel. His friends were all sitting at a long table directly overlooking the golf course. On that day, Carlyle Robbie happened to be in this group. By now, he and Hutchings had become bosom friends, having spent many evenings together.

After 45 minutes had gone by, Robbie stood up and made his way to the window. Looking out across the street, he could see the townspeople and their families gaily laughing and running in and out of the bunkers on the golf course. He imagined it must have been killing Charles not to be out there. Oh, he knew that "the Quiet One" would never break the law. It simply wasn't a part of his character. Yet, he sensed that

Sundays, curfews or not, would never stop his friend from practicing somewhere. Slowly, he turned and walked back to the table and addressed the members of the party who were still patiently waiting.

"Ladies and gentlemen," Carlyle Robbie spoke, "let us take our seats and order our food, for I don't believe we'll be seeing Mr. Charles Hutchings today."

As he took his seat, he winked at those in attendance, remarking, "My, it's too bad we can't golf on Sundays!"

The tide was going out on the North Sea that afternoon, and the sun shone brightly on the rocky beach located directly behind the ruins of the old Cathedral. Gazing out from the grassy expanse by St. Rule's tower, Hutchings saw a golden opportunity to get in some practice. It being Sunday, he couldn't play St Andrews, as the ordinance forbid anyone to play golf there on the Lord's Day. So he carried an old bag of "gutties" and his niblick and began doing what he had done so often months earlier on the coastline adjacent to the St Andrews links.

Hutchings was annoyed with himself for not having thought of this sooner. He reasoned that it must have been because he was so embarrassed from his episode with the constabulary. That had to be it. He was unnerved to the degree that he never even thought about golf on Sunday "somewhere" else!

So, there he practiced, striking ball after ball toward terns, gulls, and other seaside creatures confused by the objects that landed so close to their active gatherings.

The arrival of these spheres resulted in a great deal of squawking and shrieking when they bounced close by the feeding flocks. Indeed, many of the waterfowl insisted on inspecting the round "eggs," probably more than a little confused as to how they could fly without wings!

Hutchings was pleased with these Sunday practice sessions. He was actually relieved to have found a place where he could be alone while he ironed out the few weaknesses he possessed. There were no fellow players asking for "hints." No matches to play and money to be wagered and spent. What there was, and in great abundance, was solitude. . .

Hole 5 Hole O' Cross Out

St Andrews, site of the Royal and Ancient Golf Club, is
normally a quiet, seaside village. Citizens of the town were
justly proud of their heritage, their fine University and the fact
that golfers from all over the world recognized the "Old
Course" as the "home of golf," and came there to play.

The course, carved out of the dunes by wind, grazing
sheep and other creatures, is truly a one-of-a-kind layout. It
possesses qualities and features that can only be found in that
hallowed spot. Stories abound as to how the game originated.
Many claim it began in ancient Rome. Others attribute the
Dutch with starting the sport. It really makes no difference,
for the Scots will always lay claim to its earliest beginnings,
and the "Auld Course" it's true home.

Ever since his arrival at St Andrews, Charles Hutchings had
been designated an enigma. He dressed shabbily. He didn't
speak. His hygiene left much to be desired. He didn't have
many friends, yet he seemed content in being his own best
companion.

It's true, he became a wonderful golfer, the result of his
nonstop practice regimen no doubt. His work ethic was a tad
on the "overdone" side. Charles, additionally, proved to be an
honorable man, law-abiding and a good neighbor and friend
to all who took the time to get to know him.

As more and more residents of St Andrews learned of the
man and his strange ways, he became an object of much
curiosity and brazen speculation. For example, his fellow

golfers were never quite sure where they stood with him. If he respected someone, he would do anything to help the person. However, if you were less than a gentleman, or a fine woman, you would most assuredly be shunned by the man.

Charles Hutchings was not as complicated as some people thought. While he had the reputation of being a loner, he loved humanity. He merely wasted no time with fakes and pretenders. He treated people the way he would like to have been treated. In a Biblical sense, it reads "Do unto others, as you would have others do unto you." The Golden Rule was something Hutchings lived by, and it entered into everything he would do.

That was one of the reasons that he had taken to Andy Kirk. Kirk was a good man, liked by most, except when he offered suggestions to help his friends play better golf. Though not a great player, he would often remark that he "understood" the game better than his playing skills would indicate. He let it be known that he was available if anyone needed instruction.

Hutchings looked past his friend's particular failing and tried to improve the man's game. Like many golfers, Kirk told Charles that he wanted to improve, but he simply wouldn't do the work that was required to build a new swing. They rarely argued, although there was one time that the patrons of MacTavish's tavern will never forget.

After coming off the course one sunny, autumn afternoon, Andy was extolling the benefits of the new grip he had used in that match. Hutchings wasn't paying attention to his pal.

It seems that Kirk had been talking the entire round about how the 10-finger grip was better than the Vardon. Now, 15 minutes after the last putt had been holed, Kirk was at it again. Over and over he gave reasons why that grip was the best. Hutchings had long ago tired of Kirk's position on that issue and gave him the signal to stop. The signal consisted of Hutchings opening and closing his left hand, over and over until finally, he raised his right hand and closed his fingers quickly over the "talking" left hand. It really looked comical whenever he employed that pantomime, but apparently this time, it really infuriated Kirk.

"Hutchings, are you telling me to shut up?" Kirk inquired.

Immediately, Hutchings opened his tablet and scribbled his response, "Yes, that's what I said, shut yer yammer," and handed it to Kirk.

"Well, the nerve . . ." voiced Kirk after slowly reading Hutchings's response aloud for everyone to hear. Andy stood up and shouted, "It's an ignorant man yer becomin' Charles Hutchings."

Now, it was Hutchings's turn to show his temper. He was upset by both the comment itself and the sheer volume of Kirk's remark.

"The Quiet One" issued a loud "Ungh" and began to write sentence after sentence after sentence, one sentence to a sheet. His responses, each at a time, were quickly ripped from his tablet and piled one upon the other, three sheets, directly in front of a scowling Andy Kirk.

The sheer spectacle had drawn the attention of everyone in the tavern that night and they began to gather around the two men who were involved in a most unusual argument.

As Kirk turned over the first sheet which read, "You're annoying." He replied, "Is that so?"

Turning over the second sheet which read, "Yes, that's so, and you're a know-it-all, as well!" Kirk shot back, "Look who's talking!"

When he turned over the last sheet, which read, "I'm not talking, I'm writing, you fool!" to which Kirk responded, "What? Wait a minute. . . How did you know that I was going to respond the way I did?"

The entire room went silent and after a short pause both men stood up, face-to-face, staring at each other, eye-to-eye.

All of a sudden, both men began to laugh aloud. Amid their laughter, they began to clap each other on the back and quickly sat down in their chairs.

Hutchings mumbled a rather remorseful sounding "Ungh". His apology was matched by Kirk's, "I'm sorry, Charles, I can't imagine what got into me. Will ye forgive me actions?"

Hutchings paused, flashed an angry look in Kirk's direction and handed him another message that said, "Of course, Andy. Why ye be me best friend!"

That was that. Argument over, and since that time the two men became even closer. Golf was the glue that kept them together and they partnered up whenever possible. Of late, though, "the Quiet One" hadn't been playing as much. Indeed, Kirk began to worry about his friend when Hutchings had failed to show up for a return match against Mullen and Tolliver.

That afternoon, Andy walked over to the Robbie Rooming House. When he asked the proprietor if he could speak to Mr. Hutchings, Carlyle informed him that he had left their establishment three days ago.

"What? He never mentioned that to you?" Mr. Robbie inquired. "Why, that's bizarre, I say, because he was always writing me notes about you and him playing this team or that team. As a matter of fact, now that I think about it, I think he told me ye haven't lost a match!"

After that remark Kirk smiled, but he was concerned for his friend's strange actions, adding, "Mr. Robbie, did he happen to mention where he was going?"

"No," Robbie replied, "but I was worried about him, too. So, I had this neighborhood lad, Danny, follow him to try to find out where he might be going."

"And what did you learn?" asked a most interested Kirk.

"Well, I don't know if I should tell ye, Andy," continued Carlyle, "what if he doesn't want anyone to know where he's gone?"

"Mr. Robbie," Kirk insisted, "we've known each other for over thirty years, man. I'm only interested because he's a dear friend and I want to be certain that he's safe and healthy."

"I guess he really wouldn't mind if his friend were to somehow serendipitously run into him, would he?" Robbie joked, smiling a wry smile.

After hooking up a team of horses to his carriage, Kirk headed his team toward Pitscottie. Twenty-three minutes later found him knocking on the green door of a whitewashed stonewall cottage located some two miles off the main road. The house was situated along a gradual rise overlooking a small meadow teeming with rabbits.

Kirk stood there for several minutes and began his second round of knocking, this time much harder. Still, there was no answer. He was all ready to start back when he heard some familiar sounds being carried by the northeast wind. There could be no doubt, he reasoned, walking steadily into increasing breeze. Golf balls were being struck nearby.

As he approached the top of a small hillock, he could see the effortless power of Charles Hutchings hitting golf balls as only he could hit them. Each ball seemed to fly on the exact same trajectory, rising quickly to its apex and gently settling on a 20 by 20 foot square sand patch. It was as if Charles was carving a passage in the clear blue sky through which golf balls could travel.

Thinking he hadn't been seen, Andy sat in one of the hollows along the ridge, admiring the remarkable skills of his friend, "the Quiet One." While he was resting there, a voice behind him whispered, "Mr. Kirk, your friend can really play the game, can't he?"

Turning quickly, Kirk found himself looking into the eyes of one of the most beautiful women he had ever seen.

Extending her hand, she spoke, "Hello, we've been expecting you. By the way, you can call me Addie."

"Hello, Addie," Kirk responded, "I'm pleased to meet you."

"Ungh!", voiced Charles Hutchings, who had finished his practice session. He handed the empty practice bag to his friend and they started out to the sandy patch to gather the balls. While they were putting them back into the bag, Kirk and Hutchings went through their unique communication routine, with Kirk asking yes and no questions.

"So, Charles," Andy began, "you know why I'm here, correct?"

"Ungh!" replied "the Quiet One."

"Well, the gang at MacTavish's were wondering what happened to you," he continued, "and I offered to try to find out. By the way, is this where you will be staying?"

"Ungh!" voiced Hutchings.

"And," Kirk proceeded more slowly, "this woman, Addie. . . Are you and she, er....Never mind. . . "

Changing the subject, Kirk went on, "Charles, will you still be joining our regular match this Saturday?"

"Ungh!" Charles replied, as he picked up the last ball.

With that, both men headed back over the brae and saw Addie clipping some roses in the back garden.

When she spied them, she headed into the house and returned with three glasses of brandy.

Hutchings bowed to her and invited Andy to sit with them along the low wall extending from the cottage.

Addie started the conversation, "Charles, I think Mr. Kirk needs to know what this is all about. . . Don't you?"

Hutchings looked away for a moment, then back at Addie and Andy. He shook his head in the affirmative.

"Well, Mr. Kirk," she began, "Charles has told me all about you and if he trusts you, then I know that I can trust you."

"What are you talking about?" Kirk inquired.

"Mr. Kirk, you know that Charles is quite enamored of the game of golf. Not only does he love to play, he is quite talented in the sport. When I first heard of him, I thought that he might be able to help me, actually work with my group."

"I'm not sure I understand," offered a confused Andy Kirk.

"Let me explain, Mr. Kirk," Addie pleaded. "I am currently involved in. . . well, it's a type of law-enforcement. My group is charged with keeping a step ahead of some of the continent's most dangerous characters."

"By the way, Mr. Kirk," Addie inquired, "have you ever heard of Professor Moriarty?"

"Actually, I haven't, my good woman," replied Andy.

Shaking her head, Addie began solemnly, "Mr. Kirk, I could sit here well into the night describing only a portion of Moriarty's evil deeds. Prior to his death, he was recognized as the most dangerous man in England and the continent as well. He and his collaborators were involved in virtually every major crime that had been committed over the last several years. It was only through the efforts of Scotland Yard and other valiant law officers that his actions were somewhat curtailed."

"Thankfully, this villain can no longer threaten society." Addie continued. "He died in a struggle with our dear friend, the late Sherlock Holmes, when both men went over a cliff and were killed in the fall at Reichenbach Falls, Switzerland."

"I'd heard of Holmes," lamented Kirk, "I'm sorry to have learned of his untimely passing."

"Thank you, Andy," Addie replied. "Currently, we are trailing one of Moriarty's lackeys. He was seen recently in Edinburgh but our sources have tracked him to St Andrews."

"I'm afraid I still don't understand what you're trying to tell me," offered Kirk. "Is my friend, Charles, involved in some way?"

"As a matter of fact, yes," she continued. "You see, Mr. Kirk, we found that our target is an avid golfer and we needed someone to keep a close eye on him. When I found out about Charles Hutchings's great golfing ability, I contacted him. After explaining our plight to him, he wasted no time in agreeing to come aboard."

"Why are you telling me this?" asked the barrel-maker.

"Charles trusts you to keep his secret, and, make no mistake, his life and mine are now in your hands," explained the one called Addie.

"Furthermore," she continued, "we need to ask for your help. It's possible that we'll need a liaison in the event that anything happens to Charles. If you agree to help, you will be doing a fine thing for your country and mankind in general. Please consider joining us in our efforts to apprehend these villainous brigands."

"My goodness," Kirk offered, "you've really given me a great deal to think about. . ."

"Ungh!" Hutchings replied, shaking his head.

"Mr. Kirk," Addie responded, "I need your answer as soon as possible. But, I also must implore you to forget what you've heard today should you decide not to help us."

Kirk finished his brandy and walked back to his carriage. The horses had busied themselves on the tender shoots along the cottage wall, but were off and running with the crack of Kirk's whip, heading back home.

As the St Andrews skyline grew ever larger along the way, Kirk started to feel as though the weight of the world had been thrust upon him. He wondered why he had been placed in this position? Who was he to get involved in international schemes? He was no youngster. He was a middle-aged family man, better-suited to working with barrel staves than intrigue. How had he become involved in this? Oh, yes, he was friends with a very strange man, Charles Hutchings.

The night seemed endless for Kirk. His wife noticed his heedless behavior, but he was able to deflect her concern, saying that he was simply over-tired. When dawn arrived, he was lying in wait for it. He had made his decision and today he would meet with Addie and Charles.

After breakfast, Andy headed to his workshop. No matter how much pressure he was under, he still had to work. Ten barrels needed to be finished for shipment by three o'clock, so he found himself working right through his lunch. As the town clock tower announced four o'clock, he hooked up his team, and once more started for the white Pitscottie cottage and his meeting with Charles and Addie.

When his team pulled up to the idyllic little home, Addie and Hutchings were outside waiting for him. After tying up the horses, they entered the house and took their seats around a solid square oaken table. Addie and Charles waited patiently for Andy's answer. He could tell by the looks on their faces that his decision meant a great deal.

"Lord forgive me, I've decided to join you in your efforts to corral these culprits!" Kirk proudly announced.

"Ungh!" voiced Hutchings extending his hand to his friend.

"Mr. Kirk," Addie joined her partner's exuberance, "We are so delighted with your choice. I know it must have been very difficult when you took the time to analyze what your decision might mean to you and your family. Thank you."

"Having listened to all that you told me about these thugs and their evil ways, I could not have lived with myself knowing that you and Charles were out there trying to save lives and me sitting home doing nothing," he responded. "That's just not me."

Charles had left the table, returning with brandy to toast their new collaboration. Following the briefest of celebrations, Addie brought out a folder and started to bring Mr. Kirk up to speed, providing him with the additional information he would need to have at his disposal.

While Hutchings sat, listening attentively, Addie described the entire history of the Moriarty crime family. She listed many of the areas of daily life that have been and continue to be threatened by their activities. This included all of the major crimes one might imagine, paying special attention to robbery, extortion, murder by contract, involvement in procuring and delivering illicit drugs.

That group, Addie informed him, was now being led by a notorious scoundrel who went by the name Colonel C. M. Sebastian, although he is known to have availed himself of several other names over the years. Their mission, she continued to explain to Kirk, was to track, disrupt and finally stop this group from operating. For this to happen, she added in closing, blood might need to be shed.

When Charles and Addie had finished, they noticed a marked change in Andy Kirk's appearance. Sweat was now pouring down the sides of his gaunt face. After wiping away the perspiration, he quickly slugged down another glass of brandy. His hands began to shake as he lowered his eyes to the table, studying the descriptions and specialties of some of the criminals he might soon have to face.

Addie quietly observed Kirk's reaction to all of the information she had recently disclosed. His noticeable discomfort needed to be addressed so she offered a way out for him in a most comfortable reassuring manner.

"Andy," Addie spoke in a most calming tone, "I know that all of this information comes as a shock, for most people have no idea how detailed, depraved, disgusting, the criminal mind can be, but now you know. . . Having heard what you may be asked to do, we would certainly understand if you had a change of heart! We would only have you promise to forget all that you have heard today. . .as if that were possible. . . "

For no apparent reason, it seemed that Kirk's mood had changed dramatically. Now he was sitting up, alert and alive. He was even smiling at them.

Quickly rising from the table, he asked, "Well, I'm ready to start. So, now, when will I hear from you again? How often might we need to talk? Is this our main headquarters? What do you want me to do?"

"My word, Mr. Kirk," Addie seemed confused, continuing, "you certainly had me fooled! For a moment there, I thought we had lost you."

Charles Hutchings was genuinely pleased at his good friend's response and a warm handshake sealed the deal.

"Andy," Addie followed up, "thank you for your help. We'll keep you informed in all of our activities."

After Kirk had started back to St Andrews, Irene Adler Norton shook her head and returned to the table. Charles walked up behind her and placing his hand on her shoulder and offered, "Please don't doubt him. I would trust Andy Kirk with my life!"

Irene turned, looked up at him and announced, "I'm glad to hear you say that because you just may have to!"

Hole 6 Heathery Out

Hutchings arrived at the first tee in plenty of time for his match with Mullen and Tolliver. It was 11:10, and their starting time was listed as 11:40. Both men were busy talking to Andy Kirk and setting up the conditions of the day's game. How much would they play for?. . . How many strokes would each player receive?. . . Was it match or stroke?. . .

When they first caught sight of him, Mullen walked over and said, "Why if it isn't Mr. Charles Hutchings. . . Say now, Hutchings, are ye plannin' on playin' today or are ye a-scared of the beatin' yer gonna receive from Jimmy and me?"

Hutchings smiled amicably, knowing he deserved the harsh teasing Mullen loved to dispense. He tipped his cap in recognition of Mullen's well-aimed barb and then grabbed his clubs, wiping away some pieces of moist grass that still adhered to his niblick.

His partner, Kirk, called over, "Charles, they want to up the stakes. Can you imagine?"

Hutchings questioned the bet, responding, "Ungh?", then quickly agreed, heading to the starter's shed.

"We'll take the bet, gentlemen," Kirk offered conditionally, "provided Mullen gets one less shot this time."

"Ye, thieves," answered Mike Mullen wearing a broad incongruous smile on his face. "You're tryin' to steal the match even before a stroke's been made."

"We'll take the bet," Tolliver spoke out, "Mullen's been playing some excellent golf lately."

With stakes having been agreed to, the teams approached the tee and signed in with the starter.

While the Mullen-Tolliver team was still annoyed with "the Quiet One" for failing to appear when last they were scheduled to play, they were happy to have another chance to compete against this outstanding golfer. His reputation locally had grown by leaps and bounds and he was regularly breaking the magical number of 80! Indeed, very few players could make that claim, especially on the "Old Course."

When it was time to begin, Tolliver played first. His low-raking slider barely carried Granny Clark's Wynd, but rolled out 250 yards, leaving a mashie niblick to the pin. Partner Mullen selected a cleek and ably laced a dandy within ten yards of Tolliver's ball. Kirk's drive was foozled left, just missing an old Scot who was lining up his shot off the adjoining 18th green.

The shot was so poor that Mullen had to comment, saying, "Well, I bet you would like to have that beauty over again, now, wouldn't ye, Kirk? Well, it's too bad, cause ye can't! Haw!"

Same old Mullen, "the Quiet One" thought as he struck his usual high-arcing spoon perfectly down the left side of the seemingly endless fairway.

The hole was halved in level 4s as was the left-to-right 411 yard second, although it took a magnificent recovery from the Cheape's bunker by Tolliver to make par for his team. At Cartgate (Out), the 371-yard third hole, Hutchings's par was good enough to put his team one up. Both Mullen and Tolliver were unable to recover from the gorse that lined the entire right side of the rough.

As the teams were preparing to play their tee shots on the Ginger Beer hole, a now familiar character showed up bidding them all a most warm welcome.

"Gentlemen," Colonel C. M. Sebastian called from a short distance behind, "it's good to see you again!"

Tolliver and Mullen walked over and greeted him warmly, with Tolliver offering, "Why, Colonel, good morning to you as well. Might I inquire why you're not out enjoying this fine, brisk Scottish weather?"

"Mr. Tolliver," he replied, "let me assure you that I would love to be out here playing. It's just that I have some important meetings scheduled for the afternoon."

Kirk and Hutchings simply waved to Sebastian, believing a polite acknowledgment was all that was needed at the time.

Following the brief interruption, the match continued with all four players hitting excellent tee shots.

Kirk now found it very difficult to even look at Sebastian, having newly discovered the man's criminal history. He was so incensed that he almost acted on his feelings! What he really wanted to do was smash that blighter with his brassie!

Hutchings could sense the emotions that were stirring in his partner's soul and offered an indifferent "Ungh!" to bring him back to reality. Fortunately, it seemed to work, for nothing good could come from having Sebastian discover that Kirk and Hutchings both knew who he was.

That was all that it took, for Kirk was back on track. He understood his role in this scenario. He even began a discussion with the colonel, though it was killing him.

"Did I hear you tell Tolliver that you were to be otherwise occupied this afternoon, Colonel?" Kirk inquired. "That's most unfortunate," he commented. "It's such a fine day for the game."

"Perhaps, we can make it tomorrow, Mr. Kirk," the colonel suggested. "Can I count on you and Hutchings then?"

"Let me think," Kirk paused for a moment. "No, I'm sorry, I have thirty barrels to prepare in the next several days, although I can't speak for Charles here. . . "

Kirk caught himself and laughed aloud, "Actually, I guess I have to speak for Charles, don't I?"

At that remark, everyone laughed. . . Everyone that is, except Charles Hutchings.

Hutchings feigned anger at his partner's witticism. He scowled and began to walk faster, pretending to get away from his partner and the rather rude reference.

"There, there, Charles," Kirk continued, "I didn't mean to make you angry. Please forgive me."

Hutchings issued a loud "Ungh!" and kept walking, continuing to employ his award-winning "act" at Colonel Sebastian's expense.

"Now you've done it, Kirk!" Colonel Sebastian showed his true colors exclaiming, "Thanks to your calloused remark, I may never get to play with Hutchings."

Kirk was starting to feel rage, but he quickly composed himself, realizing that he had gotten the best of Sebastian.

When they played their second shots, only Mullen was able to reach the green. His ball had taken a hard bounce on the firm fairway and made its way up and onto the huge double-green that serves as the putting surface for both the 4th and 14th holes. After sending his first putt, a long, twisting eighty footer twelve feet past the cup, Mullen rammed the par putt into the back of the hole for a hard-earned win.

Both teams moved to the long 5th hole, a five-par over 560 yards that made its way further out from the town. All four golfers tried to hit their drives down the far left side of the fairway to avoid a cluster of six bunkers. Kirk's ball was the only one to safely find the fairway. Tolliver and Hutchings both pulled their shots finding the Hell Bunker while Mullen's ball disappeared in thick gorse bushes down the right side of the rough.

A fairly struck brassie, followed by a bellied mashie that hopped over a gaping greenside bunker, left Kirk with a short distance for his birdie effort. His two-putt par was enough to put his team one hole ahead for the second time in five holes.

The 6th hole that day was playing slightly less than 400 yards and the wind had picked up, blowing directly down the fairway. The blind tee-shot always bothered Kirk, and today was no exception. He pulled his drive down the left edge of the fairway toward the infamous Coffins bunker. Hutchings smashed another high, drawing drive that landed atop a ridge at roughly the 270-yard range and continued rolling another sixty yards.

Tolliver and Mullen both hit fine drives, Mullen, the further of the two.

When they reached Kirk's ball lying in the Coffins bunker, Mullen, again, couldn't resist the opportunity, "

"Gentlemen, let us all bow our heads," he spoke in mock solemnity, "for our poor friend, Kirk, is dead!"

Then the laughter began. Mullen and Tolliver were laughing because they really thought it was funny; Hutchings and Kirk laughed because they thought it validated Mullen's moronic ways.

When they had settled down, all Kirk could do was chop his ball out of the bunker and try to hit some type of recovery shot. Tolliver finally put two good shots together and it was lucky for his team that he did, for his partner had hit a nasty looking hosel-buster that disappeared in the whins. ***

Hutchings's drive had left him with a delicate pitch that had to fly just far enough to carry a dip in front of the green, but not reach the green itself. He appeared to have clipped his ball cleanly and began walking, anticipating a good shot.

When the group reached the putting surface, Hutchings's ball was nowhere to be seen. He walked to the back and found it sitting in some gnarly rough. What had looked like a great shot must have carried too far, landing on the middle of the green. Undeterred, his clever blast with a niblick gave him a chance for par. He only needed to convert the tricky ten-footer. Feeling some pressure after Tolliver's two-putt par, Charles studied the borrow and calmly rolled it into the cup.

High Out, the name of the seventh hole, was also playing shorter than its 372 yards that day. For the first time in the round, all four players found the fairway, with Kirk away. This had always been a tough hole for Andy. No matter what he tried, his ball had a way of finding the Shell bunker, a cavernous, gaping maw of sand that closely guarded the undulating green.

Kirk waggled his mashie, lined up for the left side of the 11th green, and took his swing. When he looked up, he could see his ball slowly sliding from left-to-right, heading off the targeted 11th green and flying toward the proper green of the hole they were playing. It looked like a beauty but as he continued watching, he noticed Shell bunker gobble it up!

"In the name of the wee man!" Kirk screamed, "Why in this world can't I ever avoid that hazard?" ***

Andy was totally scumered as he walked away from the others, still giving himself a severe talking to. ***

"Easy now, Kirk," voiced the ever-ready-to-annoy Mullen, "Yer too far away from the clubhouse to have a seizure now."

"Why, it's the last thing we want to see!" he continued. "It would be all about, hit the ball, drag Kirk, hit the ball, drag Kirk. And that would be for eleven more holes!"

Once more the foursome started to laugh. For all of his surliness, Mullen did have some funny ways of saying things.

Mullen and Hutchings both hit decent approach shots, but Tolliver struggled mightily, his short mashie niblick wound up in the same bunker as Kirk.

When the players arrived at the green complex, they were surprised to find that Tolliver's ball had somehow rolled up against Kirk's ball.

At first, it seemed quite funny, but it would take some discussion before they could decide what was to be done about the situation. Tolliver quoted one of the Rules of the Game, stating, " If your balls be found anywhere touching one another you are to lift the first ball till you play the last."

Kirk looked at him and remarked, "Why that's true enough, James, but since I'm away, you'll be the one that has to lift your ball."

Tolliver answered, "Mr. Kirk, I'll be more than pleased to lift me ball so that you can flub yer ball out of the Shell."

Shaking his head, Kirk softly replied, "Ah, Tolliver, me lad, "you haven't grasped my meaning. . ."

"Which is?" up spoke Mullen who had been quietly watching what was transpiring.

"Which means," continued Kirk, "After I've played my shot, how will Tolliver get to play his shot? Will he get to place it back in the original spot, after I've removed a goodly amount of sand, leaving him a hole in which to put his ball? Or, am I supposed to rake the area after I've hit, maybe not raking it to his satisfaction? There's also the issue as to whether he has to place the ball or drop it in the bunker as near as possible to where it originally lay?"

Some time went by as the four men gave Andy's questions careful consideration.

"I see what ye mean, Andy," an appreciative Tolliver remarked. "There are quite a few options that are not listed in the Thirteen Rules of Golf."

Hutchings had been observing and listening to the questions that had been raised but hadn't put in his "two-pence" worth, as yet.

It was Mullen that suddenly realized that fact, "Hutchings, what do you say should be done? Nobody knows the rules, or plays by them, as well as you do. What say ye?"

Quickly, Hutchings scribbled his response on a tablet sheet and handed it to Mullen.

Mullen read the suggestion aloud, saying, "Charles, here, suggests that we allow Mr. Tolliver's ball to be replaced by Mr. Kirk after Kirk has played his shot and repaired the sand to the original condition as it existed prior to his shot."

Tolliver said, "That's fine with me, Charles. If that's acceptable to you, Andy, it'll be fine with me."

So that's how it was handled. For the record, both Kirk and Tolliver played superb bunker shots, but Kirk missed his par putt and settled for bogey.

Hutchings played his next shot to within three inches and his par was conceded. After Mullen's par-putt stopped on the front edge of the hole, it was up to his partner Tolliver. His bunker shot had left him with a slippery four-footer. After careful study, he deftly stroked it into the hole for the tie.

Holes 8 through 11 were sometimes referred to as "the Loop", for they are located at the farthest distance from the clubhouse. Both teams secured pars over those four holes and they marched to the twelfth hole with Hutchings and Kirk still enjoying their one-up margin.

Mullen and Tolliver were very fortunate to still be in this match. They were not playing all that well, but, luckily, their opponents were not either! Hutchings was still playing his regular tee-to-green game, but his putting was not up to snuff. Perhaps Charles's concentration was not what it should have been. He might have been thinking of his friend Kirk's life-altering choice and worrying about that decision!

Kirk was not himself either, for he was a man newly sworn to a secret life. Throughout the round, Andy began to have reservations over his decision. Certainly, he wanted to help; of that, there could be no doubt. His main concern was about his family.

Had he thought about what would happen to them if he were to be killed? What if Sebastian's men found out about him and threatened his family? How could he ever forgive himself? When those very real possibilities were on his mind, he hated the decision he had made.

On the other hand, would he ever be the same man knowing that he could have prevented evil from happening to his fellow human beings? How could he face himself in the mirror if he allowed something to happen to his friend Charles? When these thoughts were present, he knew he had made the correct decision. He could only wonder what the next meeting with Addie would reveal.

The 12th hole's double-tiered green proved to be most difficult for the foursome. Mullen's approach left him with a long putt from the lower level. His effort, while laudable, just ran out of steam and rolled back into the same spot from which he had just putted!

Naturally, when he tried the putt again, his ball sped up the slope and didn't stop on the upper tier, but continued rolling and rolling, stopping some ten yards deep into the gorse! His putter quickly followed, landing deep in the middle of that nasty patch of flora.

Tolliver's 3-putt for six, was the best his team could put on their card, while Kirk's 2-putt bogey from twelve feet was good enough to put his team 2 up, going to the 13th hole.

It took Mullen some time to make his way into the picky gorse and extricate his putter. As he bent, stretched and lumbered in, among, and around the thorny wilderness, the occasional "ouch" and several nasty epithets could be heard coming from his pie hole.

When he finally appeared on the tee, there were tears in his outer garments and some open scratches on his wrists and arms. Still, he didn't seem to mind. He knew and lived by the old Scottish expression, "sic as ye gie, sic wull ye get." ***

Hutchings led off the group with an incredible whack, his ball easily carrying "The Coffins". Kirk's slice left him in the right side of the fairway with 220 yards still to go.

The Tolliver-Mullen team simply had to win this hole. The way Hutchings was starting to come alive meant that par would probably only tie any remaining holes. Blood dripping from his left wrist, Mullen hit a massive hook that was the equal of Hutchings's drive. Tolliver's ball, a low, scalded rat, safely stopped just short of the bunkers.

After Andy's second ball snapped left into the heather,
Tolliver's well-struck spoon ended up three feet from the cup.
Now it was Hutchings's turn. His high-flying niblick was
heading straight for the hole but it took a hard bounce and
bounded into the bunker over the green. Mullen's ball kicked
off a low ridge, just short of the green and rolled up ten feet
away. Advantage Tolliver-Mullen.

When Hutchings failed to get out of the bunker after two
tries, Tolliver's short putt was conceded and the birdie left his
team only one down going to the 14th hole. Things were
beginning to get interesting.

Both teams played the next two holes in regulation figures,
although it took a magical 40-foot downhill snaking putt for
par by Mullen to tie the fifteenth!

"Ungh!" voiced "the Quiet One" as he teased Mullen,
shaking a closed fist in his direction.

Mullen loved to give it, but, big bruiser that he was, he
loved it when somebody had the gall to give it back to him.
Over the past several weeks, Mullen and Hutchings had
developed a mutual appreciation and respect for each other.
This demonstration by Hutchings would not have been
tolerated a few weeks prior.

"What's wrong, Hutchings?" Mullen began, "Do ye think yer
the only golfer at St Andrews that can hole a putt?"

As the teams reached the sixteenth, named the "Corner of
the Dyke", there was a certain amount of tension in the air.
The wagers had been doubled for this match and that kept
everybody alert to the action that was taking place.

What no one could have expected was the reappearance of
Colonel Sebastian from behind the railroad tracks.

He greeted the golfers with an interesting proposal.

"Gentlemen, how goes the match, thus far?" he inquired,
and without waiting for a response continued, "I'm going to
offer five pounds to any team that can play the next three
holes in even par or better. That's a total of twelve shots!"

The players just looked at each other in wonder. They had never heard of an offer like that from anyone, be they golfer or gambler, for that matter!

"Why, what are ye talkin' about, Colonel?" asked Mullen as only Mullen would ask, "We've already got a fine match on the line. Why would anyone make such a strange offer, with nothing to gain and five pound sterling to lose?"

"Gentlemen," implored Sebastian, "I only want to see how you will respond if a little added pressure is applied. I really would consider it money well spent if one of your teams actually could meet my challenge!"

"Fine," responded Kirk, dryly, "we'll be happy to try and take money that you're so eager to give away.

"Kirk, there's no fear of that happening," spoke James Tolliver, "for Mullen and I will be the ones collecting the Colonel's most generous offer."

Just the sight of Sebastian curdled Kirk's blood. Before he had become aware of the colonel's true villainy, Andy had considered him a bit of a pompous buffoon. With the new information, he would just as soon slug him as look at him.

Both teams played the sixteenth well, with pars all around. Colonel Sebastian just watched silently with his entourage following closely behind. Hutchings and Kirk noticed that the colonel never traveled anywhere alone. Even at the first meeting, though he appeared to be alone, his henchman, Jennings, they now recalled, had been sitting at another table.

At the Road Hole, Tolliver and Kirk both missed the fairway. Tolliver hit his ball down the left rough in the whins, while Kirk's ball broke a second floor window at the Old Course Hotel! Mullen and "the Quiet One" hit fine drives that faded over the outbuildings of the hotel, leaving them 200 yards to the green.

Mullen had been left alone again, for Tolliver was unable to move his ball more than a few yards. His approach with a spoon found the right front fringe of the green, a very respectable shot for that hole.

Hutchings selected a cleek and his low-running, draw flew 180 yards in the air, kicked to the left and ran the remaining 20 yards up the slope and onto the putting surface. Things were not looking good for the Tolliver-Mullen duo.

Mullen surprised his group by chipping up the steep bank with a brassie, the ball rolling nicely and even striking the pin. Tolliver yelped as if he had been stung by a bee! Mullen's short par putt was conceded and he made his way to the road to observe his opponent's birdie effort.

Hutchings wasted no time. His putt broke nicely toward the hole but caught the edge and spun out some two feet away. Expecting to hear the putt was conceded, he looked around and studying the putt, knocked it in for a tying par.

The stage was now set for an exciting finish. Hutchings and Kirk were still one up with one to go. The best that Tolliver and Mullen could expect, would be to tie the match. That would be a victory for them, since they had never beaten Hutchings and Kirk before. Even so, Hutchings was back on top of his game, and there was still the "Sebastian" money to consider!

All four players hit fine tee balls over toward the first tee, the safe way to play the 18th hole. Kirk's second shot flew a bit too far, landing well into the green and chasing up into the rough. Tolliver's shot failed to make it up the slope and trundled back into the fabled "Valley of Sin", a deeply undulating swale from which it is most difficult to play a decent shot.

Hutchings played a low-running punch that landed at the base of the swale, skipped into the slope and, then releasing, rolled ten feet above the hole.

Mullen knew what he had to do. Tolliver or he needed to make three and hope that the best Hutchings and Kirk would make was a four. He opted for a clipped niblick and executed it perfectly, landing within 15 feet. Then, the unthinkable happened! His fine shot must have hit a hard spot, because the ball landed with a loud thud, bounding up and through the thick rough and out of bounds!

Mullen's mouth dropped wide open. . .

"In the name of the wee man. . ." he cried, "What in the world was that?" ***

The others were likewise dumbfounded. None had ever seen a ball behave like that one. Now it was up to Tolliver. He took his putter out, studied what he had to do and hit a wonderful putt that lipped out of the hole and rolled 4 feet past. Kirk had chipped out of the rough, but his ball never slowed down, rolling off the front of the green. It was now Hutchings's play. All that was needed was a two-putt to tie the hole and win the match.

Before he could bring his putter back, Mullen called, "Charles, pick it up.....your birdie is good!"

"That makes mine good too, doesn't it?" inquired Tolliver hopefully.

Kirk answered, "Why certainly, James. You seem very concerned about that putt. Why you don't even need to putt, your partner conceded Charles's birdie try!"

"Maybe you've forgotten, Andy," continued Tolliver, "but a par on the 18th gives Mike and me three pars coming in!"

"And your point would be?" inquired Kirk.

"Well," James Tolliver finished his point, "I believe that both teams can now claim Colonel Sebastian's five pound sterling!"

At that remark, all four gentlemen began to snicker at their good fortune. There was one person watching the finish who seemed less than excited about the result.

Colonel Sebastian had already disappeared behind the clubhouse but they knew he would be waiting for them at MacTavish's. They were all most curious to see the kind of mood he would be in after losing money to both teams!

Hole 7 High Out

It had been a long day on the course for Charles Hutchings and he was particularly happy when he opened the gate at the cottage on the outskirts of the tiny village of Pitscottie, a mere six miles west of St Andrews.

The village itself consisted only of a pub, a stable, an eatery and a few other traveler sites and, of course, the residents themselves. There was always plenty of traffic since it remained one of the main roads leading to St Andrews.

After entering the cottage, Charles sat on the window sill, gazing out of the back window toward the heather and gorse abundantly strewn over the hillocks in the distance. The cottage he had rented was a comfortable little dwelling. From the outside, its whitewashed stone walls, sitting behind flowering vines that seemed to embrace the tiny home, made for a most inviting appearance.

It had the kind of look that made you immediately most comfortable. You wanted to peer in one of the windows, not as a "Peeping Tom" but merely to see how it looked on the inside. . . .In other words, it was appealing!

The cottage consisted of an eating area, a table near to an open fireplace; a sitting room with plenty of books and reading lamps tucked on corner tables; and a bedroom with walls of vertical wooden slats, painted a soft yellow shade.

The interior design was common to the area, for people in this part of the world led simple lives. Their needs for day-to-day existence remained quite basic.

Hutchings and Mrs. Norton needed a base of operations, as well as a safe place to live, and this pretty little house served that joint purpose perfectly. Hutchings had rented this home for several months, primarily as a place for Irene to reside and she had truly made it a warm, comforting sanctuary. As he was sitting there, thinking about her, the door opened and Irene entered carrying a small basket of roses.

Irene Adler Norton, "Addie", had been waiting eagerly for his return. She wanted to hear what, if anything, Andy Kirk might have said to Charles about last night's meeting.

"No, Irene," Charles answered before she could even ask, "Andy said not a word, but I could tell his decision was weighing heavily on his mind."

"Oh, my," Irene replied, "I was afraid of something like this. He's going to change his mind, isn't he?"

"We'll find out later tonight," Hutchings continued, "I told Andy we'd meet him at the ruins of the Old Cathedral at nine o'clock."

Irene paced back and forth for several minutes finally asking, "Should we go over our plans to make certain we haven't forgotten anything?"

Charles caught her by the arm and pulled her to him, "Irene, you need to relax a bit. You've done everything that needed doing. We've only to meet with Andy and start to put our plan into effect."

"Perhaps you're right," Irene conceded, "I think I'll take a short walk over the brae and enjoy the evening breeze."

Hutchings followed her out of the cozy cottage and watched her disappear through the path along the whins.

These two had been working together for several months now. Irene Adler Norton was known far and wide as an actress, songstress and adventuress. She had appeared on stages throughout England and the Continent, usually to rave reviews. When she married Godfrey Norton, her life changed drastically, for they traveled to the United States and had settled down to life as Americans until circumstances changed radically.

Most recently, she had allied herself with Mr. Charles Hutchings, aka "the Quiet One." She had been contacted by him in the hope that she might be interested in helping capture one of Europe's most dangerous criminals. Irene accepted his offer without reservation, for she had come to know Hutchings years ago, when both were involved in an effort to avoid a most delicate international scandal.

Charles Hutchings was delighted at her acceptance of his offer, for he had been stricken by her amazing talent, courage and intellect for many years prior. Hutchings (he had chosen that name as his alias) needed someone to work in the background to put his plans into effect. He needed certain things to fall into place in order to spring a successful trap.

First, he needed a location where he could operate and put his plans into action with little notice. Second, he needed opportunity, that is, a situation had to be established where the prey would be exposed and easily captured. Third, he needed secrecy, for their plan had not been cleared by the law. Lastly, he needed backup, a cast of trustworthy individuals who shared similar beliefs and constructs.

Irene Adler Norton was one such person. They both believed that Andy Kirk was another of similar ilk. Oh, Mrs. Norton had many contacts of her own in place, for she had come to know many powerful people when she traveled across Europe performing. Those allies would also prove most useful as these plans continued unfolding.

Hutchings had conceived a plan that began with golf at St Andrews, Scotland. Although he had never played the game, it seemed to be a relatively simple way to get close to his target. He reasoned, "How hard could it be to play this game?" It sounded like child's play. There sits a ball. Get a club. Hit it!

Reality quickly entered the picture. He found that he had greatly underestimated what the game requires. Still, he stuck with it. In fact, he worked so hard learning to play, that the famed golf "addiction" had taken hold of him. Now, he was becoming more accomplished every day!

His original purpose for learning to play the game was to create a persona that would allow him to get closer to his prey. So far, so good. St Andrews and golf allowed step one to proceed as desired.

Opportunity was assured, for he had indeed been befriended by the target criminal that he was pursuing! In fact, a match was soon to be arranged whereby the final step would be taken and the world would be safer with one of its most heinous villains locked up or swinging at the end of the hangman's noose.

With the addition of Andy Kirk to their team, Irene and Charles felt certain that their plan would be successful. He was the kind of individual that could be trusted at all costs. He was a golfer and great storyteller to boot. There was nothing like listening to golf stories over a refreshing drink, especially when told by a true raconteur.

As Andy Kirk's frequent partner, Charles had seen how other players gravitated toward him, for Kirk always had a kind word for everyone. That is, unless you tried to take advantage of his kindness. Suddenly, another side of him would come to the fore and he was a match for anyone, be it verbal or physical confrontation.

Hutchings recalled how much he loved to hear Andy tell his jokes and golf stories to his many friends at MacTavish's, and he had quite a repertoire. He could tell one after another if he was in the right mood. One of his favorites was called by name, "the Niblick." The golfers would howl at Kirk's oft-heard rendition and no matter how often you heard it, you couldn't help from laughing again.

It was on one of those days, after hearing that joke, that Colonel Sebastian first took a liking to Kirk. From that day, the colonel would come around whenever he learned that Kirk

was holding court. Hutchings could still remember that day.
After a few drinks, the patrons started chanting, "Niblick,
Niblick, Niblick, Niblick". . . Then they began banging their
tankards on the bar top! This went on for several minutes
until Angus MacTavish spoke up loud and strong.

"Kirk," he cried, "in the name of the wee man, will ye please
tell the tale?"

Kirk shook his head back and forth then stood up and
inquired, "Gentlemen, you've heard this tale too many times
before to still find it funny, don't you think?"

A chorus of boos indicated that they apparently wanted to
hear him tell it again!

"That bein' the case," he said, "well, this will be the last. . ."
And with that, he began the story.

"I walked into Doctor Callahan's office the other day
to complain about a pain I had in me throat. Me voice
was quite hoarse and it hurt me to talk, I told him.
Well, he asked me how I got it.

I told him it happened at Troon. Troon, he said?
I told him it was so. Go on says he, so I continued.

Me and me group was havin' a hard time, a terrible
time that day and we was goin' far too slow. Can ye
imagine, we was so slow that we was actually holdin'
up a group of women out traipsin' around the grounds?

Me bein' a gentleman, I talked the boys to allow them
to play through. And I don't have to tell ye, the women
were both pleased and surprised.

Well, one of the girls hits one far to the right, over the
boundary fence into McGraw's farmland. I thought I had
seen it so when the woman comes over I decided to help
her find the lost ball.

We're looking and looking all over and havin' no luck
at all. Suddenly, I tells Doctor Callahan, I sees a cow
nearby and, I don't know what made me do it, but I lifts

the cow's tail, and would ye believe it, there sits a golf ball! So, what happened Doctor Callahan asked me.

Well, when I saw where it was, I called the woman over, lifted the cow's tail and said, 'Pardon me, ma'am, does this look like yours?' And she hit me in the throat with her niblick!"

Hutchings snickered a little when he recalled that day, for Colonel Sebastian was so surprised that he spit up his brandy and continued laughing for several more minutes. Many in the bar feared for his health, he laughed so hard and so long at Kirk's silly story.

Yes, that was one of Kirk's charms. For the joke, and the way it was told, opened up a line of communication with Sebastian. We now had easier access to that villain, making it easier for us to corral him.

Irene had returned from her walk and found Hutchings sitting at the table going over the plans. He was sipping his tea and whistling to himself when he heard the door close.

"Irene," he offered, "take a look at these sites. Which one looks most promising?"

"Well, each has its own strength," she answered. "For instance, St Rule's tower provides us with an excellent vantage point. We can easily see anyone approaching. A point against the tower is that we could be easily trapped should a group sneak past our sentinels."

She continued, "Now, consider the University. We could meet there in full view of everyone. I believe the expression is 'safety in numbers', but we wouldn't have much privacy if we had secret matters to discuss."

"Finally," she explained, "We have the ruins of the Old Cathedral and the walkway leading down to the shoreline. We could easily see if we were being followed, and still have plenty of space to do our work."

"So," Hutchings responded, "it really doesn't matter to you where we meet?"

"Let's discuss this later," Irene suggested, "I still have a few things to do to get ready before our meeting."

"You know, Mrs. Norton, we haven't had much time alone here in Scotland," whispered "the Quiet One." "We need to change that situation, and very soon."

"I don't know what you're talking about," Irene teased, feigning irritation over his comment.

"Oh, you don't?" he inquired. "I suppose you want me to state my intentions, which I might add, are purely dishonorable!"

"I'm not interested in your intentions, especially now, mister," Mrs. Norton responded, this time more seriously, "we have much too much to think about!"

At that remark, Hutchings had to agree that she was right. Until they had successfully completed their mission, there would be no time for any of life's more pleasant pursuits.

At 8:30 P.M., Hutchings pulled the carriage around to the front of the cottage. A few minutes later and Irene joined him for their trip to St Andrews and the appointed rendezvous with Andy Kirk. . . .

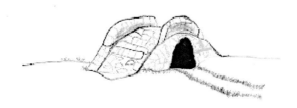

Hole 8 Short

Andy Kirk hated what he had just done. For the first time in his married life, Andy Kirk had lied to his wife. He and Agnes had just finished a wonderful plate of haggis, cleared the table and cleaned the dishes. At this time of night, Andy would usually turn to his books. An avid reader, he had lately returned to his favorite writer, Charles Dickens, but he would not be reading about Oliver Twist this night.

"Agnes, dear," he started, "I forgot to tell you that Charles wanted me to accompany him to MacTavish's tonight. It was something about some money that a mutual friend owed him and he thought it might be helpful to have a witness."

"Now Andy Kirk," his wife pleaded, "I don't like to interfere in your leisure, for the Lord knows you're a good provider, a loving husband and good father, but why do ye have to go out at this time a night?"

"Agnes," he answered, "I suppose that's the only time he could arrange this get-together. Anyway, it shouldn't take too long."

"Listen, Andrew," Agnes continued, "I wasn't born yesterday. You, Charles, Angus MacTavish, all together in his bar, with the music and the grog? . . Please, I know you'll be there for quite a while. . . . "

Andy Kirk must have had a most forlorn look upon his face after his wife's minor tirade. He was momentarily flummoxed by her attitude. Surely, this wasn't his Agnes.

"But that's all right, sweetheart," his wife concluded, "I was only teasing you. Have a good time, but be careful."

It was breaking his heart, but he couldn't tell her the truth. He gave her a quick hug and a peck on her rosy cheek and promised he'd be home as soon as possible.

Kirk took a slow walk up South Street toward the ruins of the old cathedral. These ruins, though a sad memory of a once proud period in Scottish history, had remained a popular place for visitors to the "Auld Grey Toon." However, that was during the day. At night, it was not a good place to be. What little crime occurred in that region of Scotland, usually took place at night.

As he approached the site of the meeting, he felt a cold shiver run down his spine. He supposed it was nerves. There were strange noises he had never noticed before. Kirk imagined people lurking in the shadows. Andy began fearing for the worst, but he tried to remain calm.

Turning the corner, he walked along the far wall of the old cathedral towers. He pulled out a box of matches and lit one to check his timepiece. As he examined it, the clock tower at the University told him it was precisely 9 o'clock.

The next thing he knew, Irene and Charles were alongside and all three quickly walked down the old pathway that led to the east shore and the water's edge.

"Did you know you were being followed?" Irene inquired.

"What?" Kirk replied, "you say I was followed?"

"Yes," she whispered, "let's duck down behind these dunes and we must remain very quiet!"

Charles led the way and they hid themselves behind a steep hillock covered with sea oats. In less than a minute, three men walked by, whispering among themselves.

"Can you see anything?" spoke the taller man.

"No," the shortest one replied, "what about footprints?"

"Jennings," the tall one called out, "there are too many pebbles and rocks to see footprints on this portion of the shore. The tide is returning and the water will have washed away any that were there in the first place."

Jennings, responded, "There must be some kind of secret passageway that we don't know about. I could have sworn I saw their silhouettes walking along the shoreline!"

"Well, we'll do a better job the next time," the short one spoke. "It's time we got back to the colonel."

And with that remark, they made their way back up the pathway and were gone.

"Ungh!" voiced Charles Hutchings, almost under his breath.

"You can say that again, Charles," urged Andy Kirk. "That was a close call!"

"They must have seen you when you entered the Old Cathedral ruins," Irene surmised.

"But I did everything you told me to make sure that I wasn't followed," Kirk swore. "I'm truly sorry. You know I'm not trained in this kind of cloak and dagger nonsense!"

"Kirk, I'm not accusing you of anything," soothed Irene Adler Norton. "They could have been expecting one of their own henchman. Who knows? Please don't trouble yourself over this matter. Let's move on."

The group walked along the shore, watching the tide surging in. After another five minutes, they felt safe enough to light a small fire and begin the night's work.

"Charles and I," Irene stated with deliberate assurance, "have been aware of Sebastian's plot to acquire a new and dangerous weapon."

"We have decided to intercept that delivery," she continued, "and that is where you come into the picture."

"Me?" asked the cooper. "Well, certainly. Just tell me what you want me to do!"

Charles smiled at Irene, acknowledging his friend's commitment to their plan.

"I'll go over the plan step-by-step," Mrs. Norton explained. "If you are confused by any of these directions, please let me know and we'll go over them until you feel you have a complete understanding of your role."

Kirk shook his head in agreement and Irene began to detail the plan of action.

Her sources had informed her that the package had been sent from Germany several days before. It had already arrived in Edinburgh and is supposed to be delivered tomorrow night by courier. Irene's contacts on the shipping end had planted a "mole" in Sebastian's gang, and they had assured her that all of their information was accurate.

The time of arrival was determined to be between midnight and two A.M. Information they had received also indicated that the "package" would be placed in the Road Bunker by the 17th green. It would be an easy task for Sebastian to pick it up, since he was staying at the Old Course Hotel which bordered the 17th fairway.

"Now, Andy," she spoke in a slow concise manner, "this is where you come in. . ."

"Charles and I will be out behind the wall on the other side of the road. After the drop has been made, we'll secure the package. It will be your job to drive a carriage at break-neck speed, stop by the green, pretend to load a 'counterfeit' package onto the back of the wagon and then drive off as fast as you can toward St Mary's College. When you get there, drop off the fake package at the front door of the Roundel. Is all of this plan clear to you so far?"

"I understand perfectly," Kirk stated emphatically.

"Good!" Irene continued. "Now this is very important. After you drop off your package, you'll see a young man. His name is Wiggins. He'll take the carriage. You will need to walk a block to Queen's Terrace where a black horse will be waiting

for you. Take the horse to MacTavish's and leave it there.
Then, walk straight home. Talk to no one. . . Is that clear?"

"Yes, I understand," Andy answered. "Then what?"

"Leave the rest to us," Irene responded. "We can fill you in
at a later date. The less you know about this, the better for
everyone involved. I hope you understand."

When Irene had finished, she and Charles disappeared into
the darkness, leaving Kirk alone on the shore with only the
mild lapping sound of the returning sea to disturb the silence.
Andy was careful to extinguish the fire completely. That part
of the beach would soon be covered at high tide and all
evidence of their meeting would be gone.

The next day moved swiftly, with Andy building a record
number of barrels, probably the result of the nervous energy
that he now felt surging through his being. While he was
eager to play his role in the upcoming mission, he was struck
by the harsh reality that he would be deceiving his Agnes for
the second night in a row.

That became his biggest problem. Should he tell her he
needed to take a midnight ride? No, that would never work.
His head began to throb. What if she caught him getting up at
that time of night/day? What could he say? His headache was
pounding even harder now!

Even if he somehow was able to sneak out, what could he
tell her if she found him coming in at three A.M. in the
morning. No, he was in a great deal of trouble, so much so,
that a part of him actually hoped that he would be caught by
Sebastian!

If he only knew that he had nothing to worry about. (For
Irene had thought of everything.) Imagine Andy's surprise
when Agnes approached him, and somewhat nervously
conveyed that she had to visit her sister that evening. Her
sister had wired, saying she wasn't feeling well and would

appreciate some company that night, if it wasn't too much trouble.

Andy gave her a hug, remarking, "Sweetheart, I think that it's very charitable of you to help your sister in her time of need. Just promise me that you'll be careful!"

What in the world, he thought. He sensed that somehow Mrs. Norton had made this happen. . .

Andy saw his wife to the station at 8:00 P.M. and he stood on the platform waving good-bye. The trip to Edinburgh would only take 2 ½ hours and she would be returning early tomorrow morning on the 10:40 daily.

As Kirk made his way back home, he marveled at the many facets of this elaborate plan. He found himself actually looking forward to the upcoming adventure, unaware of all of the possibilities that might arise.

At 11:50, Andy was out of his house and walking the three blocks to the Market Street livery stable. When he arrived, a team of horses was waiting for him. As he mounted the carriage, he saw a package resting on one of the seats. Looking around and seeing no one, he picked it up just to feel its weight. Deeming it to be no more than two stone, he tucked it back in its position and drove off to his appointed location.

Even a slow-moving carriage makes a great deal of noise, especially at that time of night. With every clip-clop-clip of his team's hooves, Andy felt himself grimacing. It seemed to take forever to reach the hilltop staging area one mile away from the Old Course Hotel. Andy's hands were beginning to sweat. He didn't like it, but he knew that was a good thing. He felt like a lion must feel immediately before making a deadly attack upon its prey.

The hardest part of the task, Andy imagined, would be the waiting. According to Irene and Charles, there was a two-hour block of time in which the "drop" could occur. He had been sitting there, waiting patiently for almost fifty minutes so far.

Even the horses were anxious to get started, snorting as if they were actually sensing the excitement that would soon come their way.

It was so very quiet. The only sounds to be heard were the waves washing ashore and the summertime songs of the crickets and frogs. Kirk kept watch for the signal when he heard a lone horseman riding his way toward the Old Course Hotel. He was well-hidden behind some large hedges, but he worried that his horses might give away his location. Fortunately, this was not the case as the rider sped quickly down the road, disappearing over the ridge.

His nerves were getting to him and he reached for the pistol he had stashed in his coat. That seemed to provide him with a sense of security, at least for the time being.

Seconds later, he saw the light from Hutchings's signal lantern. It was time to go! Quickly, he gave a loud crack of the whip and his team jumped forward. The carriage began to race down the hill toward his friends. While Kirk was charging toward them, Charles and Irene had retrieved the "real" package and started across the second fairway into the deep darkness of the "Old Course".

Kirk pulled his team to an abrupt stop, hopped out, ran to the Road Bunker and pretended to load something into his carriage. While he was so occupied, he could see and hear a group of men running toward him.

Jumping back into the carriage he once again cracked his whip and the horses stormed away at break-neck speed! He wanted to look behind but he decided against it when he heard a rifle shot and felt a bullet whiz past his head. Suddenly, he was really perspiring.

"Bullets?" he said aloud, "they forgot to tell me that there might be bullets!"

Two more shots rang out as he rounded the corner at City Road. He needed to travel two more blocks before he would get to South Street. It had only been five minutes, but it seemed like hours to Kirk as he drove his team helter-skelter through the sleeping city streets.

Gazing behind, he could see a wagon in hot pursuit. He simply had to reach the college or all would be lost. When he saw the street sign, he speedily turned his team up South Street nervously driving the remaining four blocks until the dark outlines of St Mary's College could be seen against a cloudless sky.

Turning into the main drive, he pulled his team to a stop in front of the Roundel. He grabbed the counterfeit package and hurriedly stowed it in the doorway. So far, so good. . . When he turned around he was startled by a young man who had been watching his every move.

"Wiggins?" inquired Kirk.

"Yes, sir, Mr. Kirk," the young man replied, tipping his cap. I'll take the team from here."

Wiggins hopped aboard the carriage and the team stormed away, rapidly rounding the sharp corner. Kirk started his brisk walk through the school grounds, breaking into a mild trot when he reached Queen's Terrace. There, just as he had been told, was a beautiful black stallion.

Wasting no time at all, Andy mounted the horse and raced across town to MacTavish's. He quickly dismounted and began his short trek back home. Along the twenty-minute walk, Andy tried to slow his beating heart. Though still shaking, he could not hold back a smile, for he had followed the directions he had received to the letter. Still, he had concerns. He worried that at any moment he might be confronted by Sebastian's followers. What about Mrs. Norton and Charles? And Wiggins too! He vividly remembered the brave young man taking up the team as Sebastian and his men chased him through the east end.

As he approached his house, Kirk noticed that the front gate was left ajar. Andy stopped and stepped behind the oak tree in his front yard. Pulling out his handgun, he made his way carefully around the back of the property and peered through the window that looked out upon the Kinness Burn.

Relieved at what he saw, he quickly put his gun back in his pocket and entered through his back door.

"Well-done, Andy," spoke a smiling Irene Norton, giving him a gentle hug. "You were wonderful!"

"Ungh!" came his friend's familiar comment.

"Uh, thank you both!" issued a very content, but still very nervous, Andy Kirk. "I'm both delighted and surprised to see the two of you!"

He was about to start asking the first of many questions that were racing through his anxious mind, but Irene was, as always, way ahead of him.

"Have a seat, Andy," she began. "I'll take you up to speed."

What followed was a detailed description of the events that had occurred from their point of view:

"When we flashed the light and you began your descent toward the 17th green, Charles and I had already taken the package. We continued running toward the second tee, hiding behind a dense patch of heather, from where we watched the rest of the action.

After you stopped, ran over to the bunker and pretended to place the package in your carriage, Sebastian's men had just started for the drop area. When they saw you speed past them and stop suddenly at the green, they began to panic. As you remember, I'm sure, some of them screamed for you to stop and then began to fire their weapons. The others had unhitched a team belonging to the hotel livery and began to chase after you.

Aside from the bullets that were fired, our plan went off perfectly. Sebastian and his men were so eager to capture you that they never bothered to look anywhere else! When they rounded the corner by the eighteenth green, Charles and I took a leisurely stroll over to your house to await your return. And, happily, here you are."

"What about Wiggins?" Andy asked after listening to Irene's account from their perspective.

"Andy," she returned, "I wouldn't worry about him. Wiggins is one of the craftiest young men I've ever known. I suspect he'll catch up to us later tonight."

Andy seemed satisfied with her response and sighed audibly. Suddenly, her final sentence took root.

"What? What do you mean catch up with us later tonight?" Andy asked most anxiously. "Aren't we finished?"

Irene paused, looked at Charles, then sauntered over to the stove to warm her tea.

"We haven't told you everything, Andy," Irene confessed. "There is still one more thing that we must do before our trap is set."

"Well," spoke Kirk, "I'm listening. . . . Please go on. . ."

"Andy, you've done more than enough," she continued, "Charles, Wiggins and I can finish the job. It's best for you if you await your wife's return tomorrow. She's going to be very upset when she finds that her sister is perfectly well and never wired her at all! Now, please get some sleep."

They closed the door behind them, leaving Andy to mull the recent events in his mind.

As Andy lay in bed, he found it very difficult to sleep. It was already four in the morning and, even though he was physically exhausted, his mind continued to race. He thought about all that he had seen, done and heard just a few hours ago, and then realized that they had never shown him the weapon! Hmmm, he thought that a bit strange for he certainly would loved to have seen the fruits of his labors. Yet, there was a wonderful sense of accomplishment as he lay there, smiling proudly, for he knew that he had done a brave thing. He was starting to feel more comfortable until. . . .

Whoops! He remembered Agnes would be coming home from her trip tomorrow. Yes, his beloved Agnes would be returning, but it would most likely be one of the following: Agnes the Annoyed, Agnes the Angry, or Agnes the Scared. He was fond of none of these last three versions and knew that she would have questions, as certainly anyone would who had been sent on a wild goose chase!

His sense of calm turned to one of desperation. How would he handle her questions? Could he even consider telling her the truth? What? Of course not, for she would be hysterical over how he had put his life in jeopardy.

The old Andy would have been terrified to see her thus outraged, but the new Andy had the solution almost instantly. Once he had learned how to lie, he saw some of the few advantages and quickly came up with a plan. For now, he was too tired to think and sleep arrived with a thud. . .

Hole 9   End

Andy awoke bright and early the next day and after eating his breakfast, washing and neatly stacking the dishes, he dressed for his trip to the station. Agnes was scheduled to be arriving shortly before eleven o'clock, and he knew when that train stopped he would have his hands full. She would either be annoyed, angered, scared or, God forbid, a little of all three!

As he waited for the train to arrive, he thought he had a suitable response prepared for every situation he might encounter. In an angry scenario, he might simply allow Agnes to blow off some steam. Then he could support her intensity, "That's right, Agnes, let the wire service come up with an explanation. Why you might even demand that they pay for your train fare!"

Should his wife appear merely miffed and inconvenienced by what had happened, Andy could give a philosophical response, "You know Agnes, aren't you glad that your sister wasn't sick?"

He was a bit concerned if Agnes ran to him, afraid that someone had purposely done such a terrible thing. His answer might be less straightforward, "You know Agnes, it could be a simple mistake, but we know there are some nasty people out there. We'll have to be less trusting in the future!"

He was comforting himself with his brilliance when the train pulled into the station. Suddenly, Andy began to quake like a willow in a hurricane, for he saw Agnes coming his way, and she didn't look too happy.

"Agnes, dear," he spoke softly grabbing her suitcase, "I'm so glad to have you back. How was your trip?"

Agnes looked up, gave him a dirty look, and shuffled off to their carriage.

So far, so good, Andy thought. She's really peeved, but this time it's not me. And with that scene safely played out, he grabbed the whip and headed his brougham back to the house, looking up to the sky, offering thanks. . . .

Last evening, after leaving Kirk's home, Irene and Charles still had much to do. They made their way to Double Dykes Road and found Wiggins waiting for them in a small buggy. He had hidden the "getaway" carriage in a shanty that had fallen into disrepair and become uninhabitable. Following the plans that were laid forth, he walked three blocks, hitched up a new team to this smaller coach and waited for Irene and Charles to arrive.

"Nice work, Wiggins," Charles said while he and Irene entered the coach, "You're as punctual as ever. Now make haste for the University museum. We've an artifact to hide and we need a good, safe spot!"

Irene smiled at those comments. They had successfully intercepted the package, but were somewhat dismayed not to find a weapon. The package, weighed down with rocks and shaped to look like some kind of square object, contained only papers and a small model that appeared to be a miniature rifle.

"Irene, our prize may seem to be only papers and a model," Charles said, "but, my dear, think, now we have an actual form of the device and can better study its workings!"

Hutchings and Mrs. Norton had had a chance to examine the papers and the miniature design at Kirk's house while they waited for him to return. The blueprints showed the design of the rifle, which at first didn't appear much different from other ordinary rifles one might see in a hunting lodge or munitions store. But this model had some features that clearly distinguished it from other weapons. They had to assume that this was the package Sebastian had been expecting. Now was not the time to study the miniature, for they still didn't know if they were in the clear!

While their transport moved ever closer to the University, Irene posed the question as to the current whereabouts of Colonel Sebastian.

Tapping Charles on the shoulder, she asked earnestly, "I need your thoughts on this question. Don't you think it a bit odd that we haven't seen or heard Sebastian or his men by now?"

She had raised a good point, for given what had happened just a few hours ago, one would imagine Colonel Sebastian's minions virtually going door-to-door looking for some clue, any clue, that might help him locate the people who robbed him of that most sought-after device.

"Mrs. Norton," Charles replied, "I share your concern, for we both know how much this item means to him. Still, your plan, brilliant in its simplicity, beg pardon, may have completely flummoxed his criminal mind."

Hutchings knew better than to look at Irene after this playful comment, but simply added, "In any event, no news is good news, or so they say. . ."

It was twenty-five after four in the morning when Wiggins brought the buggy to a stop in the alley directly behind the museum at the University of St Andrews. After Wiggins had driven away, Charles and Irene made their way across the school grounds to the back entrance of the famous museum, home to many of Scotland's most priced relics. The back door had been left ajar earlier in the evening by Wiggins, all part of the plan. Slipping inside, they had to move quickly for soon it would be dawn and they couldn't afford to be seen inside a "locked" museum.

Needing a clever hiding place for the items, they carefully sorted through many of the different collections. From Scottish jewels and historical armor, to brilliant works of early Scottish art, they searched and searched. Whenever they thought they had found a place, there were weaknesses. With sunrise approaching, Charles spotted something in a glass enclosure. It was an old steel scabbard embossed with the McLeod clan tartan. It had a lock at the top and the key was placed next to it, properly displayed.

There was no time to waste, Charles slid a sharp knife under the glass casing and pried it open. Irene grabbed the scabbard and quickly placed the rolled-up blueprints and model inside. Charles snapped the lock over the end of the scabbard, turned the key and carefully lowered the glass top back over the historic artifact.

Placing the key in his pocket, Charles took Irene's hand and they hastily made their way through the back door, locking it behind them. Together they crossed North Castle Street and followed a familiar path down to the coastline. After an hour's walk, they emerged at the far end of St Andrews Bay, just in time for breakfast at the Royal Hotel.

Following a most delightful repast, they started out through the hotel lobby, trying to appear discreet when they recognized the voice of William Davison, the hotel manager, talking to his employees.

"All of you need to pay attention," he spoke with great elation. "Next week an old friend of mine will be staying on holiday with us and I want you to be at your best."

The staff listened with rapt attention as he continued his directions, "So, when Doctor John Watson arrives, I want to be contacted immediately, do you understand?"

All of the desk staff indicated that they did indeed understand, at which time Davison clapped his hands and walked into his office.

Hutchings's face had turned an ashen white when Irene glanced at him. His legs buckled somewhat and Mrs. Norton had to hold on to him.

"Irene," he said, "I don't know if I'm delighted by what I've just heard or terrified!"

"Come, now," she said, "we've got to get back to the cottage and plan our next steps. This development doesn't change things. We have to finish what we've started."

The pair left the hotel and walked to the livery stable to get their team for the trip back to Pitscottie. It was another beautiful summer's day with a brisk wind accompanying them on their way back to the white cottage that had served them so well as both home and headquarters. They had been very fortunate to have accomplished the first part of their plan, but there was still a great deal more that needed to be done if Colonel Sebastian was to be brought to justice.

As the carriage rounded the bend, Charles noticed that the front gate was wide open. Instead of pulling his team through the open fence, he kept going as if he had no intention of stopping there in the first place.

"Steady, Irene," he spoke slowly. "Get the revolver from my jacket and stand ready."

"What?" she asked with some temerity in her voice.

"Act like you're enjoying the day," he whispered to her, "and perhaps they'll ignore our passing!"

Irene caught the squint in his eyes and understood why he had cautioned her thus.

They drove a few more miles down the road before pulling their carriage over among a forest of evergreens and poplars.

"Irene," he said, "we are discovered! Somehow the colonel has found out about you and you are now in grave danger."

"What's to be done about it?" Irene inquired. "We can still get our work done. We'll just have to find another place to make our plans."

"I'm going to contact Wiggins and have him meet us at St Rule's tower tonight at 8:00 P.M.," spoke "the Quiet One."

"What about the cottage?" Irene inquired.

"If you're up to it," Hutchings offered, "I think we can make our way through the whins to the back of the cottage unseen. If we determine that they've left, we can enter and gather what's still useful to us."

"Let's go, then," Irene spoke with great conviction, "I'm certainly up to it, especially where that man's concerned!"

It took longer than they thought to make their way through the dense heathery gorse that was so prevalent in that area of Scotland. Fortunately, luck was with them. When they peeked over the hillock, they saw Jennings and two others leave the cottage and gallop away toward St Andrews. They waited several more minutes before venturing any closer to the whitewashed dwelling, and it was Hutchings who made the first move.

He crept over the slight rise behind the rear wall which surrounded the building and made his way to the rear window. Irene was waiting for a signal from him. Peering in, she saw him shaking his head.

He stood up, turned to her and called her over to the back door. The broken latch was dangling from the door frame and they swung it open and entered their soon-to-be former home. Sadly, the place had been totally ransacked.

Irene's clothing, newspapers, and foodstuffs had been thrown all over. Her closet had been emptied, and some of her clothing had been torn beyond repair. As could have been expected, Irene hadn't left any of their "important" papers in the house. The burglars had come away empty, for the plans

Charles and Irene had made were safely hidden in the bottom
of their carriage.

Suddenly, Irene began to cry. It was not because she had
lost any important clothing. The scoundrels had not stolen
any jewelry that had any real value. No one had been hurt, at
least physically, by this break-in. Yet, this strong, intelligent,
brave adventuress found herself in tears!

"Oh dear," she said, "Please, forgive me. I don't know why
I'm crying. This makes no sense to me. . . ."

Hutchings slowly walked over to her, hugged her and said,
"Irene, what you are experiencing is totally to be expected.
It's not that you or I have lost anything important, for these
clothes and objects are easily replaced. . ."

"Then why am I so affected?" she pleaded. "Please tell me!"

Holding her even closer he said, "My dear, it's the feeling
that you've been violated. Your sanctuary, such as it was, your
home has been criminally desecrated by these thugs. It is a
perfectly normal human reaction."

"Well, be that as it may," she offered, "I'm embarrassed by
my reaction. It won't happen again."

Irene gathered some of her belongings while Charles was
getting the wagon. They decided that he would return to the
Robbie Rooming House and she would stay at the Royal Hotel
until they had finished their work.

Later that evening, Wiggins was waiting at St Rule's tower
when Charles, Irene and Andy arrived. The meeting would be
a short one, but, nevertheless, an important one.

"Irene," asked Kirk, "Do you have any further need of my
services?"

"Andy," she went on, "You, sir, have our most heartfelt
thanks for your part in last night's success. As to your
question, no, Andy, we no longer will call upon you for help."

"Ungh!" voiced his friend, Charles, shaking his hand.

"However," Irene continued, "Charles wants the two of you to remain the best of friends, both on and off the course. We would only ask that you never speak of last night to anyone. Is this agreeable to you?"

Andy bowed his head, shook hands and started to leave the tower, saying, "It was a genuine pleasure to have helped ye in any way. Remember, should ye ever need me again, ye've only to ask."

After Andy had left, Wiggins, Irene and Charles began to plot their next course of action.

Charles began, "Well, Wiggins, as you now have learned they are aware of Mrs. Norton. I still don't think they have you or me in the picture yet! My thought is that they know she has accomplices who are ready to step in when necessary. They just haven't been able to find them."

Wiggins asked, "Well, what's next? What's our next move?"

Irene began, "Wiggins, tonight we need to move the blueprints out of the museum and hide them elsewhere. I'm afraid that someone must have seen Charles and me at the museum. I only hope that we aren't too late!"

Charles continued, "Here's what we need to do. Wiggins, I had a key made for the side door of the University museum. We need to go there, grab the scabbard and move it to a more secure location. Irene has already found a spot where we can safely store the artifact until the colonel has been arrested."

Wiggins said, "I understand. Let's get on about our business, Guv'nor."

With that, the three moved quickly from the tower and over to the side door of the museum. All along the way they were careful to see that they were not being followed. With Wiggins standing guard in the shadowed doorway on a moonlit night, Charles and Irene carefully entered the building, moved to the display area, and quickly removed the scabbard from the case.

Hutchings took his key and opened the top lock. Irene slid the blueprints and the miniature rifle from the scabbard and examined them to ensure they were authentic. At that point, she quickly returned them to the sheath and tucked it under her arm. After Hutchings had replaced and locked the case, they started for the door and the sweet night air. Suddenly, Charles put his hand to his mouth and the two of them moved nearer the wall. Ever so faintly, they could hear footsteps a short distance away, coming closer and closer to the display case which had formerly held the scabbard.

Hutchings took a peek around the column behind which he and Irene had been hiding. There, not ten feet away, was a museum guard making his nightly rounds. He began to whistle to himself as he moved off in another direction continuing along his evening route.

"Whew," Irene whispered, "that was close!"

Two minutes later and they had rejoined Wiggins outside the building. He was quick to inform them that he had seen no one while they were in the museum.

"That's a good thing, Wiggins!" chirped Hutchings. "Now, let's get this thing done. Quickly, lad, take us to the Cathedral, there's no time to waste!"

Wiggins took the whip to the horses and the wagon sped away down the dark streets. . .

Once again the three shadowy figures entered the old Cathedral grounds. Irene led the way, for she had discovered an excellent hiding place. She led Hutchings and Wiggins to the other side of the historical site and stopped when they reached the ruins of the main entry. There, down in the lower left side of the first step was a most hardy hemlock bush growing right out of the wall itself. The roots were solidly attached to the rocks one foot above the ground, but the dense leaf and branch structures stretched from the ground up to a height of nearly three feet.

It was underneath the growth that Irene had hollowed out a shallow area and inserted a long box that lay under that section of the foundation. There they stored the scabbard with its precious contents, and after placing a lid atop the box, covered the area with small pebbles, dirt and other indigenous materials.

To anyone who might examine the area, there was nothing, absolutely nothing, that would suggest a hiding place.

Satisfied with the site and the work they had done, they walked back to St. Rule's tower to continue developing their plans.

After a brief discussion, it was decided that with Hutchings back at Robbie's rooming house, and Mrs. Norton now residing at the Royal Hotel, they might be safe for a while.

Wiggins had suggested that the blueprints be taken to Scotland Yard for safekeeping, but Hutchings felt that they were safe where they were. He believed that they would make an excellent bit of evidence when the colonel was finally brought to trial. He also intimated that while Scotland Yard had some competent detectives, there were very few that he would ever entrust with such a valuable piece of evidence.

Irene and Charles instructed Wiggins to begin working as a caddy for the present time. The current plan might call for his presence on the grounds of the "Old Course". They assured him that when everything was set, he would be so notified.

Charles and Irene made their way back to the hotel. They had had her clothing dropped off earlier in the day and she had checked herself in to that stately establishment just a few hours before. It would be a much safer place for her.

It was on this short walk that Charles shared a new idea he had recently developed, believing that this plan, properly executed, would lead to the capture of Colonel Sebastian.

Charles stunned Irene when he told her that he was going to involve an old acquaintance of his. . . one Doctor John Watson, a man one could count on at all times.

He outlined the plan in the following manner:

Irene would be in the lobby on the day Doctor Watson arrived at the Royal Hotel. She would be standing somewhere in the background– someplace where the good doctor might not easily spot her. It would not serve their cause if he were to notice that he was being watched!

Irene would have to surprise him. Hutchings suggested that Irene approach him and express her deep sorrow over the loss of his bosom friend, Sherlock Holmes. A conversation would naturally follow with Irene suggesting perhaps dinner together to discuss common interests, or some such notions.

After that initial contact, Irene and Hutchings would have the opportunity to secure Watson as another ally, should they need him, in their continued effort to apprehend Sebastian. Watson would learn of the plan and Mrs. Norton's involvement if, and only if, it were necessary. Hopefully, he would never need to know that Hutchings was anything more than just a golfer. Should that happen, Watson's life would be in imminent danger.

Charles concluded this initial phase of his plan, informing Irene that he would soon be in touch with her to finalize things. After seeing her safely into the hotel, Hutchings headed back to the Robbie Rooming House. . . .

End of Part I

Part II

Hole 10 About Turn

"John, I'll have no more of this. I've had it with you," my lovely wife Mary complained. "You've been carrying on now for much too long. Why you know that he himself wouldn't have approved, don't you. It's time to get yourself together!"

Although I knew she was speaking the truth, I just continued to gaze up at the rainy sky through a foggy window, not daring to respond to her urgent request. It was certainly not a topic worthy of debate, nor could I, or would I, dare interrupt her frantic pace. Totally immersed, she was scurrying about our study, tidying up the dwelling before embarking on a trip to Surrey. Mary and our two boys, Ian and Barton, had made plans to visit the cousins at their lovely estate for a fortnight and she was once again trying to shake me from my stupor.

It had been a most difficult time for me after the passing of my dear friend, Holmes, as he pursued the villainous Professor

Moriarty to his ultimate demise. Sadly, my malaise was beginning to wear on her, poor thing.

I was ready to respond to her remark when she began once more, "John, dear one, why don't you cancel some of your appointments and come with us? That might be just the thing. . . or, she hesitated briefly, walking over to me, why not a trip to St Andrews? You know how much a round or two of golf always revives your spirits."

Hmmm, golf, I thought. She may be right! I can't keep going on the way I am. Life goes on after all. Quickly, I rushed over to her, gathered her up in my arms, and kissed her tenderly.

"Why John," she questioned, "what on earth has gotten into you?"

"My sweet Mary," I answered, "that is a capital idea. I have been so selfishly preoccupied these last several months, wallowing in my own self-pity, that I have made your life most miserable. Your suggestion makes perfect sense to me. I'll cancel all of my appointments and get away to St Andrews to clear my mind. When I return home, I'll most assuredly be a much cheerier man. That is, as long as my golf game isn't too discouraging."

"That's a good lad," she replied. "The children and I will, of course, miss you, but I believe some recreation in the fresh air will do wonders for you, John."

After returning my hug, she went back to her tasks while I took a brougham to the wire service and informed each of my patients that I would be unavailable for the next several days. Thereafter, I contacted the famous Royal Hotel and secured accommodations for my stay in that grand old city. Before returning home, I purchased my rail pass for the trip which would be leaving King's Cross station at 8:20 AM on the morrow.

After dinner with the family, I excused myself and tried to get some extra sleep in anticipation of my golf excursion.

Strangely, I tossed and turned much more than I had in a long time. Visions of the beauty and challenges of the "Old Course" kept flowing through my mind. I couldn't stop thinking about the history of the place and I remembered how the "Old Course" rejuvenated me. Golf had always had that effect on me, although I never found enough time to play as much as I desired.

"John, oh John," came my morning wake-up call, "Time to greet the day, dear one."

The mellifluous sounds of my sweet Mary's voice lovingly roused me from my slumber as sunlight poured into our bedroom. Wiping my sleepy eyes, and rising from our warm bed, I found Mary up and about, dressed and packed for her trip.

"Good morning, sweet one," I whispered to my doting wife.

After a good stretch, I smiled, watching her flit about the room, making our bed.

"You know, John, the train won't wait for you even though you are the celebrated Doctor John Watson," she teased.

"What are you saying, woman?" I queried. "Why, they should be honored by the presence of the man who successfully wooed and won the hand of the most wonderful girl in all of England."

"Oh, how you go on," she replied. "Honestly, you are such a prevaricator."

"Me, tell a lie about such a thing? Why, I'm cut to the quick," I feigned being slighted by her remark.

"Well," she continued, "you can stop your sweet talk for the moment, but I expect to hear much more of it when you return from your trip."

A comforting hug followed that exchange and soon I had eaten my morning porridge, sipped my tea, grabbed my clubs and bags, kissed my family good-bye, and headed out the door for the train station.

The train departed as scheduled and I once more began my daydreaming about the "Old Course". It would be good to get away from the mundane work-a-day world for a while and try to enjoy the sheer beauty and tranquility of the linksland. I settled into my compartment and prepared for the long ride to St Andrews.

Prior to boarding, I had picked up a copy of the morning paper and browsed the headlines to see what had occurred during the past twenty-four hours. Hmmm, the Queen will entertain the Duke and Duchess of Hamlin this afternoon. That should be splendid, I joked to myself. What else? Oh, I see that they've captured the firebug who had been terrorizing Havisham Circle. That's a good thing. Let's see who has passed on in the last day or so. No, don't know that one....No, don't recognize that person....

Looks like all of my friends had made it through one more day.....Whoa, there! Ashton Price, Bradley Road Accountant, murder victim. Good Lord, he's my accountant, rather he was my accountant. Oh, dear, what a shame. He was a fine man and he had a wonderful head for numbers. Sadly, I'll have to miss his wake. Worse than that, I'll need to find another accountant!

I was ashamed of that last thought, very selfish on my part. After all, Ashton had handled my business for the last nine years. He was a good, honest, hard-working man. I'll sorely miss his friendship and his sage counsel.

Moving on to the social section, I scoured the pages for theater reviews. Alas, there were no shows that were of any interest to me. The rugby scores from last Tuesday were finally posted and I was happy to see Lancashire victorious yet again. As I continued to peruse the news, a knock on my door roused me from my comfort. It was the conductor looking to punch my ticket.

"Ridgely, I say, man, is that you?" I offered.

"You are the sharp one, now, aren't you, Doctor Watson," he replied. "I see you're on your way north. What is it this time, fishing or golf?"

"Ridgely, it's good to see you again," I said handing him my ticket. "You're correct, old boy. I'm going to play my golf at St Andrews."

"St Andrews?" he asked with a strange look on his face. "Do you mean to tell me that they would allow the likes of you to despoil such an historical golf course? Why, it's difficult for me to fathom such a thing."

"Why you old coot," I rejoined, "I could take the likes of you anytime, anywhere!"

He smiled broadly at that, "Good to see you, John. Hope the weather cooperates," he added shaking my hand.

Once he had left the compartment, I tossed the newspaper aside. I went back to my daydreaming as the old train rumbled around a sharp turn and under one of the many bridges that cross the route north. Once more, thoughts about my old friend entered my mind, for Holmes would always remain with me, while no longer in person, certainly always in spirit.

He had known that I played golf, and I always asked him to come and have a go at it. Try as I might, he always resisted my efforts to interest him in the sport. Holmes could never be coaxed into the game, which he referred to as "a complete and utterly frustrating, wasteful endeavor." Although a well-toned athletic specimen, cerebral exercises were more to his liking. Golf required much more time and patience than he could muster. Still, he knew that I was among the many who were captivated by the sport and rarely made comment when I happened to occasion the links.

As the train sped through the verdant countryside, I found myself recounting many of the adventures Holmes and I had shared over so many years. For him it was his life's calling, while for me, my profession and family remained most important. I would be lying though, if I were to state that the times spent with Holmes were not among the most enjoyable periods of my life.

He and I first met in London in 1887. At the time, I was still recuperating from injuries that I had incurred while serving with the military in Afghanistan. Sent home to recover from a bullet wound and also from an unfortunate acquisition (one of that god-forsaken land's many diseases), I needed a place to live while I was on the mend, so to speak. Finding myself on a very meager salary, I could not afford any decent lodgings at the time. While in London, I ran into a former acquaintance of mine from medical school who was kind enough to introduce me to one, Sherlock Holmes, a very "different" sort of individual, my friend had opined. I had found that his brief analysis proved to be "spot on".

After interviewing each other in an effort to determine compatibility prospects, we imagined that we could tolerate each of our unique idiosyncrasies and so paired up to split our rent at 221-B Baker Street. Initially, though cordial to each other, there was some natural tension, for we were altogether different types. He was extremely private and reclusive, or so I imagined him to be. I was slightly more outgoing, in my opinion, and believed myself to be a much more well-rounded person.

When Sherlock moved in, he seemed to spend an inordinate amount of time inside our quarters. Early on, he was most reticent to divulge his line of work and it began to wear on me. I remained most desperate to discover his occupation, for there seemed to be little activity ongoing, not counting frequent visits by apparent strangers at all hours to our modest apartments.

Looking back on those grand days, I readily admit that I should have been able to guess his line of work. It concerned me that he was able to pay his share when I never saw him working. Perhaps, I pondered, was he independently wealthy?

Might he be a violinist in the London symphony? Heavens, could this man be some sort of criminal? Hmm, early on I could only wonder!

I didn't have to wait very long to find that he was, in fact, as he later self-proclaimed, the world's "foremost consulting detective". And, yes, he certainly was all that and more, God bless his soul. . .

Holmes was a most striking individual; a tall, thin man, well over six feet. He had sharp and piercing eyes, excepting those times when he fell victim to his "habit". A thin, hawk-like nose added to his charisma. His noble chin, too, had the prominence and squareness which so often serve to identify the resolute man. For his lean appearance, he was extremely strong and athletic. When the "game was afoot," it was difficult to keep up with him!

For all his clever logic, one would imagine him to be extremely neat and orderly, especially with the records he kept on file. I fancied such people to be ever so concerned with their appearance. Strangely, Holmes could never keep his hands clean very long, for they were invariably blotted with ink and stained with chemicals. Additionally, he possessed extraordinary delicacy of touch, as I frequently had occasion to observe when I watched him playing his violin or when gathering clues at many of the crime scenes we visited. I had classified him a most gifted and, at the same time, bizarre human being. In truth, time would prove my appraisal most accurate.

The noise of the rail car rattling along the clicking tracks interrupted my thoughts for a few moments. The countryside was beautiful, even more eye-pleasing than I had remembered when last I traveled to Scotland. As the summer scenery continued to speed by as the train neared Newcastle, I renewed my reverie. So many cases came to mind. . . So many incredible solutions to seemingly unsolvable problems. . . Ah, where to begin, where to begin. . .

The first time that I was privileged to witness his brilliance on display was in the mysterious case I chronicled as "<u>A Study in Scarlet</u>." Interesting to note, in this particular case, were the startling differences between Holmes's means of solving a mystery and Scotland Yard's methodologies as practiced by Inspectors Lestrade and Gregson.

Neither of those law enforcement officials would ever own up to their true appreciation of Holmes's incredible faculties. To do so would have undoubtedly diminished their own standing in London's crime-solving circles. Oh, they might politely include a brief reference to Holmes in their case summaries, pointing out a particular fact that he was able to bring to the case. Sadly, little more, most of the time. Their jealousy of his abilities was most obvious but it scarcely bothered him at all.

Holmes was a master at his craft. An astute observer of his fellow man and possessing a keen ability to locate details so miniscule, that no one, save himself, could recognize. Only he would ever have been able to recreate many of the crimes that seemed unsolvable to the ordinary individual. On that point, it need not be mentioned, but Holmes was anything but ordinary!

The train continued northward while I gazed at the passing scenery. Much of the uninhabited landscape reminded me of our visit to the Moors and the case of the Baskervilles and that glowing "Hound from Hell." Oh, that was one I shall never forget. There were so many twists and turns in that case. How we ever survived that beast's vicious attack is truly a wonder indeed! Again, it was the incredible mental acuity of Holmes. He steadfastly refused to accede to all of the supernatural clues that constantly strained and assailed our mortal sensibilities!

As the train wound its way through a tiny village, I saw youngsters playing along the hillocks and hollows that bordered our tracks. It brought back more memories of our investigations; specifically, recollections of Holmes's special investigative team. What had become of our little group of detectives, better known as the "Baker Street Irregulars"? My, what an ingenious means of fact-finding Holmes had devised in putting this curious band to work. Imagine using young lads to search for clues. . . What ingenuity!

Oh, the workings of his incredible intellect! Imagine how easily an innocent child might gather information by carefully observing the daily goings on in a busy city. Sheer brilliance! Not even the most calculating criminal mind would ever expect youngsters serving as reconnaissance personnel.

As for their safety, Holmes had demanded total obedience to his dictums, which included traveling in numbers and always pretending to be playing some sort of game. Often their work was to scour an area, making mental notes of any and all deviance from the normal day-to-day activities in that area and report back to him. It had been a most helpful brigade, I must admit.

My imaginings were interrupted by the loud wail of our train whistle as we made our way past another small town station not scheduled on this trip. As our train chugged along, people on the station platform were gathering their packages and bags as they waited for the next train. By their anxious movements, I thought that there must be another one arriving soon.

Never a particular strong point of mine, this time my powers of deduction were rewarded when a swift locomotive came alongside our transportation heading in the opposite direction. I quickly returned to my daydreaming and decided to concentrate on the purpose of my trip –to play the "Old Course" and enjoy all of the challenges that came with it.

The scenery continued to change as the train chugged into the hill country that marked the Northeast corner of England. As we approached the highlands, our rail cars struggled mightily to remain on the tracks, for the climate variations associated with elevation changes had had an effect on the conditions of the roadbed. This area needed to be constantly monitored, and judging by the bouncing, someone must have neglected that task.

The continuous jostling accompanied by the rhythmical cadence of the clickety-clack of the train allowed my mind to recall some of my fondest memories of Scotland. Mary and I had some great times exploring many of the old castles and lochs. We particularly enjoyed visiting the magnificent city of Edinburgh with its Palace of Holyroodhouse, Scotland's official residence of the Queen. While there, we also toured famous Edinburgh Castle, experiencing the spectacular views of the storied city. Mary was very pleased when she was able to examine the lovely gardens and well-maintained grounds of that historic place. Ah, those were the days! As they say, how quickly the time passes!

A loud creaking sound, followed by a rather disquieting bounce, brought me back to reality as my train ride continued. We were proceeding nicely, and it wouldn't be much longer until we reached our destination, the pleasant little village of St Andrews. . . .

Hole 11 High In

St Andrews and the "Old Course"....I had forgotten just how
long it had been since I last had visited that fine old golf
course. My mind once again drifted back to that place. I
started to play an imaginary round. Memories of that course
were so vivid that I could actually envision each hole and many
of the obstacles that lay in wait for the errant shot.

The last time I played her, I was the guest of Commander
Joseph Lawler, a friend of Mycroft Holmes, brother to Sherlock.
Commander Lawler, a fine player from Woodbridge, was a
fellow member of the Diogenes Club, one of Mycroft's
frequent haunts. Both men were employed by "Her Majesty's
government" and shared many common interests.

When I arrived that chilly morning outside the stately
clubhouse overlooking the "Old Course" at St Andrews, I had
to change my golf shoes outside the building. I was quickly
soaked to the bone. Fortunately, I had remembered to bring
my brolly, for Scotland, and St Andrews in particular, hard by
the North Sea, was frequently met with inclement weather.
Knowing the kind of conditions I might face, I was mentally
prepared for what was to follow.

That day was a particularly rainy day with gusty winds adding to the demands of play. In Ireland though, I believe it would have been referred to as a "fine, soft day." Most, however, had chosen to remain indoors when we began our round, so we pretty much had the whole course to ourselves.

That was just as well, for I hadn't played for many months and I knew that I was capable of some truly horrendous play. Sensing that I was in for a most trying round, I tried to warn my golfing partner of the kind of play he might witness.

"Mr. Lawler," I explained, "I'm not sure if your company merits my limited skills on this God-forsaken day. Should you wish to beg out of this round, I would certainly understand."

"Doctor Watson, I'll hear nothing of the kind," spoke the experienced golfer. "We have the course open before us, two excellent caddies and a fine mist to accompany our play. Please don't worry about your skills or lack of them, I'm not too concerned with scoring today, and you shouldn't be either!"

Well, I thought, that makes it perfectly clear. The man has no idea of how poorly a game I can play, especially in less-than-ideal conditions. And off we went into the wind, rain, and, most recently a low-lying cloud bank. . .

Our caddies were bundled up for the elements and my Macintosh was to provide only the most rudimentary protection from the blustery winds and pelting rain. The umbrella offered little protection and quickly became unusable when one particularly vicious gust cracked one of the ribs holding the fabric together.

My game went as expected. I struggled with my drives, which seemed to fly higher than ever, making them all the more susceptible to the punishing winds. My poor caddy did a yeoman's job in tracking down most of my errant efforts. He even ventured into some of the heather and gorse, suffering some scratches and gouges, while attempting to retrieve my gutties.

Commander Lawler seemed to hardly notice the harsh conditions and I admired his steely manner of play. His caddy had a much better time of it since most of Lawler's shots landed safely in the short grass. Steeped in the tradition of the game, he accepted the conditions, playing the course as he found it. Not many golfers are so blessed with that type of composure.

As for me, I quickly grew agitated at both the horrid weather and the plethora of poor golf shots that plagued my psyche. I was embarrassed by the quality of my shots, but equally concerned by the quantity of them. Clearly, this would not be one of my finer rounds. I had prayed for some respite, suggesting perhaps a brief stop at a local establishment prior to completing the final few holes.

My sponsor would have none of it, explaining that conditions like this were what separated the men from the boys. After making that remark, he turned to me smiling and said, "So, are you up for it, Johnnie boy?" Too embarrassed to admit weakness I responded, "You know, Joseph, you're absolutely right. Why these added difficulties only make the day more memorable!"

That much was certainly true, for I would never forget that round and Mr. Lawler. Mercifully, the clubhouse was in sight and my travails would soon be over. I couldn't wait until I had a bowl of chicken soup and a hot toddy before me.

When we had finished our round, we were both soaked to the bone. In truth, Lawler had played remarkably well. So well, in fact, that he needed only two putts for a 77, easily one of the finest rounds I had, to that point, ever seen, and I remember that I had told him as much. He politely doffed his cap with one hand, extending his other to bid me good day.

With a wry smile he offered, "Thank you, Doctor, I appreciate your kind remarks. Hopefully, we'll get the opportunity to do this again sometime soon. In the meantime,

let's get some sustenance and warm ourselves indoors. You'll
be my guest."

I didn't know whether to laugh or cry, but I found myself
mumbling a rather contrite, "Thank you, oh, thank you. That
sounds very good....very good, indeed."

Yes, that was years ago and shortly thereafter, my golfing
days were few and far between. Much of my free time, or not
so free time, for that matter, would be spent with the world's
finest detective and the demands of a growing family. So, my
golfing was relegated to a less important status, and it was
probably just as well. To play this game, especially to play it
well, one needs plenty of time and opportunity to practice. At
that stage of my life I found I had neither.

Still, this trip would be different, different for many
reasons. The weather was much milder and those who like to
predict those things had assured those of us who read the
local news, that the temperatures in that part of the United
Kingdom would stay unseasonably warm for the next several
days. As I read that report, I smiled, thinking, "Well, that
would be very well received, but I'll believe it when I see it."

The train continued making its way through the woodlands
and open fields north, and the sylvan hills we were now
traversing were providing wonderfully scenic vistas. I began
to feel some hunger pangs for it had been a long time since
breakfast. Remembering that Mary had packed some scones
for the trip, I feasted on them and carefully washed them
down with some water I carried in my traveling flask. There
were still several hours left before I would reach St Andrews
and once more I found myself thinking about the layout I
would soon be playing.

The "Old Course" was a difficult yet fair test of golf, that is,
if you were able to keep your ball in play. Unlike many of the
parkland courses that have sprung up throughout all of
England, this course, perhaps one of the oldest in the game,

lacks clearly defined landing areas. Additionally, many hazards are difficult or impossible to see from the tee.

First-time players rarely experience much success unless they are playing extremely well, have a good caddy, are very lucky or enjoy a combination of all of the above. To be successful, the player must be careful to avoid the hazards. Each hole presents a variety of challenges to the golfer intent on playing well.

There was the Swilcan Burn guarding the green of the first hole. What a terrifying shot for the average golfer! Why your entire round could be ruined by that tiny stream. "Cheape's bunker" was the chief danger down the right side of the second hole along with the boundary fence also down the same side of the fairway.

Speaking of difficult obstacles, the "Cartgate bunker" which guards the third green, makes a drive down the right side of the fairway imperative if the player wants to have a safe shot to the flag. It's decision time when the golfer reaches the long fourth hole named "Ginger Beer." The player has to play his tee ball straight down a narrow gap or play left of a grassy ridge. That hole always seems to be most problematic to me and my limited skills. Perhaps this time I'll be more successful.

Number five is easily my favorite hole on the outward nine. Once players have safely negotiated "the Seven Sisters," a group of bunkers that lay in wait down the right side of the fairway, they still have to deal with two deep, yawning bunkers known as "the Spectacles," for obvious reasons. Having escaped these hazards, one gets to putt on possibly the most expansive putting area in the world. Sharing its surface with the thirteenth green, it's easily over 90 yards!

The sixth hole is notable for the "Coffins" and "Nicks" bunkers which lie down the left side of the hole. The former, I do admit, is aptly named, for if you land there, you're as good as dead.

What else? Ah yes, trouble awaits the player unable to avoid a large bunker called "Shell," which protects a most devious and undulating green, the seventh. I've never really been able to master the many subtle breaks of that fearsome surface! Three putts seem to have been my personal best there and I'm already concerned about how I'll do this time. What a game, what a game!

One of the finest views of the town of St Andrews is the reward given the golfer arriving at the eighth tee. A relatively short hole, it is made difficult since the player can't see the bottom of the flag because of mounds which obstruct one's vision.

Number nine brings the player to an easy four-par, barely over 300 yards. The chief dangers are two bunkers, "Boarse's" and "End Hole," which separate the ninth and tenth holes. Another feature is the blasted heather which runs the entire left side of the fairway rough.

As golfers head to the final nine, they must contend with a ridge that protects the front of the tenth hole's putting surface. A run-off to the right can send a ball trundling down and away from the short grass.

Another short hole, the eleventh, I believe it's called "High In," plays extremely difficult due to two of the most demonic bunkers on the course. Sadly, I've been victimized by both the "Strath" and "Hill" bunkers! Even if you manage to avoid them, the green is one of the slipperiest on the course. Many times I've putted my ball off the green and back into the fairway. Blast it all!

Never a long hitter of the ball, I always looked forward to playing number twelve. It's not very long for a four-par, but roughly thirteen yards shy of the green there lies a nasty little bunker that occasionally will cause problems.

More difficulties await players on "Hole 'O Cross," number thirteen, should they fail to fly their approach to the green. My ball has taken many unpredictable bounces whenever I came up short. The Captain of the Club once told me that this hole plays to an average of six in the Open Championships that have been played there!

The true challenge of the "Old Course" can all be experienced on one hole. I've found that number fourteen will expose the weakness of any golfer when you examine all of the hazards that this hole provides. Why, first of all, the hole is extremely long. It seems to go on forever! Indeed, that's the very name of the hole itself, "Long." On my first visit to number fourteen, I asked my caddy what I needed to do with my tee ball.

He told me to hit it perfectly straight, being careful to avoid the boundary marks down the right and the fabled "Beardies," a group of bunkers down the left side of the fairway. He also warned me to avoid the deadly "Hell" bunker that prominently presents itself to the golfer, advising me to play my second shot down the neighboring fifth fairway. Finally, I was told to pay close attention to my approach to the green, for there was a fiendishly steep slope there to influence my ball adversely. Hmmm, nothing to it. . .

The correct target for the drive on number fifteen, I remember, was the towering steeple farthest to the right on the town's distant horizon. The sheer length of this hole made it one of the toughest to play.

Most prominently featured on hole number sixteen, called "Corner of the Dyke," was a pair of bunkers comprising the "Principal's Nose." I learned from observing play on this hole that the best way to play it was to hit your tee ball left of the "proboscis." While it made the hole much longer, it was the correct play, the percentage play. Any ball landing in either of those bunkers would make for a difficult, if not impossible recovery shot. Still, the player must also avoid the "Wig" bunker, for that also is most tedious.

I was just preparing to play the seventeenth in my mind, when a shrill whistle echoed over the small hills that lay near to the seaside village of St Andrews. Distracted by the noise, I forgot what I had been doing and began to gather some of my bags so I would be ready when the train pulled up to the quaint old station.

After the porter opened my compartment door, I eagerly stepped down to the station's wooden platform. Before doing anything else, I found it necessary to take a deep breath to restore my senses. It had been a long ride from London, although the scenery and my memories helped to make the time go quickly.

"Doctor Watson, Doctor John Watson," called a voice I didn't recognize. It seemed to be coming from out of the shadows on the far side of the station.

Startled by the attention, I slowly proceeded toward the origin of the voice and spoke, "Hello, is someone calling me?"

"I am, sir, that is if you're Doctor Watson," came the reply from a rather diminutive hansom driver.

He continued, "I was employed to drive you to your lodgings, sir, compliments of the Royal Hotel."

"Well, well," I offered, smiling at the young man, "you've found your fare, lad. Thank you very much."

The young fellow wasted no time in getting me over to the hotel and he didn't spare the whip on the poor old roan hitched to his wagon. The quaint old town hadn't changed much, at least as far as I could tell. Before I knew it, we had rounded a corner and there, before my eager eyes, in all her splendor, was the "Old Course." Soon after, we arrived at the Royal Hotel which lay directly across the street from the Headquarters of the Royal and Ancient Society of Golfers.

Hole 12   Heathery In

It was well into the late afternoon when my carriage pulled up to the old majestic Royal Hotel. This fine inn had served as my home away from home whenever I chanced to visit the famous "Old Course." Its excellent reputation was most deserved, for it was known for its fine accommodations, outstanding service, and the scrumptious quality of its food. Located close to the St Andrews golf course, it was the perfect hotel for the avid golfer.

After alighting from the landau, I summoned the bell-captain. He quickly had my baggage and clubs removed to the interior of the ornate establishment. I stretched, took a deep breath and after climbing a few steps, turned to look out on the golf course that lay spread before me. I smiled a contented smile and allowed myself a few seconds to enjoy the strange beauty that is St Andrews. Tomorrow could not come soon enough and, at that moment, I felt the need to take a practice swing, imagining what it would feel like on the first tee. Oh, what a magical game that can lift the worries of the world from a person's shoulders, even if only temporarily. I certainly must have forgotten where I was for when I began to walk toward the hotel, I noticed that several of the guests as well as some passersby, were giving me inquisitive looks!

Upon entering the airy lobby, I immediately caught the eye of William Davison, proprietor of that grand old establishment. He seemed to be deeply engrossed with one of the hotel guests. When he saw me, he interrupted the conversation momentarily in the form of a wink in my direction. While still communicating with this patron, he waved his arm, pointing toward the hotel's main office. Returning his wave, I bowed and slowly made my way in that general direction as he courteously concluded his discussion and moved to greet me.

"Well, now, look who's made his way to St Andrews," Davison offered in a most kindly, teasing manner.

"William," spoke I, "the call of the linksland was too much for me. I simply had to return and once again try to conquer that which is unconquerable."

Laughing at my remark, he took my arm and led me into his office. I remembered that it was a most tidy room, full of bookcases and filing cabinets. A large blackboard was stationed on one side of his desk, indicating a list of hotel "things-to-do," as it were. A huge oaken desk was located in a corner, and a large window provided him with a breathtaking view of St Andrews Bay. He sat me down in a very comfortable burgundy-shaded leather chair and offered me a glass of sherry, pouring a glass for himself as well.

"John," he began, "It's good to see you. I've thought about you these last several months, wondering how you've handled your good friend Sherlock's passing."

"To tell you the truth, William," I responded, "it has taken me a while to come to terms with it all. My wife and children have seen another side of me, one of which I am not proud. I have suffered some depression and it's made things very difficult at times."

Pausing for a few seconds, my host took a long sip from his glass, rose from the chair and moved slowly toward me, rubbing his chin pensively.

"Now, John," the hotelier continued, "we all must face the harsh realities of life. Surely, Mr. Holmes would not have approved of this in the least."

"I know that you are correct," I stammered. "In fact, my wife was so sick and tired of my malaise that she insisted that I get away to my favorite place on earth. That, of course, is here at St Andrews."

"In that case," Davison spoke, "on behalf of the Royal Hotel and its staff, let me once more welcome you to St Andrews and may you have a wonderful visit. If there is anything, anything at all that I can do for you, please feel free to contact me. I want you to have a most pleasant time."

"As always, William, you are most kind," I replied. "While I have you here," I inquired, "Could you arrange several starting times for me on the 'Old Course'? I'd prefer the noon hour, if possible, but I would be happy with any times you might be able to schedule."

"Not at all, John," came the response. "The Captain always saves a few prime times for guests of the Royal Hotel and there's no one I would rather see fill those times than Doctor John Watson, London, England."

For the next several minutes, we tried to catch up on mutual friends we had come to know over the years, but soon he had to lead me to the door for he had business to conduct.

As we shook hands at the front desk, he added, "I'll make your starting times and try to join you for a drink later."

Moments later, I found myself amidst all of the noise and hubbub that so oft accompany the arrival of a group of tourist-golfers to the "Royal," as it's sometimes called. Just as I did when first I came here, they were anxiously looking about in every direction. Some were taking in many of the paintings depicting the game so dearly loved in these parts. Others were drawn to the large bay windows overlooking the quaint town and the links beyond. Some of the remaining arrivals were simply standing in line, eager to complete the registration procedure.

Everywhere the hotel personnel were flitting about, trying to cater to the newest patrons in every way imaginable. Bellhops pushed small wagons heavily laden with luggage and golf clubs which, as they moved across the tiled floors, produced a most annoying clanging and clatter as niblick and mashie brushed against each other.

Deciding to quietly observe the excitement on hand, and also to rest my weary bones, I found a most comfortable armchair in the grand lobby and positioned myself to view what continued to transpire. Desk clerks were collecting signatures, distributing room keys and explaining hotel rules and regulations with the utmost alacrity. Smiles and familiar greetings were repeated as each newcomer and returnee registered to stay in this most elegant edifice.

I was thus happily engaged, entertaining myself by trying to ascertain each new visitor's pedigree and occupation by their manner of dress and conduct, as well as the way they carried themselves. Holmes, of course, would have had no trouble in identifying any of them, I surmised. Still, I decided to try my hand, using many of the uncanny, yet simple, techniques he might have employed. And so I began. . .

My first effort proved spot on. Here, directly before me, marched, and I do mean marched, a rather tall, broad-shouldered man. Carrying a top hat in his left hand, he moved briskly to the hotel desk. Studying his tailored tweed suit, I deemed it to have been fashioned by Fainwright, Inc., one of London's finest clothiers. The man had a very pompous air about him, if I may be so bold as to insinuate! His smartly-polished black boots told me that he was possibly a horseman who had come to the quaint borough of St Andrews not for the golf, but for the bi-annual horse races.

My curiosity led me to move closer to the desk to see if I might validate my deducing. Pretending to read the local tabloid, I meandered near enough to hear the conversation between the desk clerk and this recent arrival.

"Greetings, sir," the man behind the counter politely welcomed his charge. "Welcome to St Andrews!"

"Ah, yes, ah thank you," the gentleman replied, scribbling his name and address in the registry.

Turning the book in his direction the clerk continued, "Well, Sir Thomas, I hope you will enjoy your stay with us. I heard that London is seeing more than its share of weather these days."

So far, so good, I thought.

Ignoring the clerk, Sir Thomas turned quickly and began to walk away. Suddenly, he swirled around and inquired, "Young man, would you please have one of your stable hands take care of my horses, particularly the sorrel thoroughbred in the racing silks?"

"Certainly, Sir Thomas," responded the young man. "I will personally see to it. Have no fear in that regard."

"You had better see to it!" the horseman growled, although somewhat under his breath.

Hmmm. . . I decided that Sir Thomas was a very hard, demanding man as I slowly returned to my chair. I smiled slightly, feeling that Holmes would have been pleased with my findings. With the arrival of another glass of sherry, I was preparing to continue my sleuthing when I was interrupted by a light tap on my left shoulder.

Rising from my position to investigate, I was startled by the beauty that met my glance.

"Dr. Watson," she softly spoke, "please forgive the intrusion, but I could never walk by without conveying my deepest sympathy to you on the loss of your dear friend, Mr. Sherlock Holmes."

"Thank you," I replied, bowing, "That's most kind of you, Mrs. Norton."

Irene Adler Norton, I need to state, was easily one of the most elegant, stately, beautiful women I had ever had the pleasure to have met. Her pictures, prominent on many theater marquees, though striking, could never do her justice, for all of her features were, dare I say it, flawless. And that remark was putting it mildly.

Irene was a slender woman, with long, wavy dark hair. Her well-defined figure indicated that she took some pride in her appearance, for she easily met the most demanding standards of any man's fancy! Her facial features and complexion could have been a match for the mythical beauty of Helen, whose face Homer reported, "launched a thousand ships." Those deep-set brown eyes indicated a most inquisitive and self-confident nature that made her even more interesting.

It had been said that Irene Adler Norton could quiet a room merely by entering it. I quickly found that, I, too, was caught up in admiration, though we had never formally met until this moment.

She nodded, smiling and continued, "I should have known that over so many years you might have learned his ways. But tell me, how could you have recognized me?"

"Mrs. Norton," I responded, "there isn't a playgoer in London who hasn't admired your talent, rare beauty and elegance both on and off the stage, if I may be so bold as to mention. Also, Holmes and I often discussed one of our most interesting cases involving a certain Miss Irene Adler, before she became Mrs. Godfrey Norton."

"Why Doctor Watson, you're most kind to make such generous comments," she remarked. "Those days, however, are long gone."

"Oh, yes," I interrupted her reverie, "Now that you are a married woman, you have taken on other challenges and responsibilities. I trust that all is well in your life?"

At that remark, she quickly turned away, sighing, "Sadly, it is not. Enjoy your stay, Doctor."

And, just like that, she disappeared down the long lobby hallway. I couldn't imagine why she had departed in such haste. Had I said too much? Could she have misconstrued my compliments? Perhaps she had a meeting scheduled and had noticed that the time was quickly approaching? I could only speculate.

Yet, she had made a point of coming over to me and offering condolences. Maybe she had simply decided to end the conversation? It could have been any of those things or none of them. At any rate, I decided it was now time for me to check in and find my room. The dinner hour was slowly approaching and I had yet to wash and dress. . .

When I approached my hotel room, coincidence afforded me yet another opportunity for reverie, for the bellboy opened the door to room 221. . . .Why should it have been 221, I wondered? I was struck that this hotel room should have the same number as our apartment at 221-B Baker Street. That address had been home to Holmes and me for many years prior to my marriage.

The young man unlocked the door and we proceeded inside. After he had placed my travel bag on the luggage shelf and had left the room, I suddenly felt the need to rest upon the bed. It had been a long day and the brisk clean air off the North Sea was doing its best to restore my mental state and part of that task quite naturally was regenerating my stamina.

A strange sadness once more began to envelop me as I lay there quietly. My mind turned to thoughts of Holmes and golf. Once more I regretted that I had never been able to interest my friend in this great game! How many times had I offered to introduce him to this great mysterious sport! One can only imagine the kind of golfer he might have become with his incredible powers of observation and his amazing ability to concentrate.

While he never professed to be a sterling athlete, I was always amazed at his suppleness and agility. He also, on more than one occasion, had demonstrated incredible strength when sheer power was called for. His eye-hand coordination was unmatched, for he was a top-notch fencer and, although he would argue this point, Holmes was an accomplished violinist.

As I continued to ponder these vagaries I slowly drifted away into a sound sleep....

What was that strange rapping sound? At least I imagined it to be a rapping sound. Again it came. And yet again. . . Wait a moment, where was I? I quickly tried to awaken myself from my nap and slowly made my way to the entryway.

"Who's there?" I inquired through the hardwood door.

There was no answer.

I called louder the second time, "I say, who's knocking?"

Once again, there came no reply. I continued to listen for any additional noise but the only sound I could hear was piano music that had to be coming from the main banquet room downstairs. I slowly reached for my service revolver, ever mindful of Holmes's advice, and threw open the door ready for whatever might be lying in wait for me. I saw nothing but the hallway across from my room!

Quickly, I bounded through the door, turning this way and that, prepared for what I might discover. Admittedly, I was relieved to find no one lurking. Half-amused, yet, at the same time disappointed, I started back into my room when I spied an envelope fastened to the outside of my door. After gazing around the hallway one last time I grabbed the missive and sped back to the quiet safety of my hotel room.

I was naturally anxious to rip open the sealed letter when, once more, Holmes's methods came to mind. Why he would never have succumbed to the temptation of tearing open a letter no matter how curious he might have been. He would be afraid that he would destroy some evidence that he might need for future reference. With his ways in mind, I decided to proceed with an examination of the letter as he might have. . . and so I began. . .

Turning over the item I deemed the letter to have been written on hotel stationery, not so difficult to discover since the Royal Hotel insignia was embossed into the upper left-hand corner. Brilliant! Next, I would try to ascertain the contents prior to opening the packet. What might be inside? The envelope certainly contained more than a piece of paper. One could tell simply by feeling the weight of the object. There was something sturdy inside, that much was evident.

Was there anything else that was to be gleaned prior to opening the letter? I slowly ran the envelope by my nostrils, hoping to put my olfactory sense to good use. Hmmm, there was a certain sweet perfume emanating from the paper. . . What could that mean? Perhaps, the letter came from someone of the female persuasion. . . or, perish the thought, some Scottish "dandy."

What additional information might I gather from the outside of this communique? I could wait no longer. I very carefully slipped the hotel letter opener along one side of the envelope. I momentarily peered inside, then slowly emptied the contents onto my desk.

A small, strange looking key fell out along with a brief note. I quickly saw that the note had been sent by Mrs. Norton. Before actually reading the message, I wondered if she had some kind of clandestine affair planned for the two of us? I was ashamed of such a thought and simply attributed it to my male ego at play. Not that she couldn't have been attracted to such a handsome individual as I, but surely, she must have realized that I was a most happily married husband and father. Shouldn't she?

I decided before I created any more inane fantasies that I had better examine the note. It read as follows:

"Dear Doctor Watson,
    What you now have in your possession is a most valuable piece of a puzzle. I cannot tell you at this time what it will open or why I am entrusting it to your care. Please keep it with you until I am able to meet with you again. I beg you not to speak

of it to anyone, as you might be placing your life in
great danger.

I further implore you to excuse me for not
providing any explanation at this time. All will be
revealed when next we meet. Forgive me for involving
you in this matter, but should this artifact fall into the
wrong hands, it could be calamitous! It's also of
paramount importance that the authorities be
unaware of this dilemma. I'm sure you'll understand when
you learn more. Your reputation as an upright and
trustworthy individual made you my last best hope. I
know that you will be discreet in this matter.

Gratefully,

Irene Adler Norton"

I could scarcely believe what I was reading. Piece of a
puzzle? What kind of puzzle? Why couldn't she have hidden it
somewhere safe? Perhaps she had no time to secure a safe
location to hide it? Why me? How could she so callously put
my life in danger? She said so in her missive. Why, what has
she gotten me into? And now, what have I gotten myself into?
I came to St Andrews for the purpose of relaxing and enjoying
my favorite game. Why should this matter concern me in the
least? What should I do next?

I really concentrated on trying to unravel these goings on.
Examining the strangely shaped key more closely with one of
my old magnifying lenses, I saw a number etched along the
stem. It read 1754. Hmm, 1754? Well, at least I now had a
starting point, perhaps not. I had a glimmer of hope that this
date might shed some light on a specific event. Yet, it
remained only a key, nothing more at this time. My curiosity
demanded that I find the lock for this key, but where to begin.
. . where to begin. . .

Clearly, this puzzle required attention. I poured another
glass of wine, gathered up the key and Irene's letter and

moved to a most comfortable armchair. I checked my timepiece and was startled to find that it was already 7:00 PM. Still, the night was young and I once more returned to the matter at hand.

For another 45 minutes, I thought long and hard about what this could be. I admit that I was completely baffled. Why even Holmes might have been at a loss, for there really was very little to go on. I could only sit and wonder when Mrs. Norton would contact me again.

My question was quickly answered when a knock came to my door. As I neared the door, I called out, "Who may I ask is knocking?"

"Doctor Watson," came the voice, "it is I, Graham, your bellboy. I've got a note that is to be delivered to Doctor John Watson, Room 221."

Quickly opening the door, I grabbed the note, gave the young bellboy a tip and closed the door. Ripping open the note, I lifted my eyeglasses and began to read:

"Doctor Watson, leave the hotel tonight at 11:40 PM and walk toward the ruins of the Old Cathedral. I'll meet you there at midnight.

Irene"

Hole 13   Hole O' Cross In

It was now 8 o'clock. I certainly had plenty of time to contemplate what this meeting was about. Checking my revolver, I made sure it was loaded and carefully placed it in my jacket. Next, I proceeded down to the lobby to see what was being served for dinner. I hadn't had my evening meal as yet and my stomach had no problem reminding me of that fact. Ten minutes later found me seated with Davison, both of us waiting for our meals to arrive.

Davison, old friend that he was, began to reminisce about our first meeting. He said he fondly remembered meeting my wife on our first visit to St Andrews as a married couple.

"Your Mary," he stated, "informed me that she felt that a few days away from your workday tedium would be good for you, and golf at St Andrews would be the perfect cure."

Why she had thought of St Andrews was not immediately apparent to me, I confided to him and we both laughed at the comment.

I told Davison how surprised I was when she chose a golfing getaway and I said to her, "Mary, dear, I am surprised to find that you enjoy golf!"

She answered my remark with a coy smile, and quickly informed me that she did not care for the game at all! Instead, she said that she chose St Andrews for its history and scenery. At this disclosure, Davison and I enjoyed another good laugh as we ate our evening meal.

"That was a rather long time ago. This time, William," I emphasized, "I am here for the golf only!"

"And we, at the Royal Hotel, are so much the better for that, my friend," Davison politely stated.

I didn't know whether it was the clean air or the promise of adventure that lay ahead, but that evening's fresh trout and rice were especially scrumptious. Additionally, I was more than thankful when my friend picked up the bill. After sharing a few more stories, I excused myself, promising to join him bright and early for breakfast.

Rising from the table, I thanked William for a wonderful evening, and walked from the stately dining room. As I rounded the corner, I carefully looked around the lobby before heading up the magnificent circular stairway that led to the floors above.

Scurrying up to my room, I noticed it was 11:20. There was not much time to prepare for the evening's rendezvous. Changing into more comfortable clothing, I carefully placed my service revolver in the pocket of my coat. Soon it would be time to go.

At 11:40, I slowly made my way out of a rear door of the hotel that led into a narrow walkway. Making my way to the main street, I noticed that there weren't many people on the street at that time of night. Actually, that shouldn't have surprised me. It was, after all, quite late!

While heading for the old ruins, I studied my route carefully, trying to imagine what this meeting was all about. I still had this key, this infernal key clasped firmly in my hand. What could it open? I could think of nothing else. Might it reveal a hidden treasure recently located in the ruins of the old Cathedral? Perhaps, it would open the door to a secret room, long hidden from sight by one of Scotland's famous feudal warlords of days gone by. Certainly, by the looks of it, the key must have been fashioned many, many years ago, for the detailed ornamentation was not of recent vintage.

My mind continued to race. What if this key merely opened a room in some old hotel? That would be disappointing it's true, unless someone was waiting to meet me. Hmmm, meet me. . . For what purpose, I wondered? Possibly it was sent with the note to lure me for reasons unknown; take me from the safety of my hotel room. Why it may not have come from Mrs. Norton at all! Oh how these bothersome thoughts raced through my head as I moved out onto another one of the narrow thoroughfares of the "Auld Grey Toon."

It was a pleasant enough evening though, with moonlit sky and mild summer zephyrs flowing through the quiet streets. Barking dogs and the occasional screech of sea birds broke the silence of the night. Ahead could be seen a work wagon with its team of mules plodding their way to their home stalls in preparation for the next day's chores. I find that I am always captivated by the unhurried clopping gait of the work horses as they pull their heavy loads up and down the same roads, day after day. They seem so content doing their daily, ordinary, laborious routines. All this effort for the minimal rewards of stalls and oats, and the occasional apple treat! Oh, well, it's probably enough for them, being animals, you know.

After these Clydesdales rounded a turn in the road, my mind returned to the situation at hand. Continuing along the narrow way, I renewed my vigilance as I slowly neared my destination. Observing this grand old village at night brought many thoughts to mind, but St Andrews can be a rather drab place. The dull colors of the city's buildings, while striking in their consistency, lack interest. With the onset of dusk, however, the city appeared much more inviting with street lights and lanterns illuminating the homes and taverns of this coastal town. Proceeding toward the old Cathedral, I noticed that, one by one, there were fewer and fewer lights as the clock moved slowly toward midnight. With every step I took, I became more anxious to find the answers to the many questions that had been laid before me just a few hours earlier.

I had come here for a brief respite from my daily habits, work, and my depression over Holmes's untimely and horrible death. I had been content in contemplating the "Old Course" and its many challenges. How would I fare with the "Swilcan Burn"? What about avoiding the "Principal's Nose"? Could I master the many difficulties of the "Road Hole"... Sadly, these encounters might have to wait until this new mystery was explored in greater detail.

Moving north along Primrose Road, I was suddenly aware of a low whisper coming from one of the dimly lit alcoves that are prevalent in buildings in this region.

"Psst...Psst...Dr. Watson. Over here!"

"Who's there," I stammered grabbing my revolver, quite taken aback by the urgency of the request.

"Quickly, quickly," the soft voice of Irene Norton Implored.

"You must get out of the light. You're much too visible a target!"

"I say, target?" I queried, moving at once into an alleyway near where she was standing.

"Yes, Doctor," Mrs. Norton reaffirmed, "you are now a target, thanks to my unthinking selfishness. Please forgive me for getting you involved, but now that you are at risk, you need to know all."

We continued to move toward the spectral ruins of the Cathedral. The light of the half-moon shining down behind it produced a most eerie effect from our perspective as we perambulated ever nearer the ancient edifice. Irene led the way, being careful to remain in the shadows as best she could find them. She seemed very ill at ease and I must say that I shared her condition as I tried to negotiate the serpentine path she was trailblazing, although there was no need to clear the way of anything like bushes, branches and the like.

When we finally reached the walls of the ruins, she began to tiptoe around a small dilapidated column and continued along a well-worn pathway that I, at once, recognized as the way to the coastline. I had traveled this path many times on my way down to the water's edge. Of course, that was in daylight and there was no need to maintain silence on those occasions. Irene stopped when she reached the dunes. She cleared a spot on the hill, and invited me to join her. After looking around to see if the area was secure, she began to speak.

"Dr. Watson," she began, "as I've already stated, you are in great danger and it's all because of the key I've sent you."

My silence allowed her to continue, "I know you must be very confused by all of these doings, and rightly so, for I've still told you nothing. You've been contacted by me because you are the only one I could trust with so dangerous a state of affairs. I'm about to divulge the reason for our meeting here tonight and the story behind the key that you now have in your possession."

And with that having been said, Irene Adler Norton began her tale. She sadly informed me of the death of her husband and stated that after his passing, she had felt lost in America. Most of her family and friends still resided on this side of the Atlantic and it seemed most logical to return to her home in London to try to put her life back together.

She talked of her first meeting with Holmes in one of our most famous cases, "A Scandal in Bohemia," in which her true love for her future husband was jeopardized by an earlier romance with royalty. Struck by his clever strategies, she could never forget him, especially since Holmes, as it turned out, was one of the witnesses to her marriage! "But, oh there was so much more to the man," she confessed.

Unbeknownst to me, she informed me that she had corresponded with Holmes on many occasions. They found they had so much in common, both being particularly gifted in problem solving. Holmes had asked for and received permission from her husband, Godfrey, to contact her when he needed another like-minded soul to help solve some of his most trying cases.

Irene said she was embarrassed in telling this, for she stated that Sherlock Holmes hardly needed help from anyone, his intellect was so keen. Suddenly turning red, she felt the need to qualify that remark, adding, "I meant to say, present company excluded, Doctor. Please excuse my careless comment."

I felt obligated at this point to interrupt her story, "Mrs. Norton, I must inform you that Holmes considered you one of his most brilliant challenges, never really an adversary, but simply on the opposite side of a most delicate matter."

I continued, "In fact, although what you are telling me is, quite frankly, most shocking, I am not surprised that he would have enlisted your help. My dear, he never quite got over you!"

Irene gasped, speaking with some discomfort, "Please, Doctor, I'm afraid I'm starting to blush!"

"Dr. Watson," she explained, "when I first returned to London, I received a telegram from an anonymous source informing me that my life was in great peril."

"Beg pardon, Mrs. Norton?" I inquired. "Have you no idea who might offer such a heinous threat?"

After briefly hesitating, she went on, "At first, I tried to dismiss the message as some harmless effort at revenge from perhaps a jilted lover or from an angry wife who perceived me as a potential threat to her marriage. That had little effect on me. However, there are more dangerous elements out there who would love to keep me from prying into their criminal affairs. I refer, of course, to Dr. Moriarty's followers."

"What do you mean, Mrs. Norton?" I inquired, "Dr. Moriarty is dead. He perished with Holmes in that fall at Reichenbach Falls."

Irene looked the other way, pushed her hair to one side, shook her head and said, "Yes, Doctor Watson, Moriarty is gone....but his criminal organization continues under the leadership of Colonel C. M. Sebastian, a devious man who is every bit as evil as his famous predecessor."

"Sebastian," I stammered, continuing, "the name is familiar to me, though I haven't a clue as to when or where I may have heard it."

"That's not surprising, Doctor," Mrs. Norton added, "he was always in the background, always monitoring, always complementing and supporting Moriarty as that despicable man worked his evil on his fellow man."

"Oh, my word," I responded, "I suppose Holmes must have known about him but was too concerned with Moriarty. Perhaps he would have been next on Holmes's list."

"I believe you are correct, Doctor, for Sebastian is every bit as treacherous as was his leader, Moriarty," she surmised.

"And so," she continued, "I realized that somehow he and his followers believed that I had returned to avenge Mr. Holmes's demise. Would that I might, I would do it, Doctor, for Mr. Holmes will long be remembered for his ability to thwart evil and help capture the vilest among us. I, too, believe in the importance of observing our laws and protecting the innocent. I will continue to do what I can to rid our beloved London, and indeed, all of Europe, of this hideous criminal."

"I decided to follow some leads and try to discover what Sebastian and his conspirators might be up to," she continued.

"I followed them through France and Switzerland, and believed that I had done so without having been detected until I received another telegram sent to this hotel yesterday afternoon," she stated.

Handing me the message, Mrs. Norton turned away and under the light of the moon and with the help of the light from a match I struck, I quickly read the following:

Ms. Norton,

You are placing yourself in grave danger if you do not cease and desist from interfering in something that does not concern you. Leave Scotland at once or suffer the consequences."

"Irene," I addressed her, "this is indeed a direct threat on your life. Surely, you should contact the police about this and leave the case in their hands."

"Doctor, I can trust no one but you," she replied, "for the tentacles of this organization reach far and wide, even, I'm afraid to state, to the police themselves."

"May I inquire what you expect to find?" I asked her.

Irene paused at my question and taking my hand she whispered, "I believe that they are trying to create or possibly have already created some kind of new weapon."

"A weapon? What kind of weapon?" I inquired. "Aren't there enough guns and bullets to do their evil bidding?"

"Doctor," she spoke, "I know neither the size nor scope of the weapon they are pursuing. I'm certain, though, that whatever device they conspire to obtain might change the course of history. That's how great the danger is!!!"

She paused after that remark, leaving me a little time to ponder all that she had imparted. It was almost one o'clock in the morning, and here we were on a shoreline in Scotland, with the waves of the North Sea gently breaking beyond the dunes, trying to come up with a plan to stop God knows what from occurring.

I had begun to feel the effects of a most grueling day for my mind was working overtime to try to invent the steps that could be taken to help her with this conundrum. I was just about to ask about the importance of the ancient key when, all of a sudden, Irene ducked down behind a dune and signaled for me to do the same. I did as I was instructed, but didn't understand at first.

It didn't take me long to realize what was happening, for I saw a faint light wending its way towards us. Irene pointed toward it and slowly moved further down the coastline with me right beside her. We continued our furtive flight along the ebbing waters and mild splashing of the waves until we were miles away from the old ruins.

Even from such a distance, we could still see the light continuing to move in our direction. Fortunately, we were close enough to the hotel to return to the relative safety we hoped it would provide. As we neared our accommodations, I suggested that she enter the hotel through the main entrance. Once inside, she could open the back door for me to return.

After we were both safely back inside the Royal, we agreed to meet the following evening at the same time, but this time, behind the eighteenth green of the "Old Course."

Hole 14   Long

I carefully made my way up the back stairs, checked the hallway and slipped my room key into the lock. Not knowing what I might find, I cautiously gripped my revolver and slowly entered my room. Gingerly, I scanned the open space, ready to shoot if necessary, for I had no idea of what I might find waiting for me. Fortunately, all was as it should have been and I quickly prepared for bed, truly exhausted from a long, hard, first day at St Andrews.

How could I sleep, I wondered. Especially knowing what I had just experienced! I found my pulse beginning to race. What to do about the key? Where could I place it to guarantee its safety? Certainly, I could carry it on my person. Ah, yes, but should I come under attack, the key would most assuredly be gone! Hmm....I began to look about my room. Could there be any good hiding places for such an important item? Behind the painting of the eighteenth green? Secured to the bottom of a piece of furniture? Along the window curtains? Attached to the side of the gas lamp on the far wall?

I paced back and forth for several minutes before finding the ideal location to hide the object. In fact, I dare say Holmes himself would have been hard-pressed to have come up with such an ideal spot! I was very pleased with my selection, I do confess, and I sat back in the soft chair and slowly sipped the remnants of some wine I had ordered earlier in the day. Once more I pondered this most mysterious problem.

My eyes began to tire quickly as I continued to plot some kind of strategy for the morrow. Moments later, I found my head drooping and bobbing, for it had been a most interesting but extremely tiring day. I decided to take a brief nap instead of going to bed. My plan was to get up, bright and early. Just a few minutes......a short nap....Ah, yes. That's what's required.

The early morning sunshine flickered through the half-opened curtains of my hotel room. My dreams seemed to be compounded by the alternating light and darkness which must have been dancing across my face. Suddenly, I awoke with a splitting headache, lying on the floor of my hotel room. Moving slowly, I felt my foot send a clinking object across the floor. It was the wine glass. I had carelessly fallen asleep with the glass in my clenched hand and I must have dropped it, spilling the liquid all over my trousers. I reached up to rub my throbbing noggin, trying to imagine what must have happened to me? The last thing I could remember was my brief nap in the cozy armchair.

Quickly, I looked around the room and noticed that the place had been ransacked. Covers were off the bed. My clothes were thrown everywhere. Drawers had been left open. Just as I was about to look where I had placed the key, my headache grew even more intense. How could this have happened to me, I pondered. Of course, the wine must have been laced with some type of sleeping powder, for I certainly would have known that someone had entered my room!

The key........oh no.... Could they have found it? Slowly, I moved around the room to get my revolver. Perhaps, the thieves were still here, waiting for me to show them where I had hidden the mysterious artifact. Fortunately, they were gone, and strangely enough, my service revolver was exactly where I had left it!

Now for the key.... I quickly glanced at the entry door and there it was, right where I had placed it, sitting safely and securely in the keyhole of my hotel room door! Ah, bless you, Holmes, I thought. See all that I've learned from you! For it was one of Holmes's favorite truisms, that sometimes the best hiding place is often in plain sight, since no one expects valuable items to be left out in the open!

Good Lord, I had almost forgotten about the mysterious letter! Sadly, it was gone, along with the envelope it had arrived in! Clearly, someone had found out about my meeting with Mrs. Norton. I wondered if she was all right?

I decided to immediately repair the room to its proper state and, as Irene had requested, I would certainly not report this incident to the management or authorities. There would be much too much danger in exposing Irene's involvement in such a bizarre situation.

Clearly, she had been correct in her fears that she had placed me in imminent danger. For that, I could hardly be thankful, and yet, her faith in my character was strangely comforting. That she chose to trust me made me all the more determined to see this thing through and help her in all ways possible. I would do what I could.

My next order of business was to go through the day as if nothing was amiss. Off I went to breakfast in the hotel dining room. After polishing off some kippers and scones, I made my way across the way to the links. My friend, Davison, had set up a group for me and had secured a caddy as well. Upon first glance, the lad seemed somewhat familiar to me. He smiled as I approached, doffing his cap.

"Hello, young man," I offered. "Are you ready for a splendid day on the links?"

"Indeed, I am, Dr. Watson. Indeed I am, sir," he responded, smiling a smile that I had seen many times before. I briefly turned away and scratched my noggin, wondering where I had seen this fellow before. Suddenly, it occurred to me...

"Why, Wiggins, it's you, is it?" I stammered, quite unable to hide my emotions.

"That would be me, Guv'nor," he happily replied as we warmly shook hands.

"Well, it's been a long time, lad, I must say," I continued.

"How have you been, and what in God's great world are you doing here in Scotland?"

"Yes, Doctor, we haven't seen each other since," he lowered his head and spoke, "you know, sir..."

I quickly understood his meaning for he too had been particularly close to Holmes as well, having been the chosen leader of the "Baker Street Irregulars," Holmes's rag-tag young ruffian detectives.

"Anyway," he continued, "I've taken a fancy to this wonderful game and am thinking of making it a part of me future. I thinks to meself, what better way to learn this sport than to see it played up close by expert players like yourself!"

"Ah, Wiggins, lad," I laughed, nodding back and forth, "you've got the wrong man if you think I'm a good golfer. Still, I suppose I've had my moments on rare occasions!"

"Never ye mind, Doctor, I've a good feeling about today's game. Are you ready or do you need to warm up a bit?" he inquired.

"Well," I replied, "I guess it wouldn't hurt to stretch the old muscles before tackling the 'Old Course'."

As we moved toward the fabled first tee, I grabbed my cleek and my spade mashie and, holding them together, began to swing slowly in a measured cadence. The course lay before me as I continued to pivot, pause, and release my clubs. I loosened my seasoned sinews as best I could in preparation for a great day at St Andrews. Still thinking about the past evening's adventure, I wondered what new turn this mystery might take. But for now, I was going to play the "Old Course" at St Andrews!

Turning the corner, I beamed at the thought of golfing on this wonderful piece of linksland. Wiggins had already arrived at the tee and was industriously cleaning my clubs. I was happily surprised to see Davison, the hotel manager, waiting on the tee. I wondered if he was planning on playing?

"Ah, gentlemen," he offered, "Here is my dear friend, Doctor John Watson, London, come to pay the 'Old Course' a return visit. John, meet your playing partners."

"Greetings, gentlemen," I began, "I'm very pleased to see you on this wonderful Scottish morning. And you must be the club Captain. How are you, Mr. Iverson? I'm so happy to meet you and honored to play here at the Home of Golf."

Mr. Iverson, legendary starter at St Andrews, smiled broadly and, pointing at Mr. Davison, replied, "Dr. Watson, you come most highly recommended by one of our most respected citizens. We are happy to have you come for a visit. We trust you'll enjoy your stay."

Iverson continued, "Doctor, you'll be playing with Charles Hutchings, Daniel Duncan and Ted Tait. I've taken the liberty of pairing you with Mr. Hutchings, one of our better players. You and Mr. Hutchings will have your hands full with the likes of Messrs. Duncan and Tait. Why, these two gents have only recently captured the Robinson Cup!"

"Captain Iverson," I hesitated, "I'm afraid that I'm not the golfer that you think I am, sir. I don't know if I'll be much help to Mr. Hutchings. Perhaps, these fine gentlemen would prefer to play against a stronger opponent, not that I would mind watching them play, mind you."

Mr. Duncan stepped over to shake my hand, "Doctor Watson, I'm Dan Duncan. Meet my partner, Ted Tait. Please don't let the high-fallutin' introduction by Captain Iverson put ye' off. Why Mister Tait and I are just out for a fun round, as it were, and we've been tryin' to get a game with Mr. Hutchings for several months now. This is the first time he's agreed to play with us. Furthermore, we were informed that he would only play against us if you would be his partner."

Now this was a very strange situation indeed, I thought as I shook hands with Mr. Duncan and Mr. Tait. I had never met or heard of a Mr. Hutchings and to think that he would only play against them if I would play as his partner seemed very queer to me, very queer indeed!

After I finished shaking hands with the opponents, Mr. Hutchings shuffled over and with a quiet grunt, shook my hand. He said not one word, but smiling a rather awkward smile, shook his head in a most bizarre manner.

"Don't mind Mr. Hutchings's ways," interjected Captain Iverson, "there's a man of few words, if any, but one hell of a golfer, as you're sure to discover. By the way, Duncan and Tait have the honors. Play away, gentlemen."

Stunned by all that had transpired, I must have looked quite bewildered, as indeed I was, for Davison quickly moved to my side.

As Duncan hit a high draw 240 yards down the left side of the fairway, the hotel manager informed me, "John, please take no offense in your partner's demeanor. He's rapidly become one of the finest golfers in these parts. You should know that he rarely, if ever, speaks, but communicates by gestures, much as a mime might do."

The look on my face must have indicated that I needed further reassurance for he continued, "John, he's got a reputation as a bit of a recluse, but no one hits shots the way he can. I believe you'll have a great time watching him."

While he spoke, Tait split the fairway, leaving but a mashie to the green. Wiggins, who had overheard Davison's description, handed me my spoon and, as we made our way to the teeing ground, offered some additional reassurance to Hutchings's playing ability.

"Doctor Watson," said the former Irregular, "Mr. Davison has told you the truth. I've been caddying here for the last several months and I always make time from my bag-toting to watch Mr. Hutchings practice."

"And, as for his strange behavior," he continued, "maybe it's true that them that has a 'gift'" is a bit off the beam, if ye' get me drift, that is."

"Well, Wiggins," I replied, "we'll soon find out, won't we?"

Naturally, I felt truly intimidated by the match that had been put together unbeknownst to me, and I feared that my game would really put the other golfers off their play. Still, it seemed not to matter to them in the least, or at least they said as much when I tried to beg off.

Two swift practice swings and I lofted a polite fading shot near the gorse on the right side, well short of the Swilcan Burn. In my mind, it was not a good shot, but at least I had made contact after so many years away from the sport.

I had barely left the tee when Mr. Hutchings began his routine. I've played many rounds and seen many players set up to play their shots, but Charles Hutchings had a method all his own. He took more time than most golfers I had seen, but he was so meticulous that I wondered if we could finish in daylight! It went something like this:

First, he took a pinch of sand, two-fingers high and turned his guttie number slightly to the left inside of the ball.

Swinging from the right side, he made a very deliberate practice take-away, placing his right elbow snug against his right hip and returning to his starting position. He would do this twice before playing his shot.

The actual swing featured a dramatic pause at the top of his backswing, followed by a downswing with gradual increase of club speed to and past the golf ball.

The sound of the club hitting the ball was unlike any I had ever heard before, so solidly was that ball struck.

The flight of the ball never veered left or right. It always reached the same height as is flew toward its target.

This was what I observed when he hit his first tee shot on that wonderful summer day at St Andrews. To my mind, one thing was certain. When Charles Hutchings hit his golf ball, it was almost a spiritual occurrence.

"Fine shot, Charles," called Duncan. Tait echoed his sentiment. I, for my part, was speechless as I turned to my newly-met golfing partner. Standing with mouth agape, I shook my head in approval.

Hutchings, watched his ball, smiled at me, placed his club into his bag, and the four of us, plus caddies, proceeded toward the first green. When I found my ball in the rough, I was able to chop it back into play, but I was still a good distance from the flag. My spade mashie flew low but straight, and as it approached the Burn, it took a magical bounce off an imbedded stone in the hazard, winding up on the green some 30 paces left of the hole.

Tait hit a fine spade mashie to the right side of the green while his partner, Duncan's mashie niblick finished some twelve paces pin-high to the left. Our group walked thirty more yards before reaching Hutchings's tee ball. After sizing up his distance, Hutchings clipped the ball with his niblick. The shot flew straight at the flag, landed eight paces beyond and after two hops, amazingly spun back to within inches of the cup!

As our group crossed the Swilcan Burn bridge, Tait motioned to me.

"Doctor," he whispered, "your partner is becoming quite the local legend. The golfers say he hits shots like that all the time. Can you imagine?"

"Mr. Tait," I replied wryly, "I certainly hope he continues to do just that for the rest of the day."

Tait smiled and added, "He's known around here as 'the Quiet One,' for reasons that are readily apparent."

"Well, I guess that's the way he is and I don't have any problem with that, unless," I responded, for I had suddenly realized, "I need to communicate with him."

Tait and Duncan, who had joined the conversation, just snickered and continued to the green.

Tait putted first after conceding my partner's birdie. It became clear that we would not have an easy time of it, for Ted's putt broke three yards and slowly disappeared into the cup for a fine birdie-three to tie the hole.

For the next fifteen holes, our group enjoyed the mild sea breezes and brilliant sunshine that was the day. The course had never looked finer or was in better shape than it was on that marvelous afternoon. Both teams played some great golf, though my play was nowhere near the level of my companion or our talented opponents. Whatever score our team recorded belonged to the efforts of "the Quiet One." Oh, I made a few pars and bogies along the way, but it was the play of Charles Hutchings that kept us in the game.

For their part, Dan Duncan and Ted Tait, merited their deserved reputation. Both men loved to play the game. You could see it in their every step. They were exceptional players and fine sportsmen as well. Had it not been for the outstanding shot-making of my partner, the match would have been very lopsided indeed!

Throughout the round, Wiggins and I had had plenty of time to speak of the good old days in London. Wiggins had a remarkable memory. We discussed how Holmes and he had first met. Holmes had been out for a walk along the Thames, probably pondering a particularly difficult case when they first ran into each other.

"Yes, Guv'nor, if you would like to hear the details, I'd be more than happy to supply them," Wiggins informed me. With that, my caddy began his tale.

"'I had just lifted a small bag from an older gent and was busy taking my leave, when I feels something's got a hold of me arm. Imagine my surprise when I looks up and sees 'imself. Yep, he's there with that quizzical look on his mush and me securely on the end of a mighty firm grip. I felt like a pup on a real short leash, I did.

Now, ordinarily, I would-a smashed that bloke a good 'un, but there was something about the look in his eye that suggested that that would be a mistake. A few seconds later the older gent, whose load I had just lightened, comes over and gives me a good boot in the arse. Then, he thanks Mr. Holmes for capturing me!

Holmes ups and looks at the old gentleman and, strike me dead, says to him, 'My dear man, what on earth are you talking about? This young man just wrested a purse from another lad about the same size and age, and was knocked to the ground for his efforts.'

Continuing Holmes said, 'You sir, owe this young man an apology; for your actions were not warranted, at least as far as I could see. Now here is your purse and let's hear a proper apology.'

I thought I was going daft. What was he saying? What was he doing? What was he thinking and why was he doing this?

The old man apologized profusely and, after taking back his purse, gave me tuppence, thanked me and went his way.

After the old man disappeared around the corner, Holmes sat me down on the edge of a nearby wall and began to interrogate me, 'Well, you might start off by thanking me for saving your hide.'

I'm speechless. Imagine the nerve of this stranger, I'm thinking to meself. He wants me to thank him for putting the hold on me and givin' back me hard-earned profit!

'Beg pardon, Guv'nor,' I sneered at him, 'what the devil makes you think that you saved my hide? Why, the way I sees it, you stole me night's work and give it back whence it came? How's that saving my hide, I'd like to hear!'

'Brash young man, aren't you?' Mr. Holmes said, 'Why, don't you realize that you're on the way to a life of crime? Surely, you know that it's against the law to cuff a man and steal what doesn't belong to you? What have you got to say for yourself?'

I says to him, 'To you, sir, nuffin. Nuffin at all. You've got no right to interfere, have you? Wait a minute, you're not the law are you?'

Mr. Holmes said nothing for several seconds. Then, all of a sudden, I hears the most raucous laughter comin' from him. He's about ready to burst and so I tries to get out of his grip.

'Come back you young scamp,' says he, giving me arm another good twist.

'No, I don't work for Scotland Yard or the local constabulary,' he replied, 'so just relax for a moment.'

Wiggins finished his brief story by saying, 'Doctor Watson, Mr. Holmes spent the next five minutes telling me how I could, and should, live me life. He further suggested that although I was a mere lad, he would like me to work for him from time-to-time, promising some interesting assignments if I chose to take him up on his offer. You know most of the rest of the story. I gathered up a bunch of youngsters like meself and together we joined up with you and Mr. Holmes to help with many of his cases.'"

I know that I was smiling when Wiggins finished his story, and that certainly sounded like my dear friend. He must have had a feeling about this young man and thought if he were given a chance, not an arrest, that he might be able to change his ways. I, for one, believe that Holmes made the right decision –for Wiggins had turned out to be a fine young man.

As our match approached the 17th teeing area, I looked at the Old Course Hotel which bordered that hole. Years before I had tried to hit my tee ball over the sign painted on the black sheds attached to the hotel. Sadly, my low flying slice struck the letter "o" in the word "Hotel" and bounded away into a patch of heather.

This time would be different, I thought, and it had better be different, for our match was dead level. This hole was known as "the Road Hole" due to the green's proximity to one of the roadways in the village of St Andrews. The road passes directly along the back of the green, but is considered a playable area. The green is guarded by a huge bunker that is almost impossible from which to play. Arguably, it is one of the most famous and difficult holes on any golf course.

The Tait-Duncan team had the honors, resulting from an eagle on the fourteenth hole, which the members refer to as "Long". Duncan's second shot, a high, draw with his spoon, ended up a mere three yards from the cup and his eagle putt found the hole to tie the match. Holes fifteen and sixteen were tied with pars.

"The Quiet One" was humming a merry lilt to himself while waiting his turn. I had marveled at his play for sixteen holes now, and was convinced that he was the finest ball-striker I had ever seen. Even our opponents were awed by the quality of the shots that emanated from his clubs. I had overheard them comment on his play when he had fashioned a particularly remarkable shot, which, by the way, was quite often.

Tait's drive easily flew the sheds and ended up in the right side of the fairway within cleek distance from the green. His partner Duncan smashed his drive, but a bad bounce had him in the left rough.

Hutchings had decided early in the round to let me go first for our team. He knew that he had gotten a weaker player, but it never seemed to bother him in the least. Actually, I think it made him play all the harder, knowing that he could never really rely upon my play. I had long since rid myself of any guilt complex when I saw how well he could play. I just went along and tried my best, but for some unknown reason I found that I was very much at ease with these exceptional players, in fact, particularly calm with Mr. Hutchings. None of them seemed to mind my lesser ability and I suppose I found that most comforting.

When I took my practice swings, I made up my mind to stay with the shot and not swing too hard this time. Maybe it was the amount of practice I had accrued thus far in the match, maybe it was the beautiful day, maybe I just forgot to get nervous, but my swing on the Road Hole just happened to be my best of the day. I rejoiced to see my ball flying straight and true, directly over the same "o" that had been my ill-fated target those several years ago. The smile that I wore when I left the tee box must have been contagious, for all four players and our caddies were beaming broadly.

"Great drive," said Tait.

"Nicely done, Doctor," echoed Duncan.

"U–n–n–g–g–h–h," muttered "the Quiet One."

There was none of the drama when Charles Hutchings laced his drive high over the hotel itself, drawing back into the middle of the narrow fairway, a mere mashie niblick from the green.

Wiggins winked at me, picked up my bag and we followed Hutchings up the fairway. As we moved past the structure, I imagined the many golfers who had stayed in those rooms with their incredible views of this storied linksland. I also thought about the severity of the rough on this golf course. I envisioned the possibility of serious injuries should a golfer try to do too much in an effort to extricate himself from such difficult lies. Even tramping down through the thick fescues and seaside grasses was quite the task, and it would take a seer with special faculties indeed to locate a golf ball that landed in such gnarly, thorny flora.

The sun was still high in the sky as we continued toward our drives with the gray buildings of the town getting ever closer to our foursome. My ball was sitting nicely on the left side of the fairway, but I still had a long way to go, over 200 yards! A good brassie was what was called for, but it did not answer, for my ball sailed left into the rough, still some thirty paces from the green. It would have been an acceptable shot except the deep "Road Hole" bunker lay directly between me and the flag.

Duncan could only use his spade mashie, so deeply lay his ball in the heavy grasses. It came out spinning to the right side of the fairway, also short of the green. His partner Tait had a better lie, and his cleek landed on the right front portion of the treacherous putting surface. At least he was there in two shots and that was never easy to do.

Hutchings was the last to play his second shot. His long drive enabled him to use a much shorter club, a niblick. Predictably, his ball soared high and straight and looked a good one. This time, though, a strong gust came up and caught his ball, knocking it down and into the bunker. Not just a bunker, it was the damned "Road Hole" bunker. For a moment he seemed stunned by what had just transpired.

Looking at his club, he began to examine it closely. He held it up and pointed it at the sky. Next, he tried to twist the whipping around the hosel to see if the clubhead had been loosened. Scratching his head, he then put one hand on the grip and the other on the head of the club and started to test its flexibility.

Apparently the club met his satisfaction and he placed it back with a rather loud, sad sigh accompanying its return to the bag. Shaking his head, he couldn't believe that his ball had come up short of the green.

Our group neared the green and I was the first to play. With that devilish bunker directly between me and the flag, I decided to use the putter to roll my ball up the right side of the fairway and onto the elusive surface. Surprisingly, the shot came off as planned and I was left with a slight left-to-right putt of some twenty-two feet for par. Duncan's pitch ran several feet by the flag, but his putt was straight enough. His partner, Mister Tait, lagged his putt a foot away for another solid par.

Now it was my partner's shot. His ball had come to rest in a most precarious lie in the bunker, resting on the opposite side of that terrible hazard. There was no way to stand to hit the ball to the green, for his ball was on the side closest, direction-wise, toward the tee, not the target green which was now directly behind him!

I became very nervous as I watched him prepare to play safely away toward the tee, his back to the seventeenth green. He would have to pitch in from the fairway for par. Should he miss, it would be up to me to sink my long putt for par in order to tie the hole, or we would be one hole down with one hole to play.

Hutchings saw my concern and merely winked with a rather pronounced grunt "Ungh." As he lined up for the shot he seemed to be standing in a rather odd posture. I had never seen a man lower his right shoulder so far below his left to hit a golf shot. Indeed, to describe it as accurately as I can, his left shoulder was directly perpendicular, at a 90 degree angle, to the surface and to his right shoulder! Imagine what that looked like! What in the world was he thinking?

Without much additional fanfare, Hutchings laid his niblick's face wide-open, adding as much loft to the iron as I had ever seen and took the niftiest little clip of a swing one could imagine.....resulting in his ball being softly lofted up in the air, above his head, over the lip of the bunker, landing softly on the green and stopping within one foot from the pin!!!!!

Duncan, Tait and I just stood there shocked. After a short time we all exploded in laughter at such an incredible golf shot!

Duncan remarked, slapping his cap from his head, "Why I've never seen such a golf shot in me whole life?"

Tait concurred, adding, "Well, ye've got to show me how that was done, Hutchings, or I'll start a mumblin' meself!"

Wiggins nearly swallowed his tobacco at the sight and I just about fainted from the pain I had in my stomach I laughed so hard at what I had just witnessed.

Hutchings carefully raked the trap, walked to the green and tapped in for, perhaps, the greatest par that anyone would ever see on that most difficult hole. Tossing his putter to Wiggins, "the Quiet One" proudly made his way to the tee of the home hole on the "Old Course." All of us were still smiling at the shot we had just observed. Obviously, none of us had ever seen a shot like that before. We had been privy to either lunacy or greatness. Was it pure luck or true talent that we had recently experienced?

The Tait-Duncan team still held honors and both gentlemen laced perfect tee-shots down the left side of the fairway. When I sliced my drive down the extreme right side, Wiggins indicated that I was within the course boundary. Safe, but still a long distance from the green.

As Hutchings took his practice swing, I sensed a change had come over his countenance. He was actually grinning as he began his backswing. While he moved his driver through impact, I thought I heard him make a very strange noise. It sounded like he was growling at the ball!

This time Hutchings had really caught the ball solidly. I held my breath as the shot sailed high and long, landing 40 yards from the putting surface and bounding along, gradually ending up on the 18th green.

"My God," Tait offered, "the ball is on the bloody green!"

Duncan shook his head and continued walking to his ball. Wiggins winked at me as he replaced Hutchings's driver back in the bag. He quickly dug-out the putter and handed it to "the Quiet One."

"Ungh," responded Hutchings, as he marched up to the green in an almost ceremonious manner.

While our opponents hit decent approach shots, I could see the fire go out of them. Both birdie putts missed and it only remained for Hutchings to two-putt from 11 feet to win.

After the match, we all adjourned into the men's grille, shook hands and settled the score. Our match was a straight four-ball, and even though my scores were never needed, it felt good to be on the winning side. We all enjoyed a few pints of Scotland's finest before it was time to go. I, for my part, thanked all three men for a grand time. On the way out of the door, Hutchings caught up with me for one more "Ungh" before he left the tavern.

Wiggins was waiting outside for me and he said exactly what I had been thinking.

"Doctor Watson," he said smiling, "you'll rarely, if ever, see golf played at that level again. You can trust me on that!"

"Wiggins," I replied as I paid him for his services, "of that I can be certain. Thanks for looping for me today. I hope to see you again."

Hole 15   Cartgate In

The short trip across the street from the "Old Course" to the Royal Hotel was one of the happiest walks I had taken in some time. It had been a beautiful day for a wonderful match on perhaps the finest links course in the game. I had been privileged to have been a part of one of the best-played rounds of golf I had ever witnessed. And, my team came away winning the match to boot!

Davison spotted me as I walked through the lobby, golf shoes in hand, and quickly summoned me into his office.

"Well," he asked politely, "how did it go? What did you think of Hutchings?"

"William, I'll tell you something," I continued, "I have seen many good shots by some outstanding players, but I must admit, I have never played in the same foursome with anyone that skilled."

"I thought as much," offered the hotel manager. "I had heard about him for several months, and wanted to know, first-hand, just how good he was. People were saying the most outlandish things about his ball-striking. And yet, he hardly ever plays! I was told that he would rather practice instead. Did you ever hear of such a thing?"

"It is rather an anomaly, yes," I agreed. "Tell me how I came to play with him, William. I'm certainly not in the same league as any of those players."

Hesitating somewhat, Davison, rose from his chair and as he scratched his mustache stated, "Funny you should ask, Doctor, because it was Hutchings himself who asked to be paired with you."

"What? You say that he requested to play with me?" I inquired. "Why I've never seen the man before. Why in this great world would he wish to play as my partner?"

Davison merely shrugged his shoulders saying, "John, before you trouble yourself too much in this matter, remember, Hutchings has been here for several months and we still don't know much about the man. I've no idea how he knew of you or why he wished for you to play in their foursome. Perhaps, he followed your career? Who knows? The only thing of which I'm certain is that all who have spent time with him come away confused. He certainly is a different sort of chap."

"I should say so," I replied laughing, "I've just spent 3½ hours with the gentleman, and he never spoke an intelligible word the whole time!"

"Well, John, I'd like to spend more time with you," said Davison, looking at his timepiece, "but I need to get back to work."

"Thank you, William," I offered as I headed out of his office and back toward my room. "I'll see you soon."

As I made my way up the staircase, I had the suspicion that someone was following me. After last evening's adventure, I was quite naturally nervous and anxious to reach my room. After last night, I was content to keep my service revolver with me at all times.

Making my way past the maid, I inserted my key and slowly entered hotel room 221, quickly closing the door behind me.

"Doctor Watson," someone whispered softly, "how was your golf today?"

Startled, I quickly dove behind the couch, grabbed my pistol and pointed it at the shadowy figure sitting on the edge of the bed. Still, holding my weapon, I rose, and moving ever so cautiously, lit one of the room lamps. A calm, familiar, friendly face met my anxious gaze.

"Mrs. Norton," I said, still shaking, "What in the world....." Before I could finish my sentence, she spoke again, "Doctor Watson, I didn't mean to surprise you. Please forgive me. I felt the need to finish my tale and tell you more about the key, that is if you still have it."

Oh dear, my mind began to race again. That key.... I had almost forgotten about it. I looked at my coat still hanging on the back of the door exactly where I had left it. Reaching slowly down into the inside pocket, I carefully probed for the ancient relic, found it, and moved to the mahogany rocking chair directly opposite my visitor, placing it in her hand.

"Thank God," Irene sighed. "I'm so glad we still have it!"

"Irene," I spoke with great hesitation, "I must tell you that last evening my room was thoroughly searched! Someone drugged my sherry and when I awoke, I found my hotel room had been totally ransacked!"

"And, this key?" she questioned, "Where in the world were you able to hide this key?"

Smiling smugly, I told her, "Mrs. Norton, I used one of my dear departed friend's most simple strategies. I hid the key out in the open. . . somewhere they would never think of looking."

"What?" she continued, "out in the open and they didn't find it? What are you talking about?"

"Calm down, Irene," I suggested, "You have the key in your possession. All is well. . . As to where I chose to hide it, I placed it in the lock in the door."

A look of horror appeared on her beautiful face as she shook her head angrily.

"Sir, I simply cannot believe that you were so thoughtless as to leave that key out where anyone might find it. How could you do such a thing?" she asked with much agitation.

No sooner had the words been spoken when she smiled and offered, "Doctor, forgive me. Why that was an excellent place to hide it. I should have known better than to doubt your logic. Clearly, your intimate knowledge of Holmes's clever ways have left you in good stead. You have learned much from him."

Her brief tribute to my friend meant a great deal to me, but I tried to hide the emotion that I was now feeling.

"Irene, I'm confused," I said, lifting the key from her hand and examining it further. "Didn't we agree to meet later today on the 18th green?"

She nodded her agreement, then said, "Yes, that was the plan, Doctor, but I was worried that someone might get to you before I could provide you with the importance of the key."

"You see, Doctor," she continued, "I found the plans for that most dangerous weapon and hid them in an ancient scabbard that was on display in the museum at the University of St Andrews. I was sure that no one had seen me hide the information, which I placed there after business hours, and so I felt they would be safe there for a very long time."

"Go on, Irene," I ventured. "There is more to this story. I can tell by the way you're behaving!"

"Doctor, my sponsors, the people I represent in this issue had a mole in Colonel Sebastian's organization. I was informed that Sebastian found out about the plans and sent one of his henchmen to follow me. When I learned that Sebastian knew about the museum, I had to act quickly and move the information elsewhere."

"How may I ask did you secure the case from out of the museum?" I inquired. "How were you able to, forgive me for suggesting this, 'steal' that piece from such a well-guarded location?"

"Doctor, I've already implicated you enough in this situation. You don't really need to know. You can't testify to something you don't know about," she stated. "You're going to have to continue to trust me. Please!"

She sounded so sincere and desperate that my conscience left me no choice but to accede. I shook my head in the affirmative.

"I was afraid that they would capture me or search my room and belongings so I passed the key along to you," she informed me as she concluded that portion of her tale.

"I see," I responded, reassuring her, "so now, I assume, we need to act quickly before Sebastian comes after you directly."

"That is why I came this afternoon. I am afraid that we will be followed until they find the plans," she whispered her response.

"So what is our next move?" I asked calmly.

"I think we should rendezvous at the grave site of Young Tom Morris at 10 o'clock," she suggested. "If we haven't been followed, we can go and retrieve the case containing the plans."

As she moved to the hotel room door, she warned, "Doctor, whatever you do, be sure that you are not followed."

After dinner, I had a small glass of sherry with Davison in the main lobby. There was still some time before I needed to leave, so we caught up on old times. We talked of many things, golf, politics, the weather, of course, and the upcoming Scottish horse races that were soon to be conducted at the St Andrews downs.

William said that he was glad to have me here for a few days of relaxation, further stating that he thought the rest was doing me a world of good. I smiled at that remark thinking, if he only knew....If he only knew what was really going on!

Davison was one of those rare individuals with whom a person experiences a close kinship at first meeting. Although I hadn't seen him for several years I felt extremely comfortable when in his presence. I admired his no-nonsense, stern management style. He wanted his guests to be satisfied with their stay, demanding exceptional service. That meant that he expected the same from all of his staff, from cook to maid to bookkeeper. All were expected to put forth their best efforts to keep the hotel guests happy while they visited this storied village hard by the North Sea.

I think he felt the same way about me. We had discussed my own occupation at length and I also elaborated on many of the exciting mysteries that Holmes was able to solve. He could see my pride whenever I spoke of those cases and he also complimented my writings, for I had sent him several manuscripts detailing my adventures with Holmes.

After a nightcap at the hotel bar, I took my leave and returned to my room to prepare for another exciting evening, hoping that we might find and secure the plans for that dangerous weapon. There was still some time to go, so I lit up one of the hotel cigarettes, even though I had stopped smoking several years prior. I paced nervously, wondering if I would be of any use to Irene in this matter. It hadn't been that long since Holmes's passing, yet I felt strangely out of shape, both physically and mentally. My creative brain had not been challenged since that final adventure in Europe.

At 9:35, I threw on my jacket, grabbed the key and my revolver and headed down the back stairs and out the rear door. I knew a shortcut to the town cemetery and when I arrived beside the Tom Morris monument, I was certain that I had not been followed.

As 10 o'clock approached, I thought I heard a slight rustling coming from the back of the graveyard so I crouched down with my hand securely holding my service revolver. I remained motionless for a few more minutes before I picked up the smell of Irene's perfume. A moment later and I saw her creeping up along the near wall.

"Psst....Doctor," she whispered, "is that you?"

"It had better be," I joked. "And that had better be you, as well, Mrs. Norton."

She joined me at the final resting place of Tom Morris, Jr., one of the youngest Open Golf champions who reputedly died of a broken heart after losing his young wife and their infant during childbirth.

"Doctor," she inquired, "are you certain that you weren't followed?"

"Irene," I replied, "I'm fairly certain. How about yourself?"

"Fair question, Doctor," she continued, "I believe we're safe...at least, so far! Come with me, quickly!"

Carefully, I followed her as we made our way back past the ruins of the old cathedral. It was still quite dark despite the moonlight, but after a few minutes, I could see that we were returning to that same old site by a different route. Irene was trying to see if we had been followed. When she was satisfied that we were alone, she motioned to me to lift an old branch that was lying alongside an internal wall of that famous old church ruin.

As I lifted the branch, I saw Irene frantically digging along the base of the wall. In a short time I heard a scratching sound and saw her wrestling with a long, metallic box of some kind. She turned to me and asked me to help lift it from the hole she had dug.

I found it to be a bit heavy and said so, whispering, "Irene, this is quite heavy. How did you get it here?"

"Never mind," she remarked anxiously. "Where is the key?"

"I've got it right here," I replied, handing it over to her.

She carefully placed the long box upright against the wall, removed the cover, and, finding the lock to the scabbard, inserted the ancient key.

"Click, click, click," sounded the dusty old key as it turned in the lock.

With a short, popping sound, the lock opened and we slipped the clasp, slowly opening the case. . .

Inside there was a velvet sheath in which a scroll had been carefully placed. Irene slowly slid the parchment from its covering and unraveled it in the bright moonlight.

I struck a match to a candle I had brought along, and Irene quickly examined her findings. As soon as she read it, she gasped aloud, "Oh no, we are too late!"

Still holding the scabbard, she shook it vigorously, looking for the miniature weapon design, but alas, it was empty.

Crestfallen, Irene shook her head, dropped the paper, and slowly began to walk away.

"What?" I cried, picking up the parchment, "what do you mean?"

"Read it yourself, Doctor," she suggested.

There before my eyes was a message to Irene and it read as follows:

"My Dear Mrs. Norton,

Sorry to inform you that your efforts to keep this out of my hands have failed. You should know that you never had a chance in this matter. Even had you taken possession of this blueprint, I would most certainly have gotten it away from you, by force, if necessary. Please don't interfere any further in this matter or in any other business of mine. Should you continue, I can assure you that you will be treated in a most unkind manner.

Your most humble foe,
Colonel C. M. Sebastian"

After extinguishing the candle, I headed toward Irene.

"Mrs. Norton....Irene," I called aloud. "Please wait for me. What can we do about this?"

While she waited for me to catch up to her, she hung her head and replied, "Nothing, Doctor. There is nothing more to be done. He now has the plans and he'll soon take possession of the finished weapon."

It would have done no good to try to console her that evening, for all of her clever plans had been discovered. It was all too much for such an intelligent mind to accept. She had simply been over-matched and having come to know her, I knew that could have a devastating effect on her persona.

As we entered the hotel, I told her to bar the door and try to get some sleep. We would meet for a late breakfast and plan our next step. I suggested that a good night's rest might allow us to think more clearly tomorrow.

Her disappointment was most obvious. I certainly could understand why she might be feeling so depressed. She had failed in her efforts to stop a criminal from acquiring a deadly weapon, one that she intimated could change the nature of crime! I could empathize with her about this, since I had now become a player in this drama. What struck me as odd was that I had become so angry over this matter. For I had only recently become involved in this mystery, and, to be sure, I had been an innocent party. Irene contacted me because she believed me to be a good, moral, law-abiding citizen. But there was more.....Irene had placed her faith in me because of all she had heard about me from Holmes!

Suddenly I felt a tightness in my throat. I had actually let her down, more to the point, I had let Holmes's account of me flag, as well. Surely, if this amazing woman had been so upset by this matter, it must have merited all the attention it was given and more. I found that I was now experiencing the same sad realization that she had been feeling.

Somehow we had to get those plans back...

Hole 16 Corner of the Dyke

The next morning, as we had agreed, I met Mrs. Norton for breakfast. When I entered the dining area, she was already seated near one of the hotel's bay windows overlooking North Street. I pretended not to see her at first while the maitre' d chose a table for me. As I approached my chair, Mrs. Norton caught my eye and I politely waved in her direction.

"Jeeves," I asked the hotel attendant, "would you excuse me while I chat with an old friend whom I've just noticed?"

"Doctor Watson," he deferred, "why not at all....I say, would the lady, perhaps, wish you to join her? I can inquire for you."

"Smashing, Jeeves," I replied and soon thereafter, I made my way over to Irene, talking like we had just seen each other after a great many years.

While we breakfasted, Irene and I joked about both staying in the same hotel and not even realizing it. We laughed and reminisced about things and places we had supposedly done and visited, though we never actually did them or visited them. It was a grand show for all of those present in the room. We had decided that after the last two adventures, we would need to establish some relationship if we were going to work and plan together to somehow get the weapon back in our possession.

After nodding to the concierge, I wished Mrs. Norton a fine day, adding, "I'm sure we'll see each other again. . ." loud enough for all to hear. She continued on her way out into the lavish garden with a flower shop brochure in her hand.

I had almost reached the stairs at the far side of the lobby when two gentlemen, nattily attired in Scottish tweed jackets, called over to me, "Doctor John Watson? May we have a word with you?"

Anxiously looking all about the lobby, I smiled and said, "Why, certainly gentlemen. By the way, have we met?"

The shorter of the two men responded, "Doctor, let me introduce you to Colonel C. M. Sebastian."

I suddenly felt a tingle go up my spine. My heart raced as I came face-to-face with one of Europe's greatest criminal minds. My reaction to this sudden turn of events was, if I might be so bold, extremely well-played.

"Sebastian?" I repeated the name extending my hand, "I seem to have heard that name before, but I can't for the life of me remember where."

Of course, thanks to Irene Norton and the adventures of the past few nights, I had found out a great deal about this rascal, but I tried not to let on.

Colonel Sebastian shifted his top hat to his left hand and took my hand in a firm grip, remarking "Doctor Watson, it's a pleasure to meet you. Perhaps you have heard of me, perhaps not, but I can assure you that your name is quite well-known in my circles. I know that you were a good friend and bosom companion to the famous late detective Sherlock Holmes. In fact, I believe you compiled records of his most famous cases, and did so very astutely. You must allow me to extend my sympathies for your great loss."

I studied his expression and the inflexion in his voice as he offered his condolences. He was a tall man, easily over 6 feet, and his cool dark steely eyes were set deeply behind his high cheekbones.

"That's very kind of you, Mr. Sebastian," I replied, knowing all along that he meant not a word of what he had said.

His face twitched a bit and he curtly corrected me, "It's Colonel Sebastian, Doctor, if you don't mind."

"So sorry, my good man, I didn't mean anything by it, you know," I informed the colonel.

At my "apology" he softened a bit, "You'll have to excuse me for being so abrupt, Doctor. I have a great many other things on my mind and I was very rude just now."

"Well, now, what is this meeting all about, sir?" I inquired of the men. "Surely, you don't require medical attention. . . "

"Doctor," Sebastian suggested, "why don't you join us in the tap room for a few minutes. I have an offer for you to consider."

"An offer for me to consider?" I repeated his words, smiling. "And you wish to share a drink while I ponder my decision? Well, gentlemen, I would be delighted to accede to your most interesting invitation."

The three of us entered the bar and sat near the fireplace, although there was little evidence that any fire had been lit in many days due to the extremely mild weather the area had been experiencing.

Sebastian ordered a Guinness, his crony, whose name I had learned was Jennings, had a scotch while I sipped on a mild sherry from Bordeaux. After a few moments had gone by, the colonel leaned forward from his chair and asked me what I thought about Charles Hutchings.

"Mr. Hutchings?" I replied, "Do you mean the man they call 'the Quiet One,' sir? Why do you ask, if I might be so bold?"

Sebastian laughed a bit then responded, "Well, Doctor, I've seen him play before. I've even tried to get a match with him, on several occasions. The trouble is, he won't play against me."

"Hmmm, I see", I offered, "I wonder why that might be?"

"Damned if I can understand it," Sebastian stated with a somewhat troubled expression. "Actually, Doctor, I'm a decent golfer myself and I've seen Hutchings play. He plays a wonderful game. I only want to see how my play matches up with his."

Continuing the colonel said, "You can understand that, Doctor, can't you? I mean, you're a golfer, too!"

Pausing for only a few seconds, he didn't wait for my reply, but instead reached the point of the meeting, "Doctor Watson, I know that you played as his partner in a fine match the other day. I was hoping that you might be in a position to speak on my behalf. You know, make a match for us. How about Jennings and I versus you and Mr. Charles Hutchings?"

I sat there and tapped my fingers on the mahogany table wondering why in the world this villain had this compulsive desire to play golf against this quiet, reclusive mute. . . .

Frankly, I didn't want to do anything that might help such a wanton criminal, but here he was presenting himself to a fellow golfer as just another human addicted to this incredibly interesting and aggravating game. For some reason he thought I would have better luck arranging a game with Hutchings. Why he should think so escaped me completely. I simply had to ask.

"Colonel, I must say, this is a most interesting proposition that you are suggesting," I stated somewhat restrained.

"But," I continued, "What makes you think that 'the Quiet One' would listen to me in this matter?"

Sebastian paused for a few seconds, looked at his hat, rose from his chair, signaling to Jennings, and answered, "Because he, himself, told me this very morning that he would only play with me if you, Doctor Watson, would play as his partner!"

For a brief moment I was stunned at what I had just heard, almost choking on my sherry.

"Why that's rather remarkable, Colonel," I announced, "for you see, I really don't play well at all, at least any more. . ."

Sebastian bowed, turned and began to walk toward the doorway, saying, "Doctor, please make the arrangements as soon as possible. I can be reached at the Old Course Hotel."

It took me a few minutes to compose myself over these recent events. Sitting alone, I rolled all of what had happened over and over in my mind. After finishing my drink, I was preparing to go back to my room when Mrs. Norton sat down beside me.

"Well," she spoke in a low voice, almost whispering, "what did that miserable, thieving scoundrel want?"

Smiling back at her, I quickly told her everything that had taken place prior to her recent arrival. She seemed a bit put off by the story, biting her bottom lip while she looked about the room. It was as if she was trying to reason it all out, but apparently, she could not.

"Doctor," she inquired, "why would Sebastian want to play golf with you and that strange silent person?"

"My dear, Mrs. Norton," I responded calmly, "I can assure you that it's not because of my golfing prowess..."

Irene smiled her beautiful smile, laughed politely, then continued, "Fair enough, John, but why does he feel compelled to challenge Mr. Hutchings?"

I simply shook my shoulders to indicate my own frustration over this strange episode, mildly offering, "I think it's his ego!"

Suddenly, her mood changed. She was once again, the Irene who charmed audiences all over the continent with her beauty and talent. Irene Adler Norton was once more the vivacious, clever woman who managed to outwit the greatest detective in history. The twinkle was back in her eyes and I realized, at once, that she had arrived at some kind of plan.

"Doctor," she spoke with much excitement, "don't you realize what this opportunity affords? Can't you see how providence has interceded on our behalf? This is truly serendipitous!"

Irene suddenly realized that she had to contain herself, for her animated behavior had gathered much curiosity from the other patrons of the hotel bar.

I was extremely happy for her, but I had to confess that I knew not why she was so excited about a round of golf!

The look on my face told her as much so she grabbed my hands, stared into my eyes and whispered, "Doctor Watson, think about it. If we know that Colonel Sebastian and one of his minions will be playing golf with you and Mr. Hutchings, doesn't it also mean that I'll have at least 4 hours to search his hotel room and all of his belongings?"

Then it hit me! She was right! While we were on the golf course she could be searching for the plans or, by now, even the weapon itself, for Sebastian could already have it in his possession.

We sat for a few more minutes putting the plan together. I would try to contact Charles Hutchings, set up the match and let Colonel Sebastian know the "good news". Once the starting time had been arranged, Irene could make plans to visit Sebastian's chambers and, hopefully, retrieve what had been stolen from her at the cemetery.

"Irene, there is just one thing more we have to consider," I offered. "It's very probable that Sebastian will have his room carefully being watched by other members of his gang. You may be placing yourself in even greater danger should this be the case. You simply can't go there alone. You're going to need some help!"

"Doctor, I've already considered that possibility," she informed me. "Please understand that there are others working on 'our' side. We have a band of agents who have been tirelessly monitoring Colonel Sebastian's every movement. While there is always some danger when dealing with the criminal element, you and I both have experience in preparing contingency plans to account for the unexpected."

As she rose from her place, she agreed to contact me later that night to tie up any loose ends. A moment later and Irene Norton had left the room.

When a suitable amount of time had passed, I made my way through the lobby and back to my room. Quickly, I sent a dispatch to Mr. Hutchings to see if he could make the match with us tomorrow. While I waited for his response, I found enough time to wash, change and make my way over to the starter's shed to arrange a time for the match tomorrow.

The starter informed me that the starting times had filled up early due to the favorable weather the area continued to experience. The next open time was 4:00 in the afternoon. That would never do, I informed him, thanking him for his time. As I turned to go he suddenly waved to me.

"Doctor Watson," his gruff voice announced, "I've just received word of a cancellation at 11:40. How does that suit you?"

"Bless you, kind sir!" I replied, thanking him profusely.

Two minutes later and I was making my way across North Street and opening the door to the hotel.

As I passed the registration desk, Davison called over to me, "John, John, I have a telegram for you. It's newly arrived."

"Thank you, William," I said.

"I sincerely hope that it's nothing serious, John," my friend offered.

"Oh, don't worry," I told him after I had scanned the telegram, "everything is fine."

I fairly flew up the staircase and after unlocking the door to my room, I sat on the corner of the large bed and read the message from Charles. It wasn't much, but it didn't need to say much.

Received your invitation....Stop
Glad to play with you again....Stop
Please advise me of the time....Stop
Best regards.....Hutchings....Stop

Upon reading the brief reply, I had to laugh at my first thought, "Charles always was a man of few words."

Well, my next move was to contact Sebastian. He would certainly be pleased by this accommodation, and if he agreed to play, Irene would have a wonderful opportunity to search his room.

It was just approaching sundown when I left the Royal Hotel and headed down along the fabled 18th fairway to where Colonel Sebastian was lodging. There were still several players finishing up their rounds, as I approached the heinous 17th green of the "Road Hole", perhaps the most difficult hole on the course. Continuing along the edge of the fairway, I neared the sheds belonging to the Old Course Hotel. While I rounded the last turn, I saw Sebastian anxiously looking out of his hotel room window.

He must have seen me looking up at him as I passed by, for he waved and pointed toward the hotel entryway. I nodded back at him, assuming we would meet in the main lobby inside the majestic old hotel.

I had no sooner entered the building, when Jennings escorted me to one of the establishment's side rooms. I imagined it to be a card room that was not being used on that particular afternoon.

Two other men were sitting with Jennings and me when Colonel Sebastian appeared at the doorway.

He was smiling as he spoke, "Doctor Watson, am I correct in assuming that we have a golf match?"

"We will meet you gentlemen tomorrow morning. Our starting time will be 11:40," I proudly announced, while I watched the two "newer" members of Sebastian's gang.

Noticing my inquisitive glance, Sebastian spoke up, "Doctor, these two gentlemen are friends of mine. If you don't mind, Jennings and I will be employing them as caddies."

"Mind?" I questioned his comment, "why should I mind whom you select as your caddies? Gentlemen, I'm John

Watson, MD and I hope you don't mind seeing your friends here being soundly thrashed on the course tomorrow."

That must have been the right thing to say, for Sebastian and his cronies all had a hearty laugh with my comment.

Jennings quickly replied to my jest, "Well, Doctor, we'll see how the match goes. You might be in for a real surprise!"

"Tut, Tut, now Jennings," Sebastian reprimanded him mildly.

"Doctor, I appreciate what you've done and I promise you that my partner and I will try to make tomorrow a day you and Mr. Hutchings may never forget!" Sebastian said with a much darker tone in his voice.

"Hmmmm, Colonel Sebastian," I meekly stated, "you know, dear man, that sounded eerily like a threat."

Sebastian laughed his sinister laugh, "Doctor, what are you talking about. We're all going to have a wonderful time golfing. That's all I meant. Now, I must tend to some business but I promise to see you on the first tee tomorrow. Good evening!"

Shortly thereafter, I was back at my hotel and seated with Mrs. Norton for dinner. We had become much more comfortable with each other over the last few days; so comfortable, in fact, that Davison had pulled me aside after dinner and asked me about her.

"Why what are you implying, Davison?" I inquired of my dear friend. "Do you suppose that I've forgotten that I'm a married man, husband to the most wonderful woman in the world?"

Davison slumped in his chair and remarked, "Thank God, John. I was afraid that you and Mary had had some kind of falling out and that you had surrendered to the many charms of that beautiful siren, Irene Norton, nee Irene Adler."

I wanted to laugh, but I could clearly sense that my friend was truly concerned about my relationship with Mrs. Norton.

Suddenly, I was compelled to relate how we knew each other. I told him the story about her early involvement with one of Europe's most regal families and how Holmes and I had been asked to intercede to prevent a most embarrassing situation from fomenting into a true tragedy.

"Mrs. Norton and I are merely good friends," I told him. "We share many of the same interests as well as a deep appreciation for the memory of Sherlock Holmes."

"Thank God, John," the hotel manager sighed, "I was on the verge of losing respect for one of the most decent men I had had the pleasure of knowing. Please forgive me for ever doubting you, old boy."

"Consider it done, William," I replied, somewhat chastened by his logical suspicion. "I know what it must have looked like to you, and I appreciate your concern. My wife and I are most fortunate to have such a true friend."

When I returned to my room, I was again shocked to find Irene waiting inside.

"Irene, how in the world did you manage to get into my room?" I asked, somewhat concerned about the boldness of her actions.

"Is there a problem, John?" she asked somewhat taken aback. "I had a master key made by a local locksmith. I can assure you that I only did so to make it easier for us to make our plans. It would never do if someone saw me waiting outside your door until you returned."

"Yes, of course. Please forgive the tone and gist of my interrogative," I pleaded. "By the way, the match is all set for tomorrow. We tee off at 11:40!"

"Splendid." she replied cheerily. "I've been studying the plans of the Old Course Hotel and I believe that I've found a way to get to Sebastian's room, which, by the way, is one of the hotel's premier suites."

Irene opened a small folder containing what appeared to be an architect's schematic of the hotel. I could see that she had traced out some of the hallways leading to Colonel Sebastian's room. She coolly laid out her plans for me to examine.

"Doctor," she explained, "as you can see, these drawings show all of the stairs, hallways and main rooms in the Old Course Hotel. You'll also notice that there are several dumb waiters located in certain sections of the building. According to the dimensions, I can easily fit into the dumbwaiter that leads directly into Sebastian's suite. I have only to find a way to distract the hotel staff so that I can access the elevator."

"Irene," I offered, "mind now, you'll still be in danger even if you are able to reach Sebastian's chambers. He probably will have some men guarding it, wouldn't you think?"

"I'm sure that is the case, Doctor," the adventuress added, "that is why I will have some help along with me to create the odd diversion, if and when it becomes necessary."

She paused, staring directly into my eyes, anxious to hear my impressions of her well-thought-out plan. Those brown eyes, they were indeed, magical. I found my thoughts once more drifting back to Holmes and his fascination with Irene Adler. Any man would be struck by her great beauty and grace. Along with those qualities, perhaps even above those qualities, there was her intelligence and her courage.

"Well," she inquired, "John, I'm waiting to hear what you think about the plan!"

Her intonation shocked me back into the moment, and I congratulated her on scheme, "Irene," I said, "it seems like a very sound, reasoned strategy. I applaud you."

"Now," she continued, "you, for your part, must make certain that Sebastian finishes the round. I'm afraid that if he returned too early, he might still find someone prowling around his hotel room!"

"You needn't worry about that, Madam," I advised, "it's you who needs to be careful. Oh, how I wish I could guarantee your safety!"

"Your words are most kind, John," she softened, "but I'll be fine. I have some strong allies on my side in this matter. I'll contact you tomorrow evening. Good night."

"Please be careful," I whispered as she disappeared into the hall.

Hole 17   Road

The sunrise over the North Sea seemed particularly brilliant that August morning at St Andrews. The inhabitants were industriously plying their various trades as the tiny village came to life. The pungent aromas of freshly baked scones and freshly caught "kippers" everywhere assaulted the olfactory sensory nerves. The first, most pleasing; the latter, perhaps requiring a more acquired taste. Still, for many in this region of stark beauty this was the normal morning breakfast fare.

A steady "clip-clop-clip" echoed off the gray walls so abundant in this town, as a team of huge Clydesdales set off on its daily delivery route. This would be the first of many such wagons that had to make their way through the quiet town, all in the name of commerce.

In the distance, hammers banged away as roof repair of the town hall continued. The shrieking of the water fowl were, of course, ever present; so much so, in fact, that one hardly paid attention to their constant screeches. Add to all of these sounds the ever-increasing shuffling of shoes on the pavement as villagers hurried on their way to work.

While most of the town was coming alive after a good night's rest, there were those who found themselves unable to get much sleep. Important matters had kept them awake most of the night, for the day ahead would demand precise timing and cool nerves. They were also aware that danger was in the air, should their plans fall apart.

A heavy dew was still burning off the fairways of the golf course as the clock struck ten. It was a bit unusual for fog to remain that late in the morning, but weather patterns in this part of the world were always subject to change. The clock in the square had just finished chiming out the hour when I sat down for my crumpets and tea. The breakfast looked and smelled delicious as I placed my napkin on my lap, tossing aside the newspaper that I had recently been reading.

The dining room was normally a very busy place when breakfasts were being served, but this was a late breakfast, in fact, it could have been called a lunch! I had stayed up late into the evening and early morning, trying to imagine every possible flaw with the plan that Irene had laid out the previous evening. My role was a simple one. It would be my job and responsibility to keep Sebastian and Jennings occupied on the golf course. That was easy enough, for even a quick match on the St Andrews course would take at least 2½ hours.

That was not what worried me. Irene easily had the more dangerous job. It would be she who might encounter some of Sebastian's minions, and she didn't know who they were or how many there might be! I had a bad feeling about this, and told Irene as much, several times in fact. She had thanked me for my concern, but remained adamant about her plan.

At a quarter to twelve, the plan was to go into effect. We had determined that at that time the Sebastian–Jennings team and Hutchings–Watson team, having played our tee shots, would be walking toward the first green.

Prior to the onset of play, Colonel Sebastian had made his way across the first tee to greet us. He seemed quite jovial.

"Gentlemen, I cannot tell you how much this means to me," he spoke with genuine emotion. "As you know, Hutchings, I've been trying to get a game with you for several weeks now. Thank you for agreeing to play."

Slowly, "the Quiet One" extended his hand with a suspicious look in his eye, bowed and issued his familiar "Ungh," before winking at Watson.

Turning to his left, Sebastian continued, "Doctor Watson, I am very much in your debt for arranging this match. I believe it's going to be a most memorable game. Now let us enjoy the weather, the golf and most assuredly, each other's company. Shall we?"

Jennings played first, the lefty smashing a low runner down the left side of the enormous fairway. Colonel Sebastian took a majestic practice swing which indicated that he must have received some type of formal instruction. His tee-shot flew in a high, right-to-left path that carried a long way, leaving him a mere niblick to the green.

Now it was my turn. A nervous player to begin with, I found I was even more anxious than usual. It took me three attempts to position my ball on the wet sand. When Wiggins handed me the driver, I promptly dropped it, knocking the ball from the tee.

"Really, gentlemen," I apologized, "I'm truly embarrassed. I frankly don't know what's come over me."

"Can't stand the pressure, Watson?" teased Jennings.

"Ungh," growled "the Quiet One" in Jennings's direction.

"Tut, tut, Charles," I replied, trying to calm my partner, "I'll be much more comfortable after I birdie this hole."

That remark seemed to break the tension and our small party laughed at the statement. After re-teeing, I took a quick, nervous backswing and promptly topped my ball a mere 25 yards!

Jennings and Sebastian turned away trying to stifle a grin, while Hutchings unleashed his brassie, driving his ball almost into the Swilcan Burn that fronts the green. And with that, we were off and the match had begun. . . . .

While the golfers were on their way toward the first green, there were other, more pressing issues occurring less than two hundred yards away. . .

On the second floor of the Royal Hotel, in suite 319, two women were engaged in a most important conversation. The older woman, wearing a white surplice apron over her long black dress, paced back and forth in a worrisome manner. The matter at hand could prove to be quite dangerous and required the utmost discretion and attention to detail to have any chance at success.

"My dear, she said solemnly, "I fear that you have no idea how important it is for you to follow my directions to the letter. Promise me, you'll do as I say."

The younger of the two, Gloria Wilson, listened intently and then tried to assure her friend, "Ma'am, I understand what you're saying and I can assure you that I promise to do exactly what you have laid out for me."

Irene Norton placed a dark shawl around her young aide, hugged her and then remarked, "Gloria, I know you will be careful, but I still worry for your safety!"

"Mrs. Norton," she replied, "all you have asked me to do is cover my face and take a brisk walk up North Street to the University, where I will go to the manuscript section and spend several hours taking notes about the origin of this quaint little town. That hardly sounds like a dangerous adventure to me!"

"Gloria, dear, it is most important that no one sees your face until you return to this room," insisted her mistress. "Should you be discovered, I'm afraid we are all lost!"

And with that last warning, the young woman left the room, locking it from the outside, and quickly disappeared down the main staircase, across the lobby and out into the busy, sunlit street.

Irene quietly moved to the window and carefully peered through the drawn curtains. She patiently watched "Irene

Norton," shawl wrapped over her head and face, start her walk up North Street. A cold shiver went up Mrs. Norton's spine when she saw that her aide was being followed. A thin young man, dressed in the long black trench coat Sebastian's minions seemed required to wear, was closely trailing her.

With her plan already in motion, Irene opened that same window and stepped out onto the tiny ledge that framed the entire third floor of the majestic hotel. Very carefully she made her way to the roof of an adjoining building and found an emergency ladder which helped her to the ground. She quickly made her way through an alley and lost no time in reaching the exterior of the Old Course Hotel.

Stashing her cloak in the hotel garbage bin, she dashed to the employee entrance and entered the building. Her timing could not have been better, for the kitchen area bordering the foyer, was teeming with activity. Dressed in an Old Course Hotel maid's uniform, she quickly found the laundry room and picked up a master key. Her next move was to somehow get to the dumbwaiter that led to Sebastian's custom suite.

"So far, so good," she whispered to herself, trying to recall the location of the elevator on the hotel map she had secured.

Glancing around, she suddenly spotted it along the far wall, and just as she was about to slide open the door, she heard a voice echoing down the hallway. She had to hide, but where? The voices were getting louder when she spotted a nearby laundry hamper overflowing with dirty bed linens. Quickly, she dove into the bin and began to dig down under the smelly laundry items.

"Margaret, have you seen Mary?" asked the chief waiter.

A gray head belonging to a long time hotel washer-woman peeked out from behind a rack of ironed clothing and responded, "What de ye want her fer, ye little squint?"

"Now, Margaret," he said in a soothing voice, "we don't have to speak that way, do we?"

"Oh, haud yer wheest, McLeod!" she shrieked, "She's on about her business. Dinnae fash yersel." ***

"Well, if you do see her," he continued, "please tell her that Mr. Steed, the new manager is looking for her."

"Arragh," grumbled the old woman and they started down the hallway, still arguing.

Irene quietly waited until the talking stopped, but she couldn't be certain if the employees had left the area. Phew, she would never have believed dirty linens could ever have such a terrible smell. Slowly, she peeked out from under a pile of stained bedspreads, trying to see if she could make it to the elevator without being discovered.

Luck was with her, for when she emerged from the bin, the room was empty. Irene dashed to the dumb waiter's door, slid it open and hopped inside. Slowly, ever so slowly, she pulled the unit upwards. Sebastian's room was on the third floor so she had to be extremely careful, for every time she pulled on the cable, the unit issued a tiny squeak. Up and up she went. Passing the first floor lobby was an easy task for there was plenty of activity to absorb the sounds of the noisy elevator. It wasn't as easy going past the second floor, for the cramped conveyance seemed heavier and the squeaking became louder and more frequent.

As she pulled the unit into the third floor access panel, she slowed to a snail's pace. After stopping the elevator, she sat there motionless for at least 2 minutes, trying to listen for any activity in the room. This would be the most dangerous part of the mission. It was very possible that one or two of Sebastian's cronies would be on duty guarding the suite while their leader was golfing. Irene could wait no longer. She would have to open the panel some time or the plan would obviously fail.

Closing her eyes, she made every effort to open the door, an inch at a time; slowly, slowly, slowly. . . now take a peek. . .

Seeing and hearing no one, Irene continued; slowly, slowly, slowly. . . now she took another peek. Still no indication. . . Now, she took one slow long push and opened the door, entering into Sebastian's room.

The first thing Irene did was to survey the two-room suite. Thankfully, the rooms were empty. They were, perhaps, the finest rooms in the hotel, richly adorned with dark oaken paneling. There was a stone fireplace in the outer room that would have been the envy of any castle. The ample bedroom was as large as she had ever seen and the window treatments in both rooms were done with ornate figures of golfers playing the "Old Course."

Irene quickly went to work. She peeked through the hall transit to see if the door was being guarded. It was not. Next she sidled over to a door leading onto the balcony which provided a spectacular view of the 2nd and 16th greens and the 17th tee box. She was tempted to peek out at the course, but decided against it. All hell would have broken loose had Sebastian glanced over and seen her in his suite!

Where might the plans have been hidden? Would he have hidden the weapon in the closet? Perhaps there was a secret panel that she might have to locate. There were plenty of places in those two large rooms where the item could be stowed. Irene felt the urge to simply tear into anything and everything that could have held the weapon and/or the plans, but that would have attracted more attention. If she had to leave hurriedly without locating the object, Sebastian would surely know that someone had been poking around in his room. That would make it much more difficult to wrest the object away. What about.....?

Suddenly, her plan went up in smoke as she realized the folly of her strategy. She felt foolish. Very foolish, indeed! What made her think that one of the brightest criminal minds in Europe would ever leave such a prized and valuable object in his room unattended; especially an object he had worked so long and hard to procure?

Now, she was distraught. How could she have been so stupid? She was still feeling angry with herself while starting for the hall door when she noticed a letter on the desk. As she reached for it, she almost screamed aloud. Irene sat down holding the letter, began to shake visibly. . . . for the name on the envelope belonged to Mrs. Irene Norton!

Knowing she should make a quick escape, but fighting her woman's curiosity, Irene tore open the envelope and started to read the contents:

> "My Dear Mrs. Norton,
>   Clearly you must realize that you've missed your chance. I have that which you are once more seeking.
>   I had believed you were smart enough not to be reading this letter, but, apparently, I overestimated your mental acuity!
>   Better luck next time! Sadly though, I do believe that you are of that persistent breed who will never accept the fact that they have been beaten. Consider this to be your last warning. . . ."

Irene shuddered at the thought, but after quickly regaining her composure, she grabbed a hotel quill and jotted down a message of her own.

> "Colonel Sebastian,
>   If you believe your simple warnings are enough to scare law-abiding people from doing what is right and proper, you are even more delusional than I've heard.
>   And you, sir, may be assured that you have now become the hunted instead of the hunter. Society has no place for criminals like you and your henchmen.
>   You, sir, have now been warned. . ."

Mrs. Norton left the note unsigned, hoping to create some doubt in Sebastian's mind when he returned to his room. She placed her note on the desk, walked to the door and into the hallway, still wearing her Old Course Hotel maid's uniform. Fortunately, no one saw her leave the room and she was soon back outside gathering her cloak for the short walk back to her own hotel.

As she entered the building, she spied the tall man who had followed her aide, Gloria, up North Street. Seeing her enter, he walked toward her, hesitated, bowed to her offering, "Mrs. Norton," and then continued across the lobby to the main doorway. Quickly, Irene mounted the stairs and ran to her room. Fearing the worst, she threw open the door, hoping to find her confidant, "Gloria, Gloria, are you here?" she cried aloud.

Seeing no one and fearing the worst, Irene sat down and putting her hands to her face began to sob.

"Is that you, Ma'am?" came a voice from out of the closet.

"Gloria," Irene exclaimed through her tears, "Is that you? Are you all right?"

"Why of course, Ma'am!" she cheerily replied, "now why wouldn't I be?"

After a quick reassuring hug, Irene asked her aide what had transpired at the University. Gloria told her that she had faithfully followed her directions to the letter.

"I do admit, that I was surprised that you wanted me back so soon," she said smiling, "That nice tall young man came over to my table and told me that you had finished early and that I should return at once."

The look on Irene's face said otherwise. "Gloria, we've been duped. I never sent anyone to get you. Additionally, I was unable to complete my mission."

"Oh, I'm sorry, Ma'am," Gloria uttered sincerely, "Did I do anything wrong?"

"No, dear," Mrs. Norton softened, "we'll just have to come up with another plan. I'm just happy that you're here, safe and sound."

Back to the golf match. . . .

The winds had picked up substantially as the afternoon wore on, but the golfers had no complaints. It was a truly delightful day for golf. The "Old Course" could be incredibly scenic when the weather cooperated. The day's sunny skies served to highlight the brilliant colors of the heather and gorse that framed so many of the holes at St Andrews.

There were several matches being played that day, but most spectators had elected to follow one match in particular. By now the golfing populace had heard and seen "the Quiet One" play, and they longed to see more. When word went out that he would be playing that August afternoon, a small crowd showed up to watch. Galleries were not encouraged on the course, but neither were they banned. As long as they didn't hold up play, the Royal and Ancient had no serious objections.

Earlier in the match, Sebastian's birdie on the third hole had put his team 1-up, and that team remained there until I somehow surprised the players by skipping my cleek off the side of a tiny brae on the eighth hole. The fortunate bounce left me with a short nine-inch putt that was easily conceded by our opposition.

"Ungh!" voiced my elated partner, Hutchings, for "the Quiet One" had been doing all of the playing for the first seven holes. I sensed he was happy to see me contribute.

Both teams made solid pars on holes nine and ten and by the time we had made our way to the next hole, referred to as "High (In)," the match was all square.

The short eleventh was the second of only two three-pars on the golf course. Measuring a mere 172 yards, it was still not an easy par for most players, playing into the prevailing wind coming off the Eden Estuary.

Hutchings and I still held the honors and we decided that I should play first. My mashie started on line, but a gust of wind caught the ball, knocking it into a difficult spot in the Strath bunker, a small pot bunker to the right of the green. Hutchings's spade mashie was a well-played, low draw which landed on the left side of the green and released, leaving him a delicate twenty-foot birdie putt.

Jennings took very little time playing his shot. He was a decent golfer and his swing looked the part. A natural fader of the ball, his shot struck the right side of the green and trundled down a modest slope off to the rear of the tiered putting surface.

As Sebastian stepped up to the ball, he issued the following remark to us, "Gentlemen, what say you to a special bet on this shot of mine?"

"The Quiet One" scratched his head, stretched his hands out and inquired, "Ungh?"

As his partner, I interpreted, "My partner is asking what kind of bet do you have in mind, Colonel?"

"Well," he continued, "What would you say to a bet of five pounds sterling on this shot. I say I can get within fifteen feet of the hole. Well, come on."

I looked at Hutchings, and Hutchings shook his head in the affirmative, issuing a resounding, "Ungh!"

"My partner and I will take that bet, Colonel," I proudly replied, "You're on, sir."

With that having been agreed to, Sebastian grabbed his mashie niblick and smashed a high fade that rode the wind, settling a mere seven feet from the cup.

"Fine, fine shot, Colonel," I stated with some restrained admiration, handing him the five pound note.

Jennings was beaming, complimenting his partner, "Great play, Colonel. That's showing 'em!"

The onlookers applauded, as well they should, for it was a well-struck shot.

After Jennings and I had played our second shots, it was Hutchings's turn to play. He slowly walked toward me, a ten pound note in his hand, pointing to Jennings and then to Sebastian.

I understood immediately, offering, "Colonel, my partner and I want to wager this ten pound note that we will win this hole. Are you agreeable?"

Sebastian smiled and offered, "That's a capital idea. We'll take the risk, for that is one tricky putt over the hillock. I honestly don't think your partner can make it!"

After carefully studying the break, examining the grain, and factoring in the gusts that were now haphazardly blowing in from the shore, Hutchings stepped up for his putt.

Just as he was about to address his ball, a stiff gust swept over the hillside and caught the ball, causing it to run across the top of the slope and start down to the hole. The players were stunned at what was occurring and they watched in amazement as Hutchings's ball disappeared into the hole.

I turned to Hutchings and we smiled at each other, enjoying the inordinate good fortune that we had just incurred. The crowd roared at what they had witnessed. Sebastian and Jennings just stood there in utter shock. They really didn't understand what they had happened and weren't sure what needed to be done with that holed ball. The fact that Hutchings had actually recorded a hole-in-one had never entered their minds!

"What do we do about that situation, Doctor Watson?" Sebastian inquired.

"Why, you may pick up your birdie putt, Colonel," I happily replied, "Oh, and you and Jennings may also hand over the ten pound notes you've just lost!"

"Well, I'll be scumered," Sebastian remarked. "Do you mean that Hutchings scored an ace even though he hadn't hit his putt?" ***

"That is correct, sir," I politely continued, "my partner never addressed his ball. And the wind, not being considered an outside agent, moved the ball across the green and into the hole. Since Hutchings only struck his ball one time, it counts as a hole-in-one, although a very strange hole-in-one!"

Jennings and Sebastian walked away from the green talking quietly, but when the foursome had reached the 12th tee, Sebastian spoke.

"Doctor," he said, "I'm not questioning your integrity with respect to that last hole, but Jennings and I aren't too sure that you are correct in your remarks. Would you take umbrage if we took our point to the rules official?"

"Of course not, Colonel," I responded politely, "after all, it was a very strange occurrence and, truthfully, I do not believe many golfers would know the rule. I can assure you, no offense will be taken by us in that regard."

For all of the intensity of the match, both parties played the game honestly, with Sebastian and Hutchings having a splendid match of their own, though not readily apparent to the casual observer.

With our team, Watson-Hutchings, now leading by 1 hole, much of the casual conversation dropped off, for now, both teams were very much into the match. The next five holes were halved with pars, with Jennings and I relegated to observers for the most part since Sebastian and Hutchings were both playing sterling golf.

While "the Quiet One" and I were making our way to the tee area on the next hole, I expressed my gratitude for having been asked to play.

"Mr. Hutchings, I must thank you for inviting me to partner with you again," I stated. "You are certainly aware that I'm not the golfer that I would like to be. I also know that I really don't belong playing a match with the likes of a player of your caliber and Colonel Sebastian. You both play outstanding golf. I pray that I do not distract you in any way, sir."

"The Quiet One" raised his hand and bowed to me, his way of indicating that all was well.

By chance, we saw Mr. Iverson, the St Andrews Captain, standing by the side of the sixteenth green. Knowing he was a Rule's Official, Sebastian took the opportunity to raise the issue of Hutchings's questionable "hole-in-one" on hole number eleven. After hearing an accurate description of what had occurred, Iverson remarked, "Nice ace, Mr. Hutchings!"

That was the end of that discussion, but Sebastian and Jennings took the decision like men, though begrudgingly.

We were now ready to play the Road Hole, so named because the back of the green itself lies directly along a roadway that runs adjacent to the golf course. The fascinating aspect to this hole is that the road is actually in play! Many shots that bound over the green can come to rest close to or even up against a stone wall that borders the property.

Throughout its history, this hole has been the scene of great drama. Far too many matches have been lost when marginal shots have made their way into the Road Bunker, a very treacherous, deep sand pit from which it is very difficult to recover.

Knowing that I could not reach the hole with two of my best swings, I took the safe approach by launching my tee ball toward the second fairway. Hutchings, playing as well as ever, played his drive directly over the outbuildings of the hotel. He had plenty of distance for the long carry that was required.

Jennings hooked his ball around the corner, leaving him under two-hundred yards to get to the surface. When it was Sebastian's turn, he slowly looked up toward his hotel room. A tall, thin figure was standing on the balcony waving his top hat for the Colonel to see. Smiling knowingly, Sebastian raised his club toward the window and then teed up his ball.

The resulting smooth swing easily drove the ball over the top of the hotel and back into the fairway.

Arriving for our second shots, I had the honors. My brassie advanced the ball to within eighty yards of the green.

Jennings played next and struck the ball solidly. His ball hit a hard spot, rolling over the green, crossing the road and ending up very close to the stone wall boundary.

Colonel Sebastian laced a high, drawing mashie, but it caught the top of the Road Bunker and rolled down into the bottom of the pit. When Hutchings saw where his opponents had left their shots, he went back to his bag, exchanging his spade mashie for a niblick. He knew full well that he could never reach the green with that club. He also knew that our team was 1-up in the match and he decided to play it safe, leaving himself a pitch of only thirty yards from the right side of the green. His club selection and subsequent shot landed precisely where he had planned.

I played my niblick sixteen feet beyond the flag, leaving a difficult, yet makeable, par putt. Jennings took two more shots to get on the green and still had a putt of twenty feet for his bogey five. Hutchings's pitch shot rolled up the swale and finished seven feet from the hole.

When Sebastian saw his lie, he turned away from the ball, issued an impolite comment and then grabbed his niblick from the caddie. Extracting the ball was his first priority and he did an admirable job just getting the ball out of the hazard. He was left with a fifteen foot, hard-breaking, left-to-right, downhill slider. This was not the putt anyone would want to have as a "must-make" shot!

Jennings's putt for bogey lipped out and he settled for a double-bogey, while my effort stopped a mere two inches short, much to my dismay.

Sebastian knew that he had to make the putt to have any chance of winning the match. He stalked that putt like a hunter on the trail of a hind. With an air of supreme confidence, he stepped over his ball, gave it one quick look, and then stroked it toward and into the cup.

Hutchings felt the impact of the roar of the crowd as if he had just been hit in the solar plexus. Staring at Sebastian, he issued his now familiar, "Ungh," and placed his putter behind the ball. His was a straight putt, the kind a quality player like Hutchings would make nine out of ten times. As the putter head contacted the ball, "the Quiet One" began to walk. His putt came up two feet short of the hole and, in a rare show of anger, he smashed the ball over the stone wall behind the green. The match was all square with one hole to go. . .

Shocked, I wanted to go over to my partner and try to console him, but one look told me to stay away. I had never seen this side of him before, but it told me "the Quiet One" could be nasty. . .

Jennings and Sebastian hit fine drives up the fairway of the 354 yard finishing hole. They would have short second shots into the green. My tee ball started off far to the left, but the wind, freshening from the North Sea brought it back into play. I knew that I would have a long second shot to the short hole, but at least I had a shot.

Hutchings was smiling at me as he took his practice swing. It was a steely grin, and this time his swing seemed to pack some extra "whip". He teed his ball up even higher than normal and set up for his shot. As the crowd grew quiet, Hutchings began his backswing and let it go, really let it go! The ball started off high and to the right, near the boundary stakes at first. Then, suddenly, the ball started to turn toward the green and ended up in the swale known as the "Valley of Sin." While a massive drive, Charles knew he would still have a difficult time getting his second shot close to the pin.

As we crossed Granny Clark's Wynd, the gallery, now much larger since the front nine, came up close behind us. I quickly played a low, running shot with my mashie niblick, and my ball finished on the back of the green. Jennings fluffed his second shot, barely reaching the front of the green. Sebastian was only sixty yards from the pin, but the hole was located on the first tier above the Valley of Sin. It would take quite a shot to get close, but it was obvious by his actions that he was determined to get it close.

He took his mashie, and played a low runner that flew to the front of the green, bounced into the slope, checked and released, rolling eighteen feet beyond the flag.

The stage was now set for Hutchings. He had played this shot before, many times before, so he knew what the shot called for. Reaching for his putter, he stroked the guttie just above the ball's equator and watched it hop and roll across the famous swale and begin to climb the slope. The ball seemed almost to stop as it moved to he top of the hill. However, the law of gravity was now having its effect on this putting green.

As the ball neared the cup, it looked like an eagle. The ball struck the pin softly enough to have dropped, but it bounced a foot away after striking the pin. The excited gallery once again announced its presence. An ear-splitting scream filled the air in appreciation for the excellence of the shot.

Of course the birdie had to be conceded, and Jennings did the honors, rudely knocking the ball back toward the tee. I, of course, picked up and it was now up to Colonel Sebastian to tie the match. For the first time all day, Sebastian seemed to be exhibiting some nerves.

After lining up his putt, he stood over the ball for a long time, much longer than normal. While the gallery waited for him to play, he suddenly straightened up and backed away from the putt. There were "oohs and aahs" coming from the gallery and there was a most noticeable change in Colonel Sebastian's demeanor. He took a deep breath and then went back to his routine, finally ready to putt, or so everyone thought. He looked to be struggling with himself while he prepared for his shot. Unable to take the putter back, he backed away again. . .

This time there were gasps from the observers. Colonel Sebastian, the very picture of self-confidence, appeared physically ill. Knowing it would get no better, he stepped up and stabbed at his putt. . . . leaving his eighteen foot birdie effort woefully short. . . .some six feet short of the hole!

Sebastian began to shake violently, so much so, that many were afraid that he would erupt, much like a volcano. Jennings slowly walked over to Hutchings and me and congratulated us. Hutchings and I stood on the back of the green, putting our clubs away while we watched Colonel Sebastian quickly snap his putter into four sections.

Hutchings couldn't help smiling, but he quickly turned and walked toward Sebastian. They briefly shook hands and then, suddenly, without any warning, Sebastian bolted from the green and left the grounds.

Jennings, despite his partner's actions, decided to join Hutchings and me for an after-round drink. He paid for the drinks and settled the bets like a gentleman. Weakly, he made an effort at an apology for his friend the Colonel, saying that he was such a competitive person, he had been embarrassed by his feeble effort on the last green.

Hutchings and I accepted this explanation as reasonable, for that's the kind of game this is. . . .

Shortly thereafter, I thanked "the Quiet One" for another great day, left the tavern, and crossed the road to the Royal Hotel. I surely would have enjoyed spending more time with the men, but I was extremely worried about Irene and couldn't wait to find out if her plan had succeeded. . . .

Hole 18 Tom Morris

I fairly flew back to the Royal Hotel after finishing my round. Stopping at the front desk, I picked up my mail and messages and headed up the front staircase. At first, I was tempted to go straight to Mrs. Norton's room, but I decided to be discreet, especially since we had agreed to meet for dinner.

Unlocking the door, I stepped inside my room and sat down to peruse the mail. There was a letter from my lovely wife Mary, a note from the dining room Maitre d' confirming the dinner reservation that night at 7 o'clock, and an unstamped envelope printed on Old Course Hotel stationery.

I quickly placed the reservation confirmation on the desk and holding the two other letters in both hands, tried to decide which one to open first. I knew I should open my wife's letter, but my curiosity wouldn't permit me to delay seeing what the letter from Sebastian's hotel contained.

Once more, I applied the methods I had learned from my dearly departed friend. First, I used a magnifying glass and studied the ink and handwriting style. It was fairly easy to determine the ink to be of standard hotel issue. Next, I moistened my finger and slid it along the scripted name. The ink smeared with very little pressure, indicating the letter to have been recently composed.

The actual handwriting didn't look familiar so I quickly moved to the next phase of my examination. Holding the envelope to my nose, I tried to ascertain if there was any aroma that could help me identify the sender. I thought I recognized a tobacco smell not unlike the brand smoked by Sebastian's bodyguard, Jennings. That, I thought, could have been my imagination trying to validate my hunch.

Next, I walked to the window and held the letter up to the natural light to determine if anything suspicious might be visible as light passed through the thin paper envelope. All I could see was the outline of a single sheet and, naturally, the script that I would soon be reading.

Unable to discern if any other item or material was contained within the rectangular enclosure, there seemed to be nothing left to do but open it, which I did in a typically Holmesian way. Taking the edge of a letter opener, I carefully worked the point under one of the flaps and sliced open the missive.

Without any further ado, I removed the letter from the envelope and began to read.

"Doctor Watson,
Thank you so much for arranging this morning's match. I am looking forward to enjoying a day of golf with you and Mr. Hutchings. Hopefully, we can do it again if you have the time and compunction to do so.
Oh, please give Mrs. Norton my best wishes. . .
Most Cordially,

Colonel C. M. Sebastian"

At first, I was stunned by this reference to Mrs. Norton. How, I wondered, did Sebastian know about Irene and me? I was greatly troubled by this, but then a great calm came over me when I realized that Sebastian would most certainly have had confederates all over Europe, and of course, in Scotland. Suddenly, I felt very foolish at this oversight on my part.

Folding the letter and placing it by my coat, I would discuss this with Irene at dinner, but it was time to turn my attention to the letter from my Mary.

"My Dearest John,
I hope this letter finds you well and that you are enjoying your golf. It's not the same without you. Our boys are asking for their father. I haven't received any correspondence from you and, while strange, I can accept this apparent lack of concern as long as it means that you are fully enjoying your vacation!
Please send me a letter if you have the chance. I miss you terribly! You, dear John, may always rely on my complete and total devotion.
Your loving wife,

Mary"

"Oh, what a horrible cad I have been," I thought, my mind racing. "How could I not have written a letter to my sweet Mary. What must she think? How must she feel?"

Immediately, I sat down and composed a truly caring letter to my best friend and the devoted mother to my children. In the missive, I apologized for such an appalling lack of consideration on my part and vowed to make it up to her and my boys when I returned home.

After all, I had come to St Andrews at her suggestion. It was she who had seen how depressed I was after the death of my friend Sherlock Holmes. It was Mary who appealed to me to move past this tragic episode.

What could be done? Where could I go to restore my health? She had recommended St Andrews. Knowing my keenness for the game, she had encouraged this trip. I would travel there to get some rest, enjoy my favorite game and see my old friend, Davison. That had been the plan. Sadly, as soon as I had arrived, I totally neglected the love of my life.

I was beginning to suffer guilt pangs, but then I analyzed how this could have happened. Immediately, it all made sense. For how could I obtain relief from tension, now that I had become involved in the middle of one of the most stressful adventures of my life! It was no wonder that I had forgotten to write home!

I certainly did miss my family, it was true. Yet, I had become involved in quite a complicated and dangerous set of circumstances.

While I was still deliberating about what I should do next, three sharp knocks were heard on my door. Hiding the letters, I moved toward the rapping and inquired, "Hello, who's there?"

"Quickly, John, open the door, there is no time," came the reply.

Recognizing the clear, soft voice of Irene Norton, I released the door latch, allowing her to enter.

"Mrs. Norton, what a surprise," I said. "Please tell me that all is well. How did your plan go, today?"

"Alas, Doctor," she sadly informed me, "It never had a chance. I should have seen from the very beginning that it had no chance at all. I'm such a fool!"

"Why, Irene," I tried to reassure her, "you are one of the most brilliant women I've ever met. Surely, you are being too hard on yourself. What happened?"

"Oh, Doctor, my plan was terribly elementary from the start," she confessed. "I don't know what I must have been thinking. Why would I imagine that Sebastian could ever leave such important items unguarded?"

"I catch your meaning," I replied, adding, "but where could he have left it?. . . . . .Actually, he could have hidden it anywhere. What we need to do is determine where he believes the safest hiding place would be!"

"That sounds a little too simple, John," she stated, pausing, "I don't mean anything by that remark, but. . . "

She suddenly stopped herself, continuing, "You know, you may have something there! Please be seated and I'll explain all that has happened."

She quickly narrated the entire day's events; sending her aide, Gloria, as a decoy to the University; her own dangerous walk along the hotel ledge; her dive into the dirty laundry hamper; squeezing into the Old Course Hotel dumbwaiter and finally, finding that letter addressed to her! As she read that letter to me, it was evident that Irene was still greatly annoyed that Sebastian had outmaneuvered her!

"What about you, Doctor?" she inquired. "How did your match go with that despicable human debris?"

I described the golf match, probably in too much detail, taking particular delight in describing Colonel Sebastian's reaction to his missed putt. Then, I brought my letter from Sebastian, apparently delivered while our golf match was already underway.

We sat very still for several moments, somewhat dazed. I began to quietly contemplate our next course of action.

"Irene," I inquired, "am I correct in assuming that we are still looking for the weapon and the schematics?"

"Doctor Watson," she replied, "I'm still going to continue my search. I know that your purpose for coming to St Andrews was not to help me solve this problem. I feel as though I've taken too much of your time already. . . ."

"My dear, please forgive my interruption," I interjected, "you should know very well that my golf, my comfort, my vacation, all hold very little significance for me, when compared to helping you prevent a vicious criminal from becoming even more dangerous. If you will allow me to assist, I would be most happy to continue on this quest."

Irene was deeply touched by my words, so much so that she walked over and gave me a warm embrace, expressing her thanks.

"Well, let's get back to work, then," I spoke encouragingly. "Let's see what we can come up with. . ."

"No, Doctor Watson," Irene sternly replied, "first, let us keep our seven o'clock dinner appointment. I'm famished."

Smiling softly as she moved to the door, Irene said, "It's now ten after five. I'll see you promptly at seven P.M."

The time seemed to fly. After Irene had left, I quickly drew a warm bath, washed, dressed and grabbed my note pad. I tried to put all of the facts together to see what next could be done. While I was still pondering available options, a light knock came on my hotel room door. Immediately, I tensed up, wondering what I might find in the hallway.

"May I ask who's there?" I offered.

"Ungh!" came the response.

It was Charles Hutchings who entered my room. He wasted no time in handing over a long thin package and a note which explained why he was here. I quickly scanned the contents, startled by what was contained therein. After reading his letter I smiled, thanking Hutchings profusely. Immediately afterward, he excused himself, closing the door behind him.

This unexpected interruption had delayed my dinner appointment with Irene. As I started down the stairs, I was now both excited over this latest discovery and annoyed that I would be late for dinner. I could never tolerate tardiness in others and here I was guilty of the same!

When I entered the large dining room, I tried to appear shocked to find someone sitting with Irene for dinner. As I made my way toward the table, the "guest" rose, turned and warmly greeted me.

"Doctor Watson," Colonel Sebastian continued, "it was so nice of you and Mrs. Norton to invite me to dine with you."

I acted stunned by the remark, and looked at Irene to try and alleviate her consternation.

"Doctor Watson," Irene offered, "Colonel Sebastian just now informed me that you had invited him to dine with us. I told him that you must have been keeping this secret as a wonderful surprise for me."

Blustered, flustered, and confused, at first all I could utter was, "Ah, oh, my, ah yes....surprise...."

Not my finest retort, I quickly regained my composure. As I took my seat between them I looked at Irene, winked and spoke with apparent sincerity, "Yes, I know how you love surprises! Isn't this nice?"

Sebastian wasted no time in ordering for the three of us, "Davison, quickly now, get over here! The three of us will have the Duck a l' Orange, and we would like it served over rice."

I was appalled at the way Sebastian took command and had the audacity to order meals for Irene and me.

"A minute, Mr. Davison, if you don't mind," I said, trying to ease the tension. I quickly turned back to Sebastian with an obvious edge to my look.

"Now, now, Colonel, we're in no hurry," I spoke, pausing briefly. "Actually, I would like the Sea Bass. What about you, Mrs. Norton?"

"Thank you, Doctor," she remarked sharply, "I believe I'll try the Fresh Cod a la Royal."

It was obvious that Sebastian was upset by this usurpation of his authority, but Irene and I were both very annoyed by this rather uncalled for assumption on his part.

As soon as Davison left the table, Sebastian started the conversation, "Well now, isn't this cozy? Just the three of us together having a wonderful evening together? What do you think of all this, Mrs. Norton?"

I looked at her, wondering how she might reply to such a question from her much despised quarry.

Irene Adler Norton took a sip of brandy, looked Sebastian straight in the eye and said, "Colonel, first of all, despite what the good doctor has said, I don't like surprises! Furthermore, I certainly don't like you!"

The colonel nearly spit out his wine at her remark, but quickly dabbed his dripping mustache and laughed.

"Watson, old man," Sebastian inquired, "what do you make of Mrs. Norton's rather unkind remarks about your surprise dinner guest?"

Even though I had been equally angered by this intrusion I somehow managed to remain calm, remarking, "Colonel, Mrs. Norton is certainly able and capable to speak for herself. If she finds your presence offensive, I'm of the opinion that there must be good reason for that sentiment. I daresay, that I would ask you the same question?"

I had artfully turned the tables, and Irene smiled most approvingly when I bowed in her direction.

Colonel Sebastian's face grew red and I could see the intensity building up from my clever response.

"Doctor," he began sternly, "quite frankly, I didn't appreciate her answer. I thought that we could have a nice dinner together and perhaps clear up that little issue that has been placed between us, if you understand my meaning."

"Whatever are you talking about, Sebastian?" a very demure, but agitated, Irene Norton asked.

I decided to play along, "Ah, yes Colonel, might I also ask to what you are referring?"

"All right, you, two," the colonel continued, keeping his voice very low, "let's stop all of this pretending. I know that you stole certain items that rightfully belonged to me. They have been bought and paid for. You are most fortunate that I now have them back in my possession. Why do you insist on trying to steal these items from me?"

All was on the table. There was no reason to play coy any longer. I looked at Irene and she returned his inquisitive glance.

"Colonel," Irene began, "you know perfectly well why we tried to prevent you from acquiring those plans. If that weapon should ever fall into the hands of the wrong people, the world would be a much more dangerous place."

"Ah, let me see if I have this correct," Sebastian replied, "you think it is your place to steal what belongs to me because you fear that I would turn it over to some underworld thugs? Mrs. Norton, you shock me by such an insinuation!"

The colonel stood up, placed his napkin on the table, leaned over and whispered, "I'm sorry, but I'm not comfortable breaking bread with people who accuse me of being a criminal. I'm leaving, but since you know that I already have the items secured in a very safe location, please be advised that any further attempts to interfere by either of you will be met with the most serious consequences. I bid you, adieu!"

With those final remarks, Colonel Sebastian took his leave.

Ordinary individuals might have been upset by what had just occurred. Human nature would dictate that death threats from evildoers would provoke fear and terror in most people. Irene, clearly, was not intimidated. She was an extremely brave, intelligent woman who would never succumb to the rantings of the criminal element.

When things had settled down, we calmly spent the next hour enjoying ourselves and we were treated to an excellent meal. Davison, himself, annoyed by the ill-mannered departed colonel, was kind enough to join us. I noticed that he really enjoyed his Duck a l' Orange!

Later that evening, Mrs. Norton and I agreed to meet in her room to finalize a plan to capture Colonel Sebastian. When I arrived at her door, she noticed that I was smiling. I entered the room, slowly walked over to the table, and reaching behind my back produced a golf club.

Irene wasn't sure what was going on, but she had to inquire, "What's this, Doctor? Why do you have a golf club in your hand at this time of day?"

I squirmed trying to think of something clever to say. Alas, nothing was immediately forthcoming.

Irene asked, "Am I to play in your foursome tomorrow?"

"Oh, my, oh, ah no. .no. . . not at all, I mean," I stammered, turning quite red.

When I saw her laughing, I relaxed and handed over the club, offering, "Here, Irene, take a look at this."

"Doctor," she asked, "why are you giving me this, this, what is it called, this cleek?"

"Very good, my dear," I responded. "If you look very carefully, you will notice that the leather grip is not secured to the end of the shaft. You may also observe that this golf club's shaft has a somewhat larger circumference than other golf club shafts. Come, come, do you notice anything else that may seem peculiar?"

Irene more closely examined the club and announced excitedly, "Why, Doctor, this shaft is made of Burmese bamboo. Aren't most golf shafts fashioned from hickory?"

"They most certainly are," I affirmed her conjecture.

"Why are you showing me this?" she continued, curiously.

"Mrs. Norton," I spoke solemnly, "please sit down and promise not to get too upset with me."

Irene did as I asked but she could not hide a most obvious glare in my direction.

"There's a great deal to tell you, and I don't know if an apology will be necessary on my part or not," I spoke nervously. "I only ask that you listen to all that I'm about to impart before rendering any judgment. All that you shall hear occurred a short time ago, after our meeting in my room, but before our scheduled dinner."

Following that introduction, I began my tale. . . .

"At 6:50 P.M., I was preparing to head downstairs when I heard a light knock at my door. When I opened it I found Charles Hutchings standing there. He had his hand raised to my face and pointed back to my room. Naturally, I realized that he wanted to 'talk' to me about something. It was so strange to see him here in the hotel that I knew that it must have been something very important.

He handed me a note which had obviously taken him some time to write. It was quite lengthy, so he motioned for me to sit down. As I did so, I noticed that he had a long, thin package with him. Anxiously, I opened the note and began to read its contents:

'Doctor Watson,
    Please forgive me for interfering in your business. I can't tell you how I came to know about the mission you and a certain Irene Norton have undertaken, but suffice it to say, when I heard about it, I wanted to help. Before I explain the package, I want you to know that I took the liberty of inviting Colonel Sebastian to dine with you and Mrs. Norton downstairs tonight.

    You only have to keep him occupied until 7:45 P.M. After that, you may let the conversation go where it will, for the deed will have been done.

    Inside this package is one of Sebastian's golf clubs. You will observe that it is his cleek. You probably didn't notice, but every time Sebastian needed to use his cleek in our match, he grabbed his spoon and tried to ease the shot. As you know, it's a most difficult shot.

    I first became aware of this on the fifth hole. Later in the match, on the long fourteenth, he became angry with his caddy for taking this cleek from his golf bag, and again he used his spoon instead.

    When I saw that, it became apparent to me that he was deliberately avoiding using that club for some reason. Naturally, I had to find a way to examine it.

After leaving the tavern to go and practice, I located Sebastian's golf bag and examined the cleek.

I noticed, at once, that it had a thicker shaft and was made of bamboo. The grip also seemed to be loose. I decided to give it a twist and removed it.

Peering inside the hollow shaft, I found a rolled up piece of parchment. When I examined it, I saw that it was a plan or blueprint for some type of weapon.

Upon extricating the papers from the shaft, I saw something else fall out. As you can see for yourself, it is a model or prototype of the weapon described by the plans. At that point I decided that this was what you and Mrs. Norton had been seeking.

So here it is. Although this makes me a thief, I know I've done the right thing. I'm no gunsmith, but from what I've seen of these plans, such a weapon cannot find its way into the hands of criminals! Please keep these blueprints in a safe place, and remain on guard. These men, as you know, are extremely dangerous!

You should also know that I've made a replica of this club and model and will return it to his golf bag this very evening. Hopefully, he won't notice the difference.

                    Thank you for playing golf with me,
                              Your friend,
                              Charles H.'

After reading this message, I opened the grip, examined the plans and the model, put them back inside the shaft and looked at Charles.

'Mr. Hutchings,' I said, 'It has been a genuine pleasure meeting you, and I also enjoyed watching your outstanding play. I don't know how you found out about this investigation of ours, but you are correct. We have been looking to find these plans and thanks to you, we now have them in our possession. We still need to stop Colonel Sebastian. Speaking for Mrs. Norton and myself, we will follow your plan to the letter. I think Irene and I will be able to handle your request. We will be sure to keep the Colonel busy until at least 7:45. Thank you for all that you've done.'

I finished my remarks adding, 'Charles, while what you've been able to do is most admirable, we have to consider the possibility that Sebastian has made his own copies of these plans.'

Charles seemed to agree, voicing his familiar, 'Ungh!'

With that he bowed, shook my hand and walked out of the room, leaving behind the club and the contents that you now hold in your hands."

"And that, Mrs. Norton is how we found ourselves sitting with Colonel C. M. Sebastian at dinner," I stated. "I hope you can understand why I did what I did."

Looking anxiously at Irene, I expected to see some kind of reaction to what she had just heard. I doubted that Irene Adler Norton had been rendered speechless very often, but it certainly seemed to be the case that evening.

Irene just sat there, holding the golf club as if she had just been hypnotized. Slowly, she emptied the bamboo shaft of its contents and carefully laid the blueprints on the table before her. The model, simply constructed and carved from pine, gave us a very good idea of the appearance of the finished product. A broad smile made its way across her beautiful features as she slowly turned to me.

"I can't believe it, John," the adventuress whispered, "these are the actual plans and model for the weapon, or at least a reasonable facsimile of them. Now all that remains for us to do is set the trap for that devil, Sebastian."

"We owe it all to Charles Hutchings," I contributed. "I only wonder how he found out about our dilemma? Clearly, he has friends in many quarters! Still, I'm very concerned that he had been tipped off by someone we had entrusted with our plans."

Irene quickly responded, "Doctor, I mentioned that I had many others watching over our project. Perhaps, Mr. Hutchings was also affiliated with that group. At any rate, Doctor, we need to get this information to law enforcement officials back in London, for I fear that that is where Colonel Sebastian is going to test this horrendous killing machine."

Irene paused briefly, then she quickly rolled up the plans, sliding them along with the prototype securely into the club shaft, and handed it to me.

"Doctor, I am entrusting these plans to your capable hands," she spoke with deep sincerity. "Before this night is over, we shall need to come up with a plan for their safe transport to London. One possibility we might consider could be . . ." (Kerblam – kerblam – kerblam)

Three sharp knocks on her hotel room door suddenly interrupted Mrs. Norton's plan. Quickly, I grabbed the club and looked for a hiding place. There was very little time, so I took down a picture from the hotel wall, placed it under a small pillow and hung the golf club in its place.

The knocking continued and it was quickly followed by a loud, abrasive voice, "Mrs. Norton, Mrs. Irene Norton, you need to open this door immediately!"

Stalling for time, Irene called out through the closed door, "Who are you and what gives you the right to intrude upon a guest of this establishment?"

"It's all right, Mrs. Norton," came the voice of Davison, "it is I, William Davison. With me I have the village constabulary. Please open your door."

Turning to Doctor Watson, she looked for some help, mouthing softly, "What should we do?"

I shrugged my shoulders, then pointing to the window, I carefully stepped out onto the ledge.

As soon as I had disappeared, Irene went back to the door

and opened it, speaking with some mild agitation, "Mr. Davison, what is the meaning of this?"

Standing on the ledge, I could hear the conversation that ensued when Davison and the policemen entered.

Davison explained, "Mrs. Norton, please forgive me. We received word that someone had threatened your person. May we enter?"

"Certainly," she answered calmly, "I don't understand, Mr. Davison. When did you hear of this? Doctor Watson and I had just finished a most interesting conversation a short time ago, but no one else has visited this room today except my aide, Gloria, and she is certainly beyond suspicion."

"I'm sorry to inconvenience you, Ma'am," the chief inspector politely explained, "but we will have to examine the room."

"Please do, gentlemen," Irene consented. "And while you're here, can you shed any more light on this mysterious threat?"

"The front desk found this note," Davison replied, handing it over to Irene.

Irene glanced suspiciously at Davison as she read the brief message, which stated:

> "Mrs. Norton,
>   Tonight it will be over for you. . . ."

Irene feigned fear and began to shed some tears after reading the message.

Davison quickly approached her, "There, there now, Mrs. Norton," he comforted, "we'll not let anything happen to you."

"Thank you, Mr. Davison," she whimpered, "I really don't know what I should do. I'm so afraid, and you'll be searching my room now?"

That was Irene's warning to me and I carefully moved along the ledge, turning the corner, out of sight of any inspection, should anyone peer out the window.

While the hotel manager did his best to allay her fears, a brief, but thorough search of the Norton room quickly ensued. One of the constables even went so far as to throw open her window and examine the ledge. At that, Irene flinched and readied herself to respond in case I had been discovered. No such excuse was needed, for the officer came away from the window and secured it with the window clasp.

The search ended as quickly as it had begun, and as the authorities were leaving her room Mrs. Norton stopped them in their tracks.

"Mr. Davison," Irene spoke, greatly irritated, "I demand an explanation. Might I inquire what you were hoping or expecting to find in my private quarters?"

"Mrs. Norton," Davison responded, "I know how you must be feeling, but this was just a safety precaution management had to take to ensure the protection of one of our guests."

From out of nowhere, I appeared at the open hotel door, "Davison, Irene," I pleaded, "What's happened?"

Irene answered, "Doctor, nothing has happened, thanks to the swift action taken by William and these fine policemen."

Some embarrassment among the rescuers was evident as the Inspector offered, "How very kind of you to say, Mrs. Norton. Rest assured that my men and I will be on the lookout all night long to assure your safety!"

"You can't appreciate how much better that makes me feel," swooned the talented actress. "Good evening, gentlemen, and thank you for your bravery."

When Davison and the police had left her room, I checked to be certain that they had gone. Next, I applauded, issuing, "Bravo, Irene. That was one of your finest performances!"

Bowing dutifully, Mrs. Norton replied, "Why thank you, John. It wasn't 'too' over the top, was it?"

"Well, perhaps a trifle," I answered, laughing a little.

"Tell me what you think this was all about, Irene," I inquired. "Must we really fear for your life?"

"John, I must tell you," she stated, "when I first learned of the threat, I was a bit concerned. Then I got a look at the note and I knew that I had nothing to fear."

"Whatever do you mean, Irene?" I responded impatiently. "Your life had been threatened and you say you have nothing to fear? I'm afraid that I may have underestimated your courage or overestimated your wisdom. This is a threat!"

"No, no, no, Doctor," she advised me, "I'm not that brave and hopefully, not so stupid. However, I am very observant."

"How so?" I asked, still unnerved by the threat.

"I recognized the writing and I immediately knew who sent the warning," she stated with supreme confidence.

"You do?" I inquired with some incredulity. "Might I take a look at the note?

"Of course," she responded, handing me the brief message containing the threat.

I studied it carefully, as was my Holmesian way, but I was unable to surmise from whom the message came.

"My guess, which would be an obvious one," I continued, "is that it was the work of none other than that rogue, Colonel C. M. Sebastian."

Pausing to allow me some time to reflect on my choice, Irene replied, "No, Doctor, but that is a very logical guess."

She brought over a magnifying glass that was sitting on the desk and focused it over the brief message.

"I want you to look carefully at the the writing. Do you see how it shows tiny loops above the letter 'o' that occurs 5 times in this threat," Irene suggested. "Doctor, where have we seen that writing style before?"

After looking through the lens, I responded sincerely, "Can't say that I know, Irene. Please advise me."

Irene walked over to the far wall where I had openly hidden the golf club, removed the grip and spilled the blueprints out on the table.

Placing them before me, she handed me the magnifying lens and had me check the writing atop the plans," John, do you see it? Do you see the similarity in the letter 'o'?"

I examined the writing on the plans and exclaimed, "Great Scott, they're identical. Why that would mean. . ."

Mrs. Norton interrupted, "Yes, Doctor, both the copied document and the threatening letter were written by the same person. The 'threat' came from your friend, Charles Hutchings!"

"Oh, no, Irene," I stammered, "it simply can't be. He's not that kind of person. He would never hurt you. There must be some mistake!"

Irene watched the effect her brilliant findings had had upon me. Clearly, she could see that I was very upset. She let me stew for a few more minutes before clearing everything up.

"Doctor Watson," Irene slowly explained, "please sit down and allow me to address your concerns about my findings. First of all, let's examine what he did and then, let's analyze why he did it. . ."

I was still very distraught, but agreed to listen to Irene's account of the events.

"John," she began, "I'm certain that the threatening note came from Mr. Hutchings. The writing styles are exact. What I want you to consider, is the very real possibility that Hutchings issued the message, not to harm me, but to guarantee my safety!"

"Irene," I offered, "I don't understand what you are implying."

"John," she continued, "What if Hutchings had found that Sebastian was planning to harm us, tonight? What better way would there be to guarantee our safety than to have round-the-clock police protection? An open threat would have to be addressed by the law, so Hutchings's strategy worked perfectly!"

"By Jove, Irene" I remarked, "that was a brilliant plan on his part, but it was also a magnificent deduction by you, my dear!"

"Thank you, Doctor," Mrs. Norton said modestly. "Promise me, John, that if you happen to see Hutchings, please offer him my heartfelt thanks for all that he has done on behalf of our mission to rid society of this deadly, dangerous man."

"I am planning on seeing him tomorrow morning," I informed her as I made my way to the hallway door. "I shall be honored to deliver your message."

Mrs. Norton slowly approached and voiced, "I know that you are returning home tomorrow afternoon. I want you to know how much I shall miss your friendly company and wise counsel. I feel totally confident in stating that you have more than measured up to the high praise our late friend bestowed upon you. Please be careful, for now that Sebastian knows you were involved in trying to help bring him down, he will be on your trail."

"I appreciate the kind words, Irene," I remarked. "You also deserve to know how impressed Holmes always was by you. As you have heard, he referred to you as "the woman." For whenever grace, talent, beauty and intelligence were assigned to women, Irene Adler Norton was always placed at the top of his list!"

Once more, Irene thanked me for those remarks and I started for the door, but then stopped suddenly. I had forgotten about the golf club and plans! I started to repack the model and plans back into the golf club, but we changed our plans. We decided to leave the plans and model in Irene's care, while I would keep the bamboo cleek as a souvenir of this most interesting "vacation."

"I bid you fond adieu, Mrs. Norton," I remarked, "it's been my great honor to have made your acquaintance, formally, this time. I wish you safe travel and good luck in your continued efforts to collar this criminal, for clearly this Sebastian is a son of Satan!"

The hotel clock chimed ten times as we parted for the evening. After making my way back to my room I began to pack my clothes for the trip home. Before turning out the lights, I carefully slipped Sebastian's club into my bag, still worried about what the future might hold, but too tired to think too much about it. . . .

Farewell to St Andrews

Early the next day, the residents of St Andrews were rudely awakened by the shrill whistles of the village police force. I was just finishing off my breakfast kippers when I first heard the commotion. I continued sipping the last of my morning tea when Davison came rushing in my direction.

"Morning, old chap," I said to my good friend, "I say, William, what's all the ruckus about?"

"Doctor," the hotel manager continued, "something's happened at the Old Course Hotel. Come quickly!"

I hated to leave my comfortable seat, but judging by old Davison's hasty departure I knew I had to see what was up. Together we headed down the street toward the Old Course Hotel. Upon reaching the periphery of the property, we found policemen scattered everywhere. We could go no farther.

The roads leading to the Old Course Hotel had been cordoned off and only law enforcement personnel were allowed to enter the grounds. As we stood among the gathered crowd, we watched the scenes unfolding before our eyes. William and I listened intently, trying to hear what the townspeople had to say on the matter.

Davison saw one of his acquaintances and called out to him, "Thomas, Thomas, what's happening?"

"The police have surrounded the hotel," the man reported. "They're about to make some arrests."

Sure enough, as the man was speaking, Davison and I saw a police wagon pull up to the main entrance of the lavish hotel. Several minutes later, constables were seen escorting a group of men into the paddy wagon. It was difficult to tell, but I thought that one of the men being arrested was Jennings, one of Sebastian's henchmen.

Just then, I felt a pinch on my arm. Irene Norton had sidled up beside me, "Good morning, Doctor," she said smiling that wonderful smile, "isn't this a lovely day?"

"All the better to arrest criminals," I replied, "and a wonderful day to you also, Madam. What do you think of this? It looks like they've collared Jennings."

"This could be the beginning of the end for Colonel Sebastian and his cohorts," Irene offered. "I do have a terrible feeling that we're not going to be so lucky finding him."

While we were conversing, the chief inspector spotted us and quickly made his way outside the ropes.

"Mrs. Norton, Doctor Watson," he called, "can you please come with me. One of our suspects wants to talk to you. He says that it's very important."

Following the lawman through the police line, Davison, Mrs. Norton and I were led to the back of the police wagon where Jennings had been confined.

"Well, Jennings," said the inspector, "here they are. What do you want with them?"

Jennings, now handcuffed, scowled at the lawman as he turned to us and spoke, "Mrs. Norton and Doctor Watson, I've been instructed to inform you that you are too late, much too late to prevent certain plans from taking place. I was also told to remind you of the good advice you were given. The man to whom I'm referring is perfectly willing and capable of carrying out all that he has threatened."

"What kind of gibberish is that, you rascal," the inspector responded to the criminal. "Take him away!"

The police official gave a signal, and the wagon pulled out past the throngs of people and quickly made its way for headquarters.

"I'm sorry to have bothered you with that nonsense," the officer of the law continued. "That made no sense at all, at least to me. What about you?"

Irene winked to me and agreeing with the policeman said, "Inspector, I really can't imagine what that man meant. It seemed to be a simple rant, nothing more."

"It's just as well," I chimed in. "Inspector, have you made any other arrests in this case?"

"As a matter of fact, we think we've captured the whole gang, Doctor," the inspector spoke proudly. "We received a tip that this gang had broken into the University museum the other night and absconded with a priceless old artifact from the year1754."

"Hmmm, 1754, you say," I remarked, looking at Irene suspiciously.

"Yes, Doctor," he continued, "and we found a key with the same date in the quarters of Colonel Sebastian, exactly where the informer told us it would be. Furthermore, we were given the exact location of the stolen artifact and I'm very proud to say that all is well. Our University may once more display one of its most prized possessions!"

"Bravo, Inspector," offered Mrs. Norton, "that's quite a feather in your cap, sir. Might I inquire as to the whereabouts of Colonel Sebastian?"

"Why thank you for the compliment, Mrs. Norton," spoke the lawman. "Please don't worry about Sebastian. We'll soon have him brought to justice, as well."

When she heard that last remark, Irene sadly shook her head. She knew that Sebastian had somehow escaped, and that meant that her work would have to continue.

Davison had already left the scene of the arrest, leaving Mrs. Norton and me to ourselves. We turned back toward the "Old Course" and slowly started up Links Road.

"That was very clever of you, Irene," I complimented my companion. "How did you plant the evidence in Sebastian's room?"

"Doctor," she spoke with great modesty, "it wasn't so difficult. Did you forget that I had been in Sebastian's room while your match was being played? I had only to hide the key where he would never find it."

"Just out of curiosity," I asked, "where did you hide it? Someplace clever, I'll wager."

Smiling softly, Irene proudly told him, "Why I stuck the old key in his desk's keyhole and fastened the location of the artifact behind the picture of the 17th hole on the far wall."

"You see, John," she continued, "I'm a quick study."

We both laughed at her ingenuity as we made our way past the stately old building off the first tee of the "Old Course." We only had to cross the street, to reach the grounds of the Royal Hotel.

It was time for me to prepare for my trip home. This week had passed very quickly. For me, what had been originally planned as a week of rest, relaxation and golf, had turned into an adventure much in the style of the many exploits I had shared with my late friend, Holmes. Clearly, I hadn't had much rest at all, as I think about it!

While gathering my things, I reviewed my time at St Andrews. I had only played a few rounds of golf, but all of those matches were memorable. I had met and become friends with perhaps the greatest golfer I had ever seen, one Charles Hutchings. It had been wonderful seeing and re-establishing my friendship with Davison. Above all though, what I would remember and treasure most about this trip were my adventures with Irene Adler Norton.

That Holmes had gotten to know her better and become friends with the only woman that he had ever truly respected was a source of comfort for me. Holmes's kind words about me when he had spoken to Irene, will always be a source of comfort to me. Now, that was all in the past, for I was heading home, to London and to my family.

My train was scheduled to leave at 1:50 that afternoon. I decided to spend the remainder of the morning sitting in the hotel lobby, much as I had when I first arrived. Davison and I agreed to lunch together at noon before heading off for the station. My send-off meal was most delightful.

Not long after lunch, I started down the hotel steps for the carriage that would be taking me to the depot. Just as I was about to step up into the landau, I felt a tug on my sleeve.

"Ungh," voiced "the Quiet One," clearly wishing to say good-bye. At once, I hopped down and grabbed his hand and shook it warmly, wrapping my left hand over Hutchings's firm grip.

"Well, my friend," I spoke, "thank you for everything, especially for helping Mrs. Norton and me in our efforts to try and corral Colonel Sebastian. I hope to see you again one day, Charles. Good bye, sir."

Waving to me as I walked away, Charles offered his familiar, "Ungh."

For her part, Mrs. Norton informed me that she had to remain in St Andrews for a few more days, "tiding things up" with her associates. She and some of her confederates would continue to track Sebastian, hoping that he might slip up and provide them with the opportunity to put him away for good.

That was the last time I would ever see Irene. In the short time that I had gotten to know her, I was struck by her grace, beauty and brilliance. It was clear to see why Holmes would have been so impressed by "the woman". . . .

The Denouement. . . . All Is Disclosed

Many years had passed since Watson's golfing vacation to St Andrews. Following that exciting trip, he had much to tell his patient, loving wife. He described his wonderful golf matches with a very excellent golfer; a gangly, reclusive mute, who possessed incredible talent.

He also told her of his meeting with Irene Norton and their joint efforts in trying to thwart a criminal enterprise. Watson informed his wife Mary, that Davison, the manager of the Royal Hotel had spoken kindly of her. The friendly hotelier remembered having met them when they visited St Andrews soon after their marriage, and had been most complimentary!

Watson was happy to be home with his wife and boys. It wasn't long afterward, that he went back to his medical practice. For a while he was able to rededicate his life to his craft. It was a good and noble occupation and it kept his family comfortable. Yet, it wasn't enough for him. He still longed for the excitement of the hunt! Missing was the element of danger that he had experienced for so many years.

Then, out of nowhere, a magical twist of fate made Watson's malaise quickly disappear. It wasn't too long after returning from St Andrews, that he was shocked to find that Holmes, his dear friend, had not perished at Reichenbach Falls. He had survived the incident and chose to remain out of sight for several years. Now they were back together again.

Immediately, his zest for life returned, and for many more
years, they would continue their work together solving the
unsolvable. The London crime rate was once again lowered
noticeably by the return of this crime-fighting duo.

Yes, with Holmes back in the picture, Watson was the same
old Watson. The two men fed off each other in ways that no
one could understand and their close friendship grew even
stronger over the many years until Holmes's death.

Watson remained Holmes's closest friend until that fateful
day when the news arrived that Holmes had indeed passed.
Sadly, this time it was final. Watson was once more without
his partner, but a final adventure was to come his way in the
form of a package.

Now for the rest of the tale. . . .

The Package

I remember that I had just finished a fine breakfast on a
cool, sunny morning in late September when there came a
knock upon my front door. Rising slowly, I made my way to
the entry and glanced through the window. Looking out upon
the busy downtown London street, I saw no one waiting on my
front stoop. I thought that a bit strange, but believed perhaps
it could have been a youngster's innocent prank.

Curious, after unlatching my door, I stepped out into the
sunshine to see if anyone was stirring. There was no one save
a milkman making his rounds. As I started back inside, my
eyes caught sight of a small package sitting beside the door.
Cautiously, I gathered it up and returned to my kitchen table.

After adjusting my reading glasses, I slowly began to
examine the writing. Immediately, I realized that it was
written in the unmistakable style of my recently departed
comrade-in-arms, Sherlock Holmes. Naturally, I was shocked
to have received correspondence from my deceased friend. At
first, I had an impulsive desire to rip open the contents. That

urge, however, was tempered by my knowledge of the way Holmes would have investigated such a mysterious item. So, I decided to conduct my own study of the exterior of the package, using the observational techniques that perhaps Holmes might have employed.

Magnifier in hand, I checked the covering, determining it to be of the same material, Finlay matte, that Holmes used for storing his case notes. That made sense. I proceeded to examine the ink used, blotting the writing with a drop of saline solution to loosen the stain from the label. A quick analysis indicated that the ink was the very same found in Holmes's inkwell at 221–B Baker Street, our former address.

The postage had been dated a mere seven days ago, bearing the seal of the Wembley branch office. I pondered momentarily how this could be, for we buried our dear friend over three months ago! Still, it could have been the work of some mutual friend acting in accordance with his wishes. This person would have followed Holmes's directions by delivering this package to me.

I was about to examine the glue holding the contents together but I could wait no longer. Carefully, I slit the package open along one of the edges. Turning it over, I watched two smaller parcels emerge and rest upon the table. Quickly, I opened the smaller one, which contained a folded letter addressed to me. Anxiously, I began to read:

"Watson, old friend, as you have now received this parcel, as directed by my will, I am most certainly gone from this earthly existence. Where I am now, only our God truly knows, but realize that I was the most fortunate of mortals to have been blessed with as noble, honest and straightforward a friend as you, my dear fellow.

There will be no return from the depths of the Aare, as occurred years ago, when you were so shocked to see me. Alas, would that it could happen thus. . . Take heart though.

When next we meet, I believe it will be in the hereafter or some other such setting. Rest assured, I will be very pleased to see you once again!

Till then, it is good-bye and farewell, Watson. Do not spend your time dwelling upon my passing, for as a man skilled in the healing arts, you know the finality of death. Live your days to the fullest, my good man. Please do so knowing that the person you honored in your writings, one Sherlock Holmes, considered you to be one of the most decent humans to have inhabited our spinning orb.

Yes, it's hail and farewell, John, my friend, until we meet again. . .

Oh, and I must apologize and sincerely do beg your forgiveness for keeping you in the dark about the deception you are about to discover. Please do not think ill of my handling of this matter, particularly in the way that the events have transpired. All will be revealed in the documents accompanying this letter.

Though not as gifted as you, dear friend, in the art of storytelling, I must admit to a certain level of proficiency in that department. Still, as to that remark, it will be for you to judge. As you will see, this case, albeit mundane compared to many others, provided some truly unusual quandaries that had to be solved if we were to come to a satisfactory and just conclusion. Your role in this adventure, although you were totally unaware of parts of it, was crucial to its solution. Please try to understand why I needed to deceive you. You will soon see why I did so, and I trust you will find it in your heart to forgive me.

Feel free to include this case, should you deem it worthy, in your collection of our shared adventures.

'Til our next adventure, I remain...

Your friend and admirer,

Holmes"

You must imagine the shock upon my system after reading this letter! Could such a state of affairs have actually existed? Was it possible that I could have helped Holmes solve a mystery and not have known anything about it? If that were the case, how daft a person must I have been not to have noticed? What was he hiding from me? If he was hiding something, I needed to know what and why!

Suddenly, my thoughts were not kind ones, and I found myself angry that I, his bosom friend, had not been deemed trustworthy in this instance. More and more questions raged through my mind. I was livid. This was mortifying to me! How could he have done such an unkindness? ? ?

Clearly, I would find my answer in this, his own recreation of the events as they occurred. I began to calm down, reassuring myself that my friend must have had his reasons for not divulging this information and not actively seeking my total involvement in this case, whatever it was. Several minutes later found me deeply engrossed in his tale. Hours went by quickly as I delved into one of the strangest investigations we had ever conducted.

What follows is a brief summary of the most salient points of his manuscript:

Holmes began by reconstructing the dramatic incident at Reichenbach Falls. It was much the same as he had told me the first time, when I included his return in the <u>Adventure of the Empty House</u>. This version, however, more fully detailed how and where he had spent those several "missing" years when all of England, save for the criminal element, had been mourning his loss.

Holmes informed me that while he did spend time traveling around the world, trying to remain invisible, he had been putting together a plan to capture one of Moriarty's most villainous henchmen, a man called Moran. As long as Moran was still at large, Holmes knew his life and the lives of his friends were in grave danger.

Needing an ally to help with his plans, Holmes had kept his brother Mycroft informed of his movements, so that monies could be wired to keep him solvent as he moved from place to place. He described much of his itinerary, especially his visit to Lhassa and his chat with the Lama. He also cited several interesting adventures while traveling under the name of Sigerson, a Norwegian adventurer. Some of those tales proved to be rather amusing.

Many of those details I had previously learned upon his return from the Reichenbach Falls occurrence, but here, began the twist that I certainly would have never guessed had I been offered a million opportunities to surmise.

What follows are the highlights of his untold story, spun in his own inimitable style. . .

"Watson, it is here that I will begin to disclose some of the hitherto hidden incidents that I chose to keep from you, my good fellow. As the facts are laid bare, please try to reserve judgment on my keeping you in the dark until all of the information has been laid forth.

You are doubtlessly aware of the effect that 'the woman' had upon me in our dealings with the King of Bohemia. Although I never showed any interest for affairs of the heart, and you know this to be true, there was something about her. Try as I might, I could never forget Irene Adler. Long after she became Mrs. Godfrey Norton and moved to the colonies, I must confess that I continued thinking about her. The woman had it all, Watson; beauty, brains, wit, talent, and a bit of whimsy. At least that's how I perceived her to be.

What you did not know, at least until now, was that I contacted her shortly after my 'death.' From that point forward, I was constantly being shadowed night and day by Moriarty's followers, in particular, the earlier mentioned

Moran. From time to time I was able to escape their surveillance, but they always seemed to find me. Again and again, I would try to outmaneuver them. I was finding it more and more difficult to remain hidden for long periods of time, so deep was their network of evil.

Obviously, I needed to confide in someone besides my brother Mycroft, who has never been in particularly good health. Watson, if you were to have known that I was still alive, it would have put your life at great risk. As you will come to know, Moran was watching your every move, hoping that I would contact you. Until the day we finally captured him, he had commissioned his minions to observe you, around the clock. Though I longed to reveal all, it was not the thing to do. I only hope you can understand that I would never put your life at risk under any circumstances!

As I stated, there was a need for me to share my concerns with a kindred spirit; someone with whom I could compare notes, share theories and ideas; someone to help me finalize a viable plan of action. There certainly weren't many people to whom I would entrust such a complicated mission, but neither could I do it alone. Who might pass muster? Irene Adler Norton quickly came to mind.

I don't know how I found the courage, but I decided to inquire if she would be interested in coming to my assistance. It was bold of me to even consider contacting her, but I mailed the letter. Can you conceive what she must have thought of such a strange request from a virtual stranger?

I regretted my actions almost immediately. Had I lost my mind? How could I have actually done such a thing. . . What woman would leave her husband and comfortable home for such dangerous business? And for what? Who was I to her? Oh, Watson, I had never felt so foolish and so inane!

Imagine my surprise and delight when a missive from Mrs. Irene Adler Norton arrived at my camp in Mecca, addressed to my alias, Sigerson. After taking all of my regular steps, if only to validate from whence the letter had come, I quickly tore it open, eager to read her response. As I read the letter, the whole fabric of my being was suddenly stricken to the core with incalculable sorrow for this fine woman.

You see, Watson, in her letter, Mrs. Norton informed me of the untimely death of her husband, Godfrey. Unknown to me, he had recently died in a train derailment on his way home from a business trip. Obviously, had I known, I would never have intruded upon her grief.

She continued, stating that she was doing her best to live without him, admitting how difficult it was. She further confided that the loneliness seemed sometimes overwhelming.

Watson, she indicated her surprise at my invitation, and at first, she told me that she was amazed at my nerve to think that she would consider leaving her position to help a perfect stranger, indeed, a former adversary! Help me? Certainly not! She further stated that my audacity bordered on being brazenly discourteous and patently offensive!

As I continued reading, I must admit I was somewhat hurt by her remarks, but I admired her choice of verbiage as she put me in my place. She was absolutely correct in her analysis of my affront to her. While I was still swooning from this rebuke, she seemed to soften her position. What follows is an excerpt in her very own words. . .

"'Still, Mr. Holmes, an urgent request coming from such a distinguished individual certainly merits some consideration. I should be, I could be, and, as a matter of fact, I am truly flattered by your confidence that I am worthy of your trust in such a dangerous endeavor. I have had my own 'run-ins' with the late Professor Moriarty and his thugs and would welcome any opportunity to help put his cronies safely behind bars'".

She ended her letter by saying that she would be staying at the Royals Hotel in Bashira in three weeks time. She further stated that she looked forward to working with me and was pleased to act in any way possible to help put an end to Professor Moriarty's criminal organization.

Watson, I was stunned, needless to say. I quickly made plans to meet her and begin working together to achieve our common goal.

On the night of February 13th, I found her sitting in the dining room of one of that region's most famous establishments. The Royals was one of the finest hotels in the Middle East, a pleasant tourist stop for travelers visiting that area. It had the added advantage of being far enough off the beaten path to afford us the safety and seclusion so important to the successful formulation of any plan of action we might be able to conceive.

When I approached her table, she invited me to join her for dinner. After exchanging pleasantries we sat down to a lovely meal. I thanked her for having traveled so far to help someone she hardly knew. I also told her how grateful I was for her collaboration, expressing embarrassment over the boldness of my initial request. Of course, I took the opportunity to offer my most sincere sympathies over the loss of her husband.

Mrs. Norton graciously acknowledged my remarks, indicating how much her life had changed with Godfrey's passing. She further informed me that she looked forward to working together, adding that perhaps, she could learn something from me. (What an intriguing comment!)

With that meeting, our connection had been made. An agreement was reached whereby she would provide counsel when needed, and support when necessary. We worked closely together for six days until we had finished the initial details of our plan. All was going well, Watson, but there were strange feelings at play.

For the first time in my existence, I found that I had some difficulty concentrating on the tasks at hand. Irene, in addition to her physical attractiveness, possessed an inner beauty and sense of propriety that was truly rare. I had a most troubling time separating the gifted mind from her immeasurable beauty.

Whenever I was in her presence, my mind was not as focused as it should have been. The worst part of it all was that I didn't care. Could it have been the beginnings of love? Were such emotions available to me, Watson? I wondered.

Mrs. Norton and I tried to imagine when and where our plan could be put into action. We were able to use some of her old friends to supply us with information as to the whereabouts and doings of Moran. Without these individuals we could never have developed the plan which I now will lay before you, Watson.

I'm sure you will be surprised to find that Moran was a champion golfer, inexplicably addicted to that infernal, dare I call it, sport! (I can tell you that it certainly made no sense to me, at least when I first heard of his obsession with the game.) Checking into it we found that yes, it was so. When he and his minions were not pilfering, mugging, or murdering the citizens of our dear country, he would turn to his favorite pastime. Mind you, not just casual play, but intense devotion to the game. . . tournament play! Such rubbish. . . What a colossal waste of time and effort.

You long have known of my distaste for such a mindlessly, frivolous activity, so you realize how difficult it was for me to believe that such a brilliant, though criminal, mind could have fallen so low. . . It was totally beyond my understanding!

The silver lining of Moran's golf dabbling, however, would become the main component of our plan. Irene had learned from her sources that Moran was planning to compete at St Andrews in the 1895 Open. Yes, the Open Championship! Furthermore, he made yearly trips to that part of the world to become more familiar with the golf course.

We learned that Moran was going to be in the 'Auld Grey Toon' for a month's time in 1894, continuing his preparation.

I was dumbstruck. Here we have, perhaps, the world's most dangerous criminal mind, caught up in one of mankind's silliest endeavors. Unfathomable!

Happily, this information provided a wonderful opportunity for Irene and me to firm up our plans, for we now knew both a time and a location for the trap we would devise to capture this blight to society. Using her contacts in Scotland we were able to obtain accommodations several kilometers due west of the village of St Andrews. And so it was that we ended up in that pleasant part of Scotland, where we began to implement our scheme to stop the devilish Moran.

When I first arrived in St Andrews, I decided to take up a disguise as an odd Englishman from London who was bound and determined to learn to play the game of golf. Now you must be laughing right now because of all of the guff I've given you for years and years about such a time-wasting activity. The truth is, until I seriously applied myself to that zany enterprise, I truly believed that it was perhaps the worst use of anyone's time that had thus far ever been imagined.

To be fair, I believed that I only needed to learn to play a little.....you must know what I mean. I only needed to learn to hit the ball forward, roll the ball toward the hole, look like a golfer. I never expected or intended to play decently. Golf was my opportunity to get close to Moran. I certainly never intended to take it seriously. But then something happened.

I suppose you warned me long ago that this could happen to me, just as it's happened and will continue to happen to any man, woman or child that actually gives the bloody game half a chance. Yes, I'll admit it. I actually became addicted to the silly sport. Addicted to the extent, that it made my other bad 'habit' pale in comparison. My golf highs, I found, were the equal or better than my 'medicinal' ones! At any rate, I was hooked on the game. I practiced morning, noon and night to improve. I studied the swing in all its myriad aspects, trying to master the basic skills needed to play well.

In order to maintain my anonymity, I chose to become a very quiet, reclusive sort. It would help protect my identity from those who had knowledge that I was still breathing. Since you were always well aware of my clever disguises, I had to create an entirely new personality. Have you caught on yet, my dear Watson? By now you must have realized that 'the Quiet One' was yours truly, and that C. M. Sebastian was, in fact, the Colonel Sebastian Moran that you and I finally apprehended in that empty house!

All of these things I needed to keep from you, dear friend, to protect you from the most vicious band of murderous cutthroats that the world has ever known. If Moran had found me, he doubtless would have used you. In this instance, you, dear fellow, would have made a most valuable pawn, to draw me from, dare I say it, 'hiding.'

As you know by now, Irene and I were trying to stop Moran from acquiring a newly created deadly weapon. I had heard rumors of an air gun invented by Von Herder, a blind German mechanic. It had been said that Professor Moriarty had contracted him to build it. Irene had determined the location of the plans, but at the time we still hadn't learned if it had been built.

When Irene and I learned that you were vacationing at the Royal Hotel to get some rest and play some golf, we wondered if you might be of some assistance. Irene would try to recruit you to help her find the weapon and its design, but that was only if you wished to help! You can't imagine how delighted I was when she told me you had agreed. I had previously mentioned to her that I would have expected nothing less, knowing what a brave, courageous and honorable man you have always been.

After Moriarty's death, Moran informed his gang that he had asked Von Herder to show him the plans. That way he could see for himself if such a weapon was worth pursuing. The plans were smuggled into Scotland instead of London, for security reasons. Irene and I were aware of the drop off point and we beat them to the punch. Moran's team was right on our heels, but we managed to hide the items in an artifacts exhibit at the University of St Andrews.

We sensed that Moran had somehow found our hiding spot, so we broke into the museum the following evening and moved the blueprints and model to another location, near the ruins of the cathedral. It was there that we hid the plans for a second time, planning to retrieve them as soon as it was safe to do so. We were sure that no one had witnessed our actions, but despite all of the precautions we had taken, we had been watched. For when Mrs. Norton and you went to retrieve them, they were gone, leaving only a note for Irene. Yes, as you now know, Moran's henchmen had removed them before we had any opportunity to properly study them.

You know what happened after that. 'The Quiet One' was able to locate Moran's hiding place. Voila! I made a copies of the blueprints, the wooden model, and the bamboo club, and gave them to you and Irene with Moran suspecting nothing.

Yes, we secured those blueprints for that deadly device, and you, dear friend, played a major role in all of it.

Sadly, as you know, Moran was able to slip through our nets, even though the police of St Andrews did a tip-top job in capturing many of his cohorts.

Had it not been for your efforts, Watson, and I'm talking about your golfing efforts as well as your keen reasoning skills, and personal courage, we might not have captured this evil creature for months or years later. I know that it all must be beginning to make sense to you, Watson.

Recall how I surprised you when I appeared, disguised as the old proprietor of a bookstore. I remember your reaction when you realized that Moriarty had not taken me over the falls after all! Though you were still in shock over my return, you agreed that same night to join me on the very adventure that led to the capture of that treacherous scoundrel, Colonel

Sebastian Moran. By the way, your narrative of that event, <u>The Adventure of the Empty House</u>, was brilliant!

Now, dear friend, 'the Quiet One' once more begs your forgiveness for keeping you in the dark for so long. Irene and I remained friends, actually very close friends, for several years until her untimely demise while traversing the Himalayas to meet with the Dali Lama.

A final twist for you, my good fellow, you who have known me as well as anyone. Please understand that it vexed me to no end to have kept you in the dark about the St Andrews adventure. For the sake of your safety it simply had to be done.

One last item for you to ponder. I would suggest that you go back in the newspaper archives and read the article detailing the final results of the 1902 British Amateur Golf Championship at Royal Liverpool. There, an older gentleman from London was able to capture that coveted prize over a talented field of much younger players. His name was Charles Hutchings!"

*** Note: True "Sherlock Holmes" aficionados will notice that there may be several inaccuracies in the story time-line in my efforts to portray events in the story as having taken place between Holmes's "death" at Reichenbach Falls and his return in <u>The Adventure of the Empty House</u>. Hopefully, they won't detract from the story.

About the Author:

Bill Lawler is a retired elementary-middle-school teacher who is also an avid amateur golfer. He and wife, Gloria, also a retired educator, reside in West Wyoming, PA.

Having become enamored of golf very early in life, Bill has managed to garner his share of Northeastern Pennsylvania tournament trophies. Over the last several years, Bill has enjoyed spending his free time writing golf books.

His first effort, Rank Amateur, A Selection of Musings and Vague Recollections of a Passionate Golfer, was warmly received by golfers throughout Northeastern Pennsylvania and in many regions along the east coast of the United States. Following up on the heels of that endeavor, Bill wrote Rank Amateur II, the Saga Continues, a sequel of sorts, as it serves to tie up some loose ends and answer some unfinished questions from his prior work. These books were aimed at those individuals who love and appreciate golf for all that it offers.

In this his third effort, Mystery at St Andrews, Lawler has decided to try his hand at fiction with this novel taking place at the home of golf, the" Old Course" at St Andrews, Scotland. Try it, you'll like it!

Glossary:

***Scottish Expressions/Sayings:

p. 14	shoogle = shake
p. 70 & 77	In the name of the wee man = Oh, for goodness sakes!
	scumered. = I'm fed up with something
p. 73	Sic as ye gie, sic wull ye get.
	= You'll get out of life as much as you put in.
p.186	Haud yer wheest! = Be quiet!
	Dinnae fash yersel. = Don't trouble yourself.

Scottish Vocabulary:

Auld	old
aye	yes
bonnie	good, pretty
brae	hill
foozle	mishit a golf shot
ken	know
kirk	church
wee	tiny or young
whins	small scrubby bush
ye	you, singular or plural
yon	that
Pitscottie	village near St Andrews

Old Names for Golf Clubs

Driver	1-wood or Driver
Brassie	2-wood
Spoon	3-wood
Cleek	2-iron
Mashie	5-iron
Spade Mashie	6-iron
Mashie Niblick	7-iron
Niblick	8-iron or 9- iron

Acknowledgments:

I would like to express my thanks for all of the help and support I have received from my lovely wife, Gloria, and the rest of my family and friends. Some of my close friends allowed me to use their names as characters in the story and it was fun to include them in my tale. . .

While writing this mystery in the style of Sir Arthur Conan Doyle, I attempted to "fit" it into a time frame when Holmes went missing. (After his "death" and before his return in The Empty House)

Also, I wish to thank the following for their use and permissions:

The Conan Doyle Estate, Ltd.

The Bedside Companion to Sherlock Holmes by Riley & McAllister

Phil J. Pirages, Fine Books & Medieval Manuscripts

- - - The Keen Hand, The Golfer's Manual, by Henry Farnie

Wikipedia for general information/facts on St Andrews

Sleeping Bear Press– St Andrews and The Open

Thirteen Rules of Golf by The Honourable Company of Edinburgh Golfers

Credits:

I am extremely grateful to all of my friends and family who continue to support me in my writing. I am particularly appreciative for the contributions made by the following individuals who have done an excellent job in helping to edit this book.

Len Coleman
Maripat Coleman
Andy Kuffa
Gloria Lawler
Joe Lawler
Ted Merli
Joe Sharaba

Also from MX Publishing

Winners of the 2011 Howlett Literary Award (Sherlock Holmes
book of the year) for 'The Norwood Author'

From the world's largest Sherlock Holmes publishers dozens
of new novels from the top Holmes authors.
www.mxpublishing.com

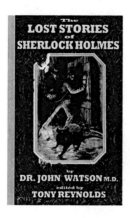 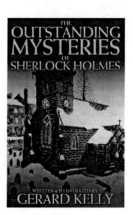

Including our bestselling short story collections 'Lost Stories
of Sherlock Holmes' , 'The Outstanding Mysteries of Sherlock
Holmes', 'Untold Adventures of Sherlock Holmes' and
'Sherlock Holmes in Pursuit'.

Sherlock Holmes Travel Guides

 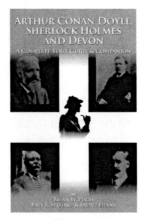

London   Devon

In ebook (stunning on the iPad) an interactive guide to London

400 locations linked to Google Street View.

Also from MX Publishing

Cross over fiction featuring great villans from history

and military history Holmes thrillers

 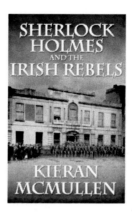

Also from MX Publishing

Fantasy Sherlock Holmes

 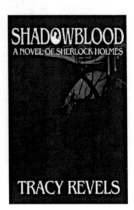

And epic novels

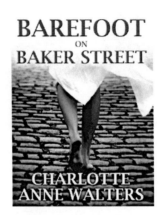

Also from MX Publishing

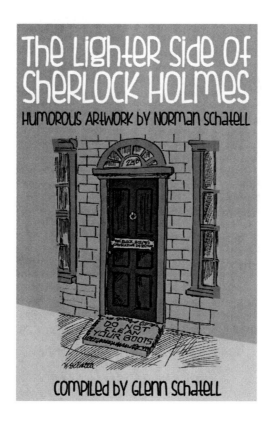

In paperback and hardback, 300 wonderful Holmes cartoons.

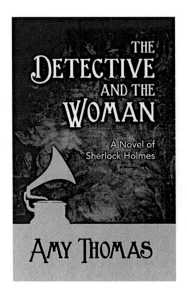 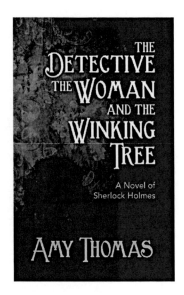

Two acclaimed novels featuring 'The Woman', Irene Adler
teaming up with Sherlock Holmes

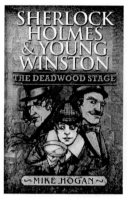  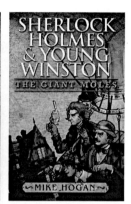

"Everything about this book, whether it be plot, casting, characters or dialogue is spot on. Mr Hogan, quite simply, does not put a foot wrong with volume, roll on the next two!"
The Baker Street Society

Three books in the Sherlock Holmes and Young Winston series from Mike Hogan.

Audio Books

www.audiogo.co.uk

 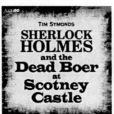 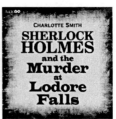

Links

The Publishers support the Save Undershaw campaign – the campaign to save and restore Sir Arthur Conan Doyle's former home. Undershaw is where he brought Sherlock Holmes back to life, and should be preserved for future generations of Holmes fans.

Save Undershaw   www.saveundershaw.com

Sherlockology   www.sherlockology.com

MX Publishing   www.mxpublishing.com

You can read more about Sir Arthur Conan Doyle and Undershaw in Alistair Duncan's book (share of royalties to the Undershaw Preservation Trust) – An Entirely New Country and in the amazing compilation Sherlock's Home – The Empty House (all royalties to the Trust).

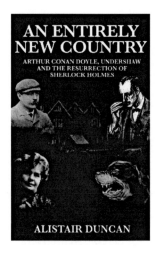

Lightning Source UK Ltd.
Milton Keynes UK
UKOW03f0326081113

220621UK00001B/33/P